HIGHLAND SLAYER

A Scottish Medieval Romance
Part of the Highland Legion Series

By Kathryn Le Veque

Every family has legends behind it, but no family more so than the dun Tarh clan.

Tucked deep in the Highlands of Scotland and relatives to the MacKenzie clan, the family is said to have been spawned from the lost Roman legion, the elite Ninth Hispania. For generations, the family was known for their dark men, quick-to-temper, fierce fighters with comely looks. They were greatly respected in the Highlands until Lares Rayan dun Tarh, a former priest who had fallen from grace, became the head of the family.

Lucifer, they called him.

And his sons were known as Lucifer's Highland Legion.

Welcome to Book 3 in the Highland Legion series.

A fighting order of nuns… a mysterious woman from the sea… and a sexy Highlander come together in this blowout adventure romance set in Scotland!

Love enemies-to-lover tropes? Love strong-women tropes? Then this is the tale for you!

Scotland is awash with legends, but there is no greater legend than the warrior nuns of St. Margaret's of Loch Doom. Founded by an order of persecuted nuns, they learned to face persecution with rage. They learned to fight those who condemned them and, two hundred years later, all of Scotland knows about the *Na Ban-Teamplairean*…

The Templar nuns.

The Templar nuns are also protectors of women and children, of those who cannot help themselves, giving the nuns a paradoxical existence. They are good to the poor and the needy, but they fight like men. But one thing is for certain—males who cross their paths don't often survive.

Estevan dun Tarh is well aware of these fighting nuns as he travels from one of his brother's home back to the Highlands. He's aware of them because in order to get to the gambling house known as The Butchery in a nearby town, he must pass through lands belonging to St. Margaret's. He ends up going well out of his way, traveling along a lonely beach, until he comes across a woman in distress. Given that the order of St. Margaret's helps women and children, he has little choice but to deliver the injured woman to their doorstep.

And nearly gets his head cut off in the process.

Anaxandra dun Muir is part of the Templar nuns. An orphan, she has lived with them since birth. It is Anaxandra who nearly kills Estevan, but soon enough, his mission becomes clear. But what isn't clear is the identity of the mysterious woman, who speaks in a different tongue. She continues to draw images of serpents in the dirt, trying to communicate, but by the time Estevan and Anaxandra realize what she is saying, danger has already arrived.

And it is deadly.

Join the most mismatched couple in Scotland as their discovery of the mysterious woman takes them through myths and legends, heartache, and finally a blazing romance that cannot be quenched.

HOUSE OF DUN TARH MOTTO

Numquam vici, semper timui

Never conquered, always feared

DUN TARH FAMILY TREE

*Children of Lares dun Tarh and Mabel Coleby de Waverton**

Aurelius

Darien

Estevan "Stevan"

Lilliana

Caelus

Kaladin "Kal"

Lucan

Leandro

Cruz

Zora

- *Mabel is a descendant of Ajax de Velt through his son, Cole*

Castle Hydra Floor Plan

"Castle Hydra"
also known as "The Hydra"

Author's Note

Well, here we are again with another adventurous Highland Legion novel!

This time, it's brother Estevan's turn. He has appeared pretty heavily in the first two novels—*Highland Born* and *Highland Destroyer*—and now he's got his own action-packed book with a strange and wonderful plot.

Strange how? You'll find out, but suffice it to say we've got an abbey full of warrior nuns. You've heard of warrior poets and warrior priests? Yep, we've got an entire abbey full of warrior nuns, only not all is as it seems. There's some strange stuff going on. It develops more as the story goes along.

We've also got some really strange people from the Isle of Man involved. I used the monsters in the epic poem *Beowulf* as my muse(s) for this tribe of brutal people who raise freshwater eels and use the body parts of their enemies to feed them. In my research, I discovered that the Island of Man, in Medieval times, was called the same thing, only a different spelling—Mann. The entire story takes place in the Lowlands of Scotland, in a place with a great name. You're going to love it. We've got Estevan, his brother Kaladin, and three new sidekicks to drool over. But it wouldn't be a story without Lares and Mabel, so keep an eye out for them, too!

Something that took a bit of a subplot in this book is more de Wolfe descendants. We're now about five generations after Willem de Wolfe, so the current Earl of Warenton is mentioned in this book, as well as his son. The current earl is Andrew de

Wolfe, son of Will de Wolfe (*WolfeLord*) and Lily de Lohr de Wolfe, so Andrew has both de Wolfe and de Lohr bloodlines. Andrew, if you recall, was named after Will's brother, who drowned alongside his mother, Athena. Athena was Paris de Norville's daughter (if you've read *WolfeLord*, then you know how Will and Athena got together. If you haven't read it, you must!).

That means that Andrew is Willem and Paris' great-grandson, and Christopher de Lohr's great-great-grandson. How's that for a lineage! Willem de Wolfe is about a generation after Christopher de Lohr (*Rise of the Defender*), since Christopher and Willem's father, Edward, were contemporaries. I've always wondered who Andrew would take after, and I'm pleased/sorry to say that he mostly takes after Paris. I'm not sure Willem (or even Christopher) would appreciate that—and that just makes me laugh. But Andrew's son, Titan, is all Willem and all Christopher. Keep an eye out for Titan de Wolfe—he's one to watch. Not only because he's got the bloodlines of Willem and Paris and Christopher in him, but he also has the bloodlines of someone else we know and love—Jax de Velt. His mother is a de Velt. No wonder his name is Titan.

Lastly, one of our players is Mateo de Wolfe. Mateo was born at the end of *Wolfeheart*, with his twin brother Magnar. As a tribute to his grandfather, Patrick de Wolfe, he bears the nickname of Matty.

But I digress.

There's really nothing more of note in the tale other than it will move very swiftly and has a lot of moving parts to come together, so sit back with your drink of choice and enjoy a bit of a complex tale. Those dun Tarh boys really seem to attract trouble—but that's what makes them fun!

Now, just FYI, the first few pages of the book are the story of how Mabel and Lares met, as is tradition in every Highland

Legion book, so if you already know the story, feel free to skip over. If not, feel free to read—it's important to the understanding of the book.

Here we go with the usual pronunciation guide:

Anaxandra—that's the heroine's name. It's pronounced like Alexandra, except there's an "N" where the "L" usually is. Literally—Ann-ax-andra. Or Annex-andra. Say it a few times. You'll get used to it.

Rodion—ROW-dee-un (believe it or not, this is a real name. Actor Basil Rathbone of Sherlock Holmes fame had a son named Rodion). I've heard it pronounced both ways—ROW-dion and ROD-ion, but I'm going with Row-dee-un.

And with that—on with the tale of Estevan and Anaxandra!

Happy Reading!

THE MEETING OF LARES AND MABEL

(EXCERPT FROM HIGHLAND BORN)

Camerton Abbey
Year of Our Lord 1315

PRETTY AND PERFECT, with golden-red hair and eyes of green, Lady Mabel Coleby Douglas-de Waverton peered from the window of the fortified carriage she and her mother were riding in, spying the rambling, rather large abbey in the distance. It was early morning on a fine day after weeks of rain, and the sky above the abbey was streaked with purplish, bruised clouds. Against the backdrop of the sky and the bright sunlight, it made for dramatic scenery.

"Is that it, Mama?" she asked, pointing to the monastery on the rise. "Camerton?"

Mabel's mother, Lady Irene, leaned over to see what her daughter was pointing at. "Aye," she said after a moment. "That must be the one. Your brother is somewhere in that monastery, and we must bring him home."

Mabel didn't ask why. She didn't ask questions. She knew

her wayward brother, George, had ended up at the monastery because he'd been traveling far from where he'd told his parents he would be and ended up breaking a leg when his horse spooked. He'd been in a remote area of Cumbria, to the southwest of Carlisle, and he'd been taken in by the priests at Camerton Abbey. A physic had been summoned, the same physic who had sent word to Lord and Lady de Waverton on George's mishap. George, in fact, hadn't sent them word at all, and Mabel had heard her father raging about her vagabond brother with no sense of responsibility. He was so angry that he sent his wife and daughter, one hundred soldiers, and two wagons to fetch George.

And that was why they were here.

Truly, Mabel was glad for the adventure. Nothing much happened in her rather sheltered life, and her father wasn't a social man, so friends and visitors were infrequent at their home of Wigton. That was in great contrast to her brother, who loved to visit and loved to travel. George the Elder, their father, didn't even like to venture out of his home, so that was why he'd sent his wife and daughter. It hadn't been because he was too angry to come, but simply that he could not come.

But George the Elder's refusal to travel was Mabel's gain. And it was probably better for her brother, whom she loved. He was sweet and kind and thoughtful, but her father was correct—he had no sense of responsibility. He was bright, but he didn't want the stress and troubles of the lordship he would inherit someday. That meant he traveled around, visited friends and family, and spent his father's money wherever he went. George the Elder paid his son's debts begrudgingly and threatened not to pay anything more that his son incurred.

But he always did.

This was simply another one of George's follies in a long line of them.

Mabel and her mother hadn't spoken much on the journey from Wigton to Camerton. It had been an overnight journey, and they'd spent the previous night in a tavern where everyone seemed to either be drunk or fighting. Mabel thought it was all great fun, but her mother wasn't under the same impression. In fact, it had put the woman in a sour mood, so there hadn't been much conversation in general.

As the carriage lurched over the muddy road that was more puddle than actual road, the rain began to fall again from those purple clouds. It was brief, just enough to dampen the men, who peered at the sky with discontent. The carriage hit a particularly deep rut and got stuck, but Lady de Waverton refused to get out of the carriage because it was so muddy, and she and Mabel remained in the carriage as the soldiers managed to free them from the hole.

After that, the dirty carriage lurched and bumped all the way to the abbey.

"Mama," Mabel said, a little green because of all of the swaying and violent bumps. "May I please get out and walk the rest of the way? It doesn't seem to be so muddy here at the top of the rise. All of the water seems to have run down the road."

Irene caught a glimpse of the big abbey ahead. They had already entered what looked like a small village area, with small cottages and fields of cabbages and turnips. She could see it along the side of the road along with men working them, more than likely pledges or wards of the abbey.

"I do not think so," she said, peering at the edge of the road. "It is still quite muddy."

Thinking she might become sick, Mabel hiked up her skirt

to show her mother the boots she was wearing. "I am properly attired," she said, taking a deep breath. "I really must walk before I become ill."

With that, she pushed her shoulder into the door of the cab, and it swung open. She was out of the carriage before her mother could stop her. She was in a heavy wool traveling dress, one that came with breeches underneath for protection and comfort, and they were tucked into her boots. Mabel began walking, holding her skirt up to keep it out of the mud as she headed off across a field on a diagonal toward the abbey.

"Mabel!" her mother called after her. "Go straight to the abbey! Do not stray!"

There weren't many places for her to stray to. Mabel simply waved her mother off, trudging across the field, trying to shake off the motion sickness. The soldiers didn't follow her because they could see her clearly as she walked through the field of cabbages. They simply followed the carriage as Mabel crossed the field toward the abbey. Fortunately, it wasn't too terribly muddy here because it was at the top of a rise. Off to her left, a few men were working the cabbages, harvesting them because they were quite large. The wind was starting to pick up a little, blustery after the rains, and Mabel fought with her skirts to keep them from blowing around. She was paying attention to her dress, not where she was stepping, and she ended up slipping on a slick spot and going down on her arse, twisting her ankle.

"Damnation," she said.

Hand to her aching ankle, she looked off toward the road only to see that it must have angled away from the abbey before coming around again to the entry. The escort was moving away from her. Realizing there was going to be no help from her father's men, she tried to get to her feet, but her ankle hurt a great deal. Still, she managed to stand, putting most of her weight on her good ankle, as a deep voice spoke from behind.

"I saw ye fall, m'lady," he said. "Did ye hurt yerself?"

Startled, Mabel turned to see a big man with shoulder-length dark hair and dark eyes. He wasn't much older than she was, and she realized with a twinge of interest that he was quite handsome. But he was dressed in clothing better suited to a peasant and carrying a farming implement in one hand. In fact, that twinge of interest turned into one of suspicion, because he'd come up behind her and she'd never heard a sound.

That made her leery.

"If you think to assault me, know that all I have to do is scream and you'll have a hundred furious soldiers down upon you," she said. "Put the shovel down."

He did, immediately. "I dinna mean tae startle ye," he said. "'Tis only that I saw ye fall. I thought ye might need help."

She tried to take a step and almost went down again. "It would seem so," she said. "I have evidently hurt my ankle."

The man moved close to her, going to one knee as he lifted her skirt to get a look at her ankle. Before Mabel could protest, he put his big hands around her booted ankle and gave a gentle squeeze.

Mabel yelped.

"Ah," he said, peering up at her. "I think ye have, indeed. Can ye put any weight on it?"

She shook her head. "I do not think so," she said, trying to use the injured joint, but she ended up nearly tumbling onto him as she walked. "Damnation. Utter *damnation!*"

He grinned at her, a charming gesture. "I've never heard a lady use such language."

She frowned at him. "And you probably never will," she said. "Unfortunately, I have a mouth like my father, and he swears constantly."

That made his grin broaden. "'Tis nothing tae be ashamed of, m'lady," he said as he stood up. "It simply means ye're passionate about the things that mean something tae ye."

She eyed him, finally breaking down in a reluctant smile. "It means my mother is constantly admonishing me," she said. "She does not share your view."

His eyes were twinkling at her. "I know something about a parent not sharing a child's view," he said, his smile fading. "My father dinna share mine, either. And if it wouldna be too bold, I'll introduce myself. My name is Lares."

That was indeed a bold move, as he suggested. Introductions were made with mutual acquaintances or friends or family, but since there was no one of that position around, perhaps it wasn't bold as it was necessary, so at least they would know whom they were speaking with.

"My name is Mabel de Waverton," she said, looking him over. "You're Scots?"

"Aye."

"Are you a farmer?"

He shook his head. "Not by trade," he said. "But by circumstances."

She wasn't sure what he meant. "What circumstances?"

He gestured toward the church. "I live there," he said. "Everyone must have a task. This is mine."

She thought she understood. "Then you are a priest," she said. "Are you even allowed to speak with a woman?"

He was shaking his head before the words were out of her mouth. "I am *not* a priest," he said. "I'm a ward, although the spineless bastards would be very happy tae see me take my vows."

His eyes widened when he realized he had sworn in front of her, and she giggled. "You have a mouth like my father, too," she said.

He put up his hands in apology. "Forgive me, m'lady," he said. "But I suppose we have that in common—we speak passionately about things."

She was smiling openly at him. "I do not think that is a bad thing," she said. "More people should say what they feel. The world might be better for it."

He chuckled. "Ye think so, do ye?" he said. "I think if the Scots said what they thought, we'd have constant wars, all across Scotland."

She giggled again. "I suppose you are right," she said. "Isn't it men saying what they feel that starts wars in the first place?"

"That is my belief."

Distant shouting caught their attention, and they both turned to see that the de Waverton carriage had made its way to the front of the abbey. Irene had climbed out and was shouting at her daughter, waving an arm.

Mabel waved back.

"That is my mother," she said, not entirely happily. "She is waiting for me."

Lares could see that. "Have ye come on business?"

She shook her head, trying to put weight on the ankle again but faltering. He grabbed her arm so she wouldn't fall, bracing his other arm around her waist to keep her upright as she tried to walk.

"Thank you," she said in reference to his help. "To answer your question, we are not here on business. We are here to collect my brother, George. Do you know him?"

Lares held her as she took another step and ended up hopping because she couldn't put any weight on her leg. "George?" he said curiously. "Is he a priest?"

"Nay," she said, coming to a halt because she couldn't walk any further. "He broke his leg and the priests have tended him. We've come to collect him."

That brought recognition. "Ah," he said. "*That* George. The lad in the dormitory. Aye, I've spoken tae him, but he calls himself Georgie. He's quite lively, which is something that vexes the priests, I think. But I've enjoyed him."

Mabel appreciated the kind words about her brother. "He's a darling man," she said, but her smile soon faded. "I hate to trouble you, but could you tell my mother I need help? She'll send a couple of soldiers to assist me."

Lares' response was to bend over and swiftly pick her up. Abruptly aloft in the man's arms, Mabel grasped his neck for support, realizing very quickly that their faces were quite close together. Now she could see him up close, and he was a prize specimen. She had been startled by his action at first, but now that she was in his arms, something else was happening.

A sweet little flutter, deep in her belly.

She rather liked it.

"No need for the soldiers, m'lady," he said as he continued across the field. "'Tis my pleasure tae help Georgie's sister, though I will admit I'm sorry ye've come tae take him home. He was a bright spot in an otherwise lonely life."

"I'm sorry we must, but he should go home."

"Of course he should," Lares said. "I simply meant I'll miss speaking tae him. But I suppose it does not matter, because I'm going home as well."

"Are you?" Mabel said, trying to ignore the giddy trembling in her belly. "When do you leave?"

"Soon," Lares said. "The priests know they must release me now that my da has died. I've been called home."

"Is that so?" Mabel said with some concern. "I'm sorry that it will be a sad homecoming for you."

They were nearing the edge of the field, and Lares could see Mabel's mother waving frantically to a few soldiers, pointing to her daughter. They started heading in their direction.

"Not a sad homecoming," he said quietly, eyeing the soldiers who were still some distance away, but by nature he had an aversion to English soldiers. "Truthfully, I'm glad tae be rid of this place. I'm glad tae have the opportunity tae live a normal life again and not exist at this wretched purgatory."

"Has it been so awful?"

He looked to the abbey and its dark, tall walls with moss growing on the north side of the building. "Awful enough," he said. "But, then again, I will return tae my family's home, which isna much better."

"Where is it?"

"Far tae the north, in the Highlands," he said. "A place called Castle Hydra."

She was curious. "That's quite a name," she said. "Why is it called that?"

He shrugged. "No one really knows," he said. "It has always been called that. The home we live in has been there for hundreds of years, but before that, there was a wooden fort built by the tribes who used tae inhabit the land. It sits on the edge of an inlet that leads out tae sea, and my father thinks they called it the Hydra because there really was a sea serpent in the inlet in days long past. He thinks the original building on the site used tae be a temple tae the serpent. But who truly knows how things get their name? Men are strange creatures sometimes."

Mabel nodded. "True enough," she said. "Then your home has been in existence for many years?"

He nodded, looking at her with those dark, twinkling eyes. "My ancestors are Romans," he said. "Ye've heard tale that the Romans once conquered the English? They tried tae come tae Scotland, but we ran them off or forced them tae live among us. Those are my ancestors. They built the temple tae the serpent. And they settled the land and married intae the tribes."

She smiled faintly. "I had a tutor who spoke of the Romans and the Greeks," she said. "But I do not remember much about them."

He was forced to turn away from her so that he could watch where he was going now that they were near the end of the field. "'Tis nothing for a finely bred lass tae know," he said. "The Romans were conquerors. They came tae the shores of England and Scotland, back in the old days, and they forced men tae serve their empire."

"Sounds fearsome."

He gave her a half-grin. "We are."

"Is that where you get your name? I've never heard it before."

He nodded. "All men in my family are given Roman or Aragon names," he said. "The Romans we descend from were men from Aragon. Therefore, our son will have a name of my choosing. Possibly after a Roman king or an Aragon prince."

Her eyes widened, and she couldn't help the snort that escaped. "*Our* son?" she said. "Are we having a son together, then?"

All he did was cast her a sidelong glance, grinning, and

Mabel's heart nearly beat right out of her chest. Something about that expression suggested he meant what he'd said, and, strangely, she believed him. She wasn't sure why, but she did. Few were actually men of their word, but Mabel suspected Lares was one of them. Out in the middle of a lightly traveled area of Cumbria, working in a field of cabbages, was a man who spoke the truth.

He meant every word.

Pondering that very thing, Mabel was prevented from answering because the soldiers were upon them at this point. Her father's heavily armed men had come to collect her, and she batted them away.

"Leave me alone," she scolded them. "He's perfectly capable of helping me."

The soldiers weren't happy about it. Irene wasn't happy about it. But Mabel tightened her arms around Lares' neck and grinned at him as a gaggle of soldiers stood by, unsure what to do. By this time, there were a pair of priests who had come forth to greet the visitors, and they were all watching with various expressions of concern and outrage as Lares carried Mabel out of the field and headed toward her mother.

Lares wasn't unaware of the battery of condescending stares, either.

He knew he was going to get an earful.

"I fear our acquaintance is coming tae a close, m'lady," he said, his gaze on the mother in particular. "'Twas an honor tae meet ye, and I'll miss George when he leaves. Should I wish tae call upon ye, where do ye live?"

Mabel looked at him. She found that she was quite sorry they would soon be parted. "Slow your walk," she said quietly. When he looked at her curiously, she smiled. "The faster you walk, the faster you must put me down."

A smile spread across his lips, and he immediately slowed. "That was a bold suggestion, m'lady."

"Then walk quickly if you do not agree."

His dark eyes studied her. "I slowed down, dinna I?"

Mabel chuckled. "You did," she said. "But my mother will be furious that I've spoken to a farmer. Look at her—she is already having fits."

"Would she have fits if ye spoke with an earl?"

Mabel wasn't sure what he meant. "Of course not," she said. "But that is different. A man of higher standing and she'd probably throw me into his arms herself."

The smile on his lips grew. "I said I wasna a priest," he said. "Nor am I a farmer, but that is my task here at Camerton. I was sent here by my da because... Well, it does not matter why. But know that I'm not a priest nor a farmer. I was born my father's heir."

"What does that mean?"

He told her.

☳

"He's a *what*?"

Irene was close to being irate as she watched the tall, handsome man in peasant clothing carry her daughter toward the abbey entry. She'd demanded to know who he was, but a few words from the priest had her turning to the man in shock.

"Say that again," she demanded. "He's the *what*?"

"He is the Earl of Torridon." The priest, a thin man with bad teeth, was looking at her rather fearfully. "That young man who has been working our fields."

Irene's mouth popped open, briefly, in astonishment. "The

Earl of Torridon is working your fields?"

The priest seemed nervous as he spoke. "Lares dun Tarh has only just become the Earl of Torridon," he clarified. "We received word two days ago that his father has passed away, and Lares was his heir. He is now the earl and, as such, is preparing to return home."

Irene's astonishment took on a hint of interest. She returned her focus to the tall, dark-haired man emerging from the field of cabbages with her daughter in his arms, and she could see all manner of possibilities. Not that she wasn't selective about whom her daughter should marry, but Mabel had been difficult when it came to finding her a husband. At her age, she should be betrothed at the very least, but she wasn't. Any man that came to call upon her, either by his own initiative or by invitation, had been found wanting in Mabel's eyes. She was bright and stubborn, and had a very strong idea about the man she wished to marry.

Irene, however, wasn't so selective. If she could garner a titled lord for her daughter—an earl, no less—then she would do it. She would do what it took.

Even if the earl was Scots.

"Tell me about him," she said to the priest just as Lares and her daughter came out of the field. "Why was he here at the abbey? Does he mean to be a priest?"

The priest shook his head. "Nay, my lady," he said. "As I said, his father him sent here after the lad was caught trying to marry a lady without permission, but also…"

He trailed off, causing Irene to look at him curiously. "Also *what*?"

The priest was hesitant as he lowered his voice. "He was sent here to save his soul," he muttered. "He was caught summoning demons, and his father sent him here to purge the demons from him. Rumors said that he was becoming Lucifer himself. But since his arrival two years ago, he's slept little, read the Bible for hours every day, and worked the fields rigorously to purge the devil from him. God shall prevail in the end."

Irene's expression had a hint of horror to it as she listened. "Nonsense," she finally scoffed. "There are no demons in that man."

"We have worked hard to ensure that there are none, my lady."

"He looks perfectly normal to me."

"I hope so, my lady."

Irene wasn't sure what more to say to that. Her daughter and the man in question, now an earl, were coming closer, and as they drew near, Irene went out to meet them.

"What happened?" she said to her daughter. "Did you fall? You foolish child, I told you to be careful. I knew you would hurt yourself."

Mabel had little patience with her mother. "I slipped in the mud and twisted my ankle a little," she said. "But I assure you, I'm perfectly well."

"If you are well, then let me see you stand."

"I'm not *that* well."

Irene growled in frustration. "First your brother, now you," she said dramatically. "We are here to bring your brother home because he broke his leg, and now you are injured as well. Your father will be quite angry!"

Annoyed, Mabel squirmed with the intention of climbing out of Lares' arms, so he lowered her to the ground carefully. She stood on both feet, but the truth was that she was mostly balancing on her left foot.

"See?" she said. "I can stand. I will be completely well by the time we return home, so you needn't worry about Papa. Right now, we should be more worried about George. Have you asked to see him?"

Irene hadn't. She'd been so concerned with her headstrong daughter that the very reason they were here had completely slipped her mind.

But she wasn't going to admit that.

"Of course I have," she said, turning to the priest. "Why have you not taken me to my son yet? I demand that you take me to George immediately."

The priest had no idea what she meant, and he looked at her with surprise first and then fear. "My lady?" he stammered. "Your… your son?"

Irene threw an imperious finger toward the abbey. "I *told* you," she said, though she knew full well that she hadn't. "We've come for the young man who has broken his leg. I am Lady Irene de Waverton, and my son is inside the abbey. Take me to him immediately."

The priest darted inside with Irene following. Mabel was left standing there, or rather balancing there, as everyone seemed to be moving into the abbey. As her father's soldiers wandered back over to the escort, she looked at Lares.

"I do believe they have left us alone," she said.

The corners of his mouth twitched. "It would seem so, m'lady."

"Would you be so kind as to help me inside?" she said. "I hate to ask, but I fear that I lied to my mother when I told her that I was well. My ankle hurts a great deal."

Lares had suspected as much. "We should tend tae yer ankle before it grows worse," he said. "If ye'll allow, I can help."

Mabel smiled at his kindness. "You've helped quite a lot already," she said. "But mayhap you can help me inside. I should like to see my brother."

Without a word, he bent over and picked her up again, carrying her into the dark, cool innards of Camerton. It smelled of cold earth and dust, and of the incense the priests were so fond of that came from mysterious places across the sea. While Lares was fairly certain he could become quite used to his arms around Mabel, she was thinking that she could become quite used to being carried around. By him. As he followed the voices into the dormitory where George was exclaiming his delight at seeing his mother, Mabel found her gaze lingering on Lares, only to flush and turn away when he caught her staring at him.

It was a game they played more than once. She would look, he would catch her, and before they entered the dormitory, he was looking and she caught him. Lares had gone from a simple rescue mission to a game of interest fairly quickly.

And so had Mabel.

But no more interested than Lady Irene. She didn't even care when Lares entered the dormitory carrying her daughter for a second time. Nay, she didn't mind at all because before the day was through, she'd come to know Lares dun Tarh and the tale of his remote, but evidently rich, earldom. By the next morning—for they did remain at the abbey overnight—she was to return home with two very important things: her son for one and a betrothal for the other. Lares dun Tarh had surrendered without a fight.

When their first son, Aurelius, was born a year later, and a second son, Darien, not quite two years after that, it was the beginning of the legend of Lucifer's Highland Legion.

PART ONE

PROLOGUE

Year of Our Lord 1353
Scotland

THE MOON WAS full.

Hovering over the sea on a strangely calm night, it seemed to be watching every move she made. She could feel the cold stare against her back, silent judgment against what she'd done.

Of what she'd had to do.

The moon could be cold and insincere comfort.

But she thanked the moon, or the gods above, or whoever was in command of the sea on this cold and clear night, that she'd made it this far. She wasn't entirely sure she would. She had no idea what had become of the boat she'd been traveling in, a tiny skiff she'd stolen and had taken to sea. Her people were from the sea, for centuries they ruled the salty deep, so she knew her way around a boat of any size.

A tiny little boat that had brought her this far but no further.

She'd had to swim her way to shore.

The water lapped gently around her knees as she struggled onto the rocky, silty shore. There were gently rolling banks around, but there were rocks jutting out of the sea, and it was those rocks that smashed her little skiff when she'd accidentally run aground. She'd ended up in the water to her waist but managed to walk ashore, pulling the damaged boat with her.

Feeling the firm earth beneath her feet was the greatest feeling in the world.

But she wasn't safe.

Not in the least.

Her body felt as if it weighed more than the rocks on the cliffs that were looming on either side of her. Breathing was difficult. Moving was worse. But she had to make it onto shore, so she struggled through the sand and rocks until she reached what seemed to be sandy soil. There was even grass just a little further on, and then trees. Dark, forbidding trees. God only knew what lay in wait for her there.

But at least here, on the shore, she was still in the moon-light, an illusion of safety even if it was only fleeting. She'd escaped those bastards who had stolen her from her home, who had kept her for their own pleasure or torment, whatever suited them at the moment. She was a princess to her people, a woman of great breeding and bloodlines, but for the past several months, she'd been no better than the horses in the stable. Something to be used and fed and beaten.

Until she'd stolen the boat and sailed away.

The problem was that she knew they would be tracking her. They wouldn't know exactly where she'd gone, but several of them would go out and follow the sea to the north and the south and the west, trying to trace her movements. She'd gone south because that was the opposite direction of her home. The seas were rougher in that direction and there was more of a chance that she would be caught, so she'd gone south, with the flow of the water. She'd slept on the little boat and eaten what she'd managed to bring with her, but those provisions had run out two days ago. She hadn't eaten nor drunk anything since. God help her, she had to find food. She had to find help. She knew that those who had enslaved her were on her tail.

And that was her last conscious thought before the world around her went black.

Pitching face-first into the dirt and sand, the white-haired woman collapsed.

CHAPTER ONE

South of Dumfries, Scotland
Near the mouth of the River Nith where it meets the Solway Firth

"HOW FAR ARE we from the butchery?"
Though it seemed like a normal question, the answer wasn't quite so simple. In fact, at the head of a group of several knights and warriors plodding their way through Galloway, the only answer the man received was to have someone hissing dramatically at him.

"Hush!" A man with a heavy Scots burr waved a sharp hand at his English-accented friend. "Keep yer voice down."

The English knight frowned. "Why?" he said, looking around the green and lush, sloping landscape that surrounded them. "Christ, Estevan, who is to hear us? There is no one around. Probably for miles. You insisted on taking this shortcut to the nearest town, so I will once again ask you—where is the butchery?"

Estevan dun Tarh hissed again, only this time he was joined by his younger brother, Kaladin, who went so far as to continue hissing and waving his hand in a silencing gesture.

"Quiet, Titan de Wolfe, if ye know what's good for ye," Estevan said with severity. "And it's not 'the butchery.' 'Tis called The Butcher's, and if ye say it too loud, my mother will hear ye and she'll rain hell and fire upon us."

Titan, heir to the Earldom of Warenton, grinned at Estevan's statement. "Your mother is back at Ashkirk Castle," he said, jabbing a big finger behind them. "She has sent us on ahead to your family seat of Hydra Castle and will join us there in a few weeks because she's not finished enjoying the summer at Ashkirk yet. And do not forget your father's new acquisition of Hollee Castle to the north. That alone should have your mother in good spirits because it means more income. She'll not care about a gambling house."

"Have ye *met* my mother?" Estevan said incredulously. "If ye have, then ye wouldna make such a statement."

Titan shook his head, amused at the fear demonstrated by a grown man. "The point is this—your mother is nowhere near us," he said. "I promise, she will not hear us speaking of The Butcher's."

Hydra Castle, or "the Hydra," was the dun Tarh stronghold, far north in the Highlands of Scotland. It would take them a few weeks simply to reach it, and Lares dun Tarh and his wife, Mabel, were at their Lowlands property of Ashkirk Castle they'd spent most of the summer. Even now, they were days away from it, but that wasn't good enough for Estevan.

He was certain she could still hear them.

In fact, it was Kaladin who seemed to have the fear of God cast into him with that very same thought. No matter what Titan said, the man was living a fool's dream. He started to groan and shake his head.

"Ye dunna know my mother," he said. "Mabel dun Tarh

knows all and sees all. Most especially, she hears all, and if she had the smallest hint that we're going tae The Butcher's, she'd fly over from Ashkirk and beat us all like incorrigible children. Dunna think she'll leave yer de Wolfe arse untouched, for ye would be wrong if ye did. She'd blister ye just like the rest of us."

Titan, an enormous man whose name suited him, started laughing. He turned to the men behind him, both English knights, to see that they were laughing also. He'd known them both all his life, much as he'd known the dun Tarh lads most of his life. They were all intertwined because their families had all married into one another over the years. Mateo de Wolfe, off to his left, was a cousin because their grandfathers had been brothers, and Rodion de Velt was a cousin to the dun Tarh brothers, as their mother, the infamous Mabel, was a de Velt.

And that was why the three English knights were heading north.

It was a sort of exchange program that the northern English warlords had with the Earls of Torridon in the Highlands of Scotland. Lares dun Tarh, father to Estevan and Kaladin and several other sons, also happened to be the Earl of Torridon. They were deeply intermingled with the Houses of de Wolfe and de Velt, and there were times when Lares would send his sons south to spend time with the English houses, gaining experience, and then the English warlords would do the same and send some of their sons and men into the Highlands to gain experience and learn about the Scots.

It was something they'd been doing for several years, ever since Lares and Mabel's first son, Aurelius, went to foster with the House of de Wolfe. Because Mabel was English, meaning their sons were half English, Lares had given his sons the choice of training as English knights, but so far, Aurelius was the only one who had actually earned his spurs.

However, Kaladin, now coming of age, was a permanent fixture at Castle Questing, seat of the House of de Wolfe, and he had decided to earn his spurs also. Baby Bull, as Kaladin was called, was already an astonishingly good knight and had inherited the de Velt trait, through his mother, of two-colored eyes. One eye was brown while the other, though mostly brown, had a big spot of green in it. That gave him a most fearsome appearance.

A de Velt with a thick Scottish brogue.

But today, Kaladin as well as his brother and three cousins were heading home to Castle Hydra before the winter set in. Castle Hydra was seat of the dun Tarh clan, and they were mostly eager to go home, but it was Kaladin himself who had come up with the idea of visiting one of the most notorious gambling dens in Scotland, a place called The Butcher's, on their way north. They would be passing so close to it that it was truly a crime—Kaladin's own words—not to spend a little time there. Games were good fun and Kaladin had a love for them.

So, here they were.

Big, strong men hoping their mummy wouldn't find out what they were doing.

The Butcher's had quite a history. It had started off as a gathering of friends in an old cottage on the outskirts of Dumfries, men who wanted to gamble and drink away from their women, but the news of the place had spread and others had joined in. The little cottage had other rooms built onto it, stone chambers for more games and more men, which would seem surprising given the somewhat remote location, but it seemed that no man in Scotland—or northern England, for that matter—gave a second thought to traveling a few days to such a place for the opportunity to gamble and drink and perhaps even seek companionship from a lass or two. It had become *that* kind of a place, too.

The name *The Butcher's* had come from the man who had founded the establishment, a member of the Douglas clan, because when his wife asked him where he was going as he headed out for the day, he would tell her "the butcher's." Now, the group of five warriors were heading for The Butcher's in spite of the fear of Mabel lurking around the nearest corner.

Some things were worth the risk.

"If I am jeopardizing my arse, this had better be worth it," Titan said dryly. "But we should be in Dumfries by now. Where *are* we, Estevan?"

Estevan looked around, to the mouth of the River Nith to his left and the endless green sea beyond. "This was supposed tae be a shortcut," he said. "If we take the main road, we end up passing through Archibald Douglas' lands, and he and my da are not friendly, so this is a shorter route."

"It's *not* a shorter route," Kaladin said. "But it's a safer one."

Estevan merely shrugged to his brother's comment. "We should be in Dumfries by nightfall if we keep up this pace," he said. Then he looked off to the west, where dark clouds were gathering over the waters. "Mayhap we should move a little faster. I dunna think any of us wishes tae be caught in what will soon be upon us."

He indicated the clouds in the distance. Rodion, who had been bringing up the rear of the group, reined his big horse over toward the mouth of the river where it met with the Solway Firth. Far to the south was England and further to the west was the Irish Sea and Ireland. A cold wind blew off the water, smelling of salt and sea, rippling through the sea grass that Rodion was treading upon.

"'Tis vast here," he said, reining his horse onto a small rise overlooking the river. "One gets a great sense of earth and sky, of air and existence. I've always thought that about Scotland."

Estevan, who had pulled his horse to a pause, turned to look at him. "Ah," he said. "The great poet speaks. Paint us a picture with yer words, Rody. Ye're good at that."

Rodion smiled faintly at his cousin. Much like Kaladin, he, too, bore the de Velt trait of two-colored eyes, only his were oddly less pronounced than Kaladin's were. He was a direct descendant of the great Ajax de Velt through his eldest son, Cole, but he didn't have nearly the pronounced eye difference that Kaladin had. It was true that Mabel also descended from Ajax de Velt through a daughter, but in their family, the women seemed to be far less affected by the eye-color trait than the males.

Something else Rodion possessed was the soul of a poet, something quite foreign to any male with the de Velt name. The de Velts, as a rule, were fearsome warlords. Ajax de Velt had been the most feared warlord in all of England during his lifetime, so the name was associated with death and warfare. But Rodion, for all of his skill as a knight, had a side to him that some men could consider weak.

As Estevan said, he painted pictures with words.

"I simply mean that everything in the world comes together in this space," he said, indicating the river as it ran into the sea. "The water, the sky, the earth, and the air. A place like this gave birth to men, to the world we live in. It's where Time and God collide. I feel reverence here, I suppose."

"Ye should," Kaladin said. "God is here, for certain."

Rodion looked at him. "What do you mean?"

Kaladin cocked a dark eyebrow. "The most infamous abbey in Scotland is nearby," he said. "Ye should also feel fear as well as reverence."

"Fear for what?"

"*Na Ban-Teamplairean.*"

It took Rodion a moment to realize what he was saying because he wasn't as good with Gaelic as others were. He was literate and educated, but he'd never taken to the Gaelic language. In fact, it was Mateo who spoke first.

"The Templar nuns," he muttered. "Bloody Christ, are those abominations around here?"

All eyes turned to the enormous knight with dark hair and pale eyes. His grandfather, Patrick de Wolfe, had possessed legendary height. There were few men taller in England, if not the entire world, than Patrick had been. Mateo was a twin, son of Patrick's eldest son, Markus, and he'd lived a rather solitary life. He'd been married, once, but he'd lost her in childbirth about twenty years earlier and had never remarried. He was a bit of an enigma because he kept to himself for the most part, a quiet man who was highly intelligent. That meant that when the man spoke in that deep, raspy voice, men listened.

Like now.

He always sounded ominous.

"Aye, they're around here," Kaladin said, pointing off to the east. "St. Margaret's of Loch Doom is that way, over that rise."

Mateo's gaze moved in that direction. "I hope we do not run into any of them."

"They keep tae themselves," Kaladin said. "I dunna think they go beyond their walls, seeking trouble."

"I've heard stories about them," Titan said. "They were

founded by a woman whose husband had been killed in battle. Legend says she prayed for forty days and forty nights before St. Margaret appeared to her and told her to start a fighting order of widows in her name."

"And she had forty widows right away, one for each day she prayed," Mateo finished. "I know because I've heard the legend, too. We all have. True or not, that was over two hundred years ago, and now all they have are a group of nuns who have been known to fight battles when their sanctuary is threatened. They have a foundling home there, you know. They protect those children rabidly."

"I heard they never let the children leave," Kaladin said. "At least, they never let the girl children leave. They throw the lads tae the wolves when they come of age, but they keep the girls."

"Then they must have a lot of girls," Titan said. "My father said he saw the Douglas summon them for a border skirmish against Carlisle Castle, and he said the nuns fought like men. They were more effective, too, because a knight is sworn to protect not only the church, but women in general. Their appearance caused a great deal of confusion because no one wanted to engage them."

"It probably caused some deaths, I would imagine," Mateo said.

Titan glanced at him. "You disapprove of a fighting woman?"

Mateo shook his head. "They have their place," he said. "I was married to a woman who took up arms, and she was fearsome. I have great admiration for a woman who can fight."

"Then why disapprove of the nuns?"

Mateo frowned. "Because they are nuns," he said. "They are women of God. It seems to me that if they can be summoned by a clan to fight for their cause, then they are *not* fighting for God. They are fighting for men. There is something inherently self-serving about that."

Titan didn't have an argument for him. He couldn't disagree that nuns, by virtue of their holy vows, probably shouldn't take up arms, and most especially not fight other men's battles. He was about to say so when they heard a shout from Rodion, who was still riding on the crest overlooking the river. When everyone turned to look at him, he pointed toward the water.

"There!" he shouted. "There is something there!"

He spurred his horse toward the river and they lost sight of him. That brought Titan and Mateo charging after him with Estevan and Kaladin bringing up the rear, all of them thundering over the rise only to see a dirty, rocky belt that ran alongside the river as it dumped into the firth.

But there was indeed something on that sand.

A body.

Rodion was the first one on the scene. He dismounted his horse swiftly and went to the body, bending over it but not touching it. He was a man with a knowledge of healing, so he knew what to look for. As he was visually inspecting it, as it was lying face down, Titan and Mateo arrived. They hit the ground running, so to speak, moving swiftly to the body and kicking up sand as they went. Titan reached down and yanked on an arm, pulling the figure onto its back.

It was a woman.

Her face and hair were covered with dirt and filth. Rodion knelt beside her, feeling on her wrist for a pulse to see if she was even alive. She certainly didn't look like it, pasty and gray like the dirt surrounding her.

"She's alive," he muttered. Then he lifted his head and

looked around, up and down the riverbank. "Is she alone? Does anyone see wreckage of any kind?"

That had the knights looking around, heads bobbing. "Nay," Estevan said. "No wreckage that I can see. Kal, ride down the bank, toward the sea. There may be something down there, sunken so we canna see it."

Kaladin was already heading in the direction his brother had indicated. He and his cream-colored stallion raced down the riverbank. As he headed south, Estevan brushed some of the dirt away from the woman's face and nose, making sure it wasn't impeding her breathing. She was wet, but he didn't have anything to cover her with. In silence, they waited until Kaladin returned, which was nearly a half-hour. The could see him thundering back in their direction.

"There's some wreckage down that way," Kaladin shouted as he came near, reining the horse to a rough stop as the animal kicked up clods of dirt in its haste. "The tide has gone out, but I could see a small boat that has been badly damaged. It must be hers."

Estevan nodded, returning his attention to the woman at his feet. Titan and Mateo were gazing down at her, also, watching Rodion assess her condition. It didn't take long for him to figure it out.

"The woman is near death," he said grimly. "She will not survive if we do not find someone to tend her."

"A physic?" Estevan said, turning his attention northward. "Dumfries would have the nearest physic, but we are an hour or more away."

"What about the nuns?" Mateo asked.

Everyone looked at him. "They are a fighting order," Estevan pointed out. "They dunna heal."

But Mateo shook his head. "If they are a fighting order, then they must also have knowledge of healing," he said. "I am certain they would not let a male physic touch them should they be wounded, so it stands to reason that if they fight, they heal."

His logic was sound. As Estevan sighed heavily, trying to determine what to do, Rodion spoke.

"How far is the abbey?" he asked.

Estevan gestured toward the east. "Not far," he said. "A mile or two at most."

"Then we should put this woman on their doorstep and continue on our way," Rodion said. "We cannot simply leave her to die. Let us take her and be done with it."

It seemed the reasonable course of action, but unfortunately, no one seemed particularly eager to make the first step. No one wanted to go near the Templar nuns, their fierce legend perhaps larger than the actual truth. Sometimes things like that happened, when stories told from man to man took on a life of their own with each successive telling. They'd just finished speaking about the mysterious nuns of the order of St. Margaret of Loch Doom and now they were facing the very real possibility of actually having contact with them.

A far different destination than the gambling den.

"Matty, collect the woman," Rodion said when no one else seemed willing to move. "We must get moving. We'll take her to the nuns and then continue on to The Butcher's."

"Mayhap taking pity on the lady will erase the sin of gambling," Kaladin muttered. "Mayhap it is penitence for what we're about tae do."

Mateo heaved the sandy, wet, limp woman over his shoulder. "Then let us get about it," he said. "I do not need another stain against my immortal soul. If this will eliminate one, then I am keen to do it."

That seemed to make the decision for everyone. They found a ready cause for absolution for their future gambling sins right in front of them, so no one questioned it. They began to run for their horses as Estevan helped Mateo get the woman onto his horse. When she was finally secure and Mateo mounted, the five men made haste for the lair of the Templar nuns.

And for one of them, a distinct date with destiny.

CHAPTER TWO

St. Margaret's of Loch Doom

S ISTER HILDEGARDE WAS coming again.

She could tell by the woman's footsteps, which weren't so much footsteps as they were concussions of impending trouble.

The sound always made her heart race, just a little.

It had for as long as she could remember. From her very earliest memories as a foundling, a ward of St. Margaret's, she could remember the sound of Sister Hildegarde's footsteps and how all of the children would stiffen with fear. Strange thing, however, was that Sister Hildegarde never hit anyone. Not a strike nor a slap. She was not a warm woman, but she was a fair one. It was simply her expression and words that struck terror into the most stalwart child, and even now, as a young woman, she still felt that familiar fright.

This time, however, there was no reason to.

She and Sister Hildegarde were comrades these days, no longer pupil and teacher. It was a relationship that had matured over the years, just as she had matured, and nowadays, there was even ground between them. Whispers in the cloisters said that she was Sister Hildegarde's favorite child, a child now a woman, but a woman who had grown into something strong and magnificent.

"Ana!"

Now, Sister Hildegarde was shouting along with those thunderous footsteps. Anaxandra dun Muir looked up from the enormous bowl full of vegetables that she had been washing.

"Sister?" she called out. "In here."

Sister Hildegarde, as stout and strong as a Scottish pine, appeared in the doorway of the chamber used to prepare meals for the abbey. It was both kitchen and greenhouse. Outside, in the kitchen yard, two sisters were roasting a pig that had been slaughtered, and the smell of pork wafted in through the windows.

It would be a good supper of pork and beans tonight.

"There you are," Sister Hildegarde said in her stiff English accent. "You are supposed to be in the garden with the children."

Anaxandra picked up one of the turnips she'd just washed off and set it on the clean table beside her. "I left Christiana watching over the children," she said, her accent much the same because she'd practically been raised by the woman and picked up her speech patterns. "These were too heavy for them to carry in, so I did it. Why? Is something amiss?"

Sister Hildegarde frowned. "Aye," she said, pointing toward the ceiling. "What is amiss is that you have missed your time on the wall. Sister Cecelia has been waiting for you."

Frowning, Anaxandra rushed to the windows overlooking the garden, peering up at the angle of the sun. "My apologies," she said, quickly rushing back to the table with the turnips. "I did not realize it was so late. I lost track of the time."

"That is not unusual with you."

"I will try to do better, sister."

"God is watching and so am I. You'd better."

That was most definitely a threat, something not taken lightly. Punishment at St. Margaret's was for any infraction deemed serious enough. Knuckles slapped with a switch, or reading the Bible for hours on end, or any number of uncomfortable repercussions. Anaxandra had faced them before because she was a woman who spoke her mind at times and wasn't afraid of a confrontation.

That had worked against her in times past.

However, as serious as a threat of punishment could be, the truth was that Sister Hildegarde was more bark than bite, at least with Anaxandra. Part of the fun of their relationship was Anaxandra allowing Sister Hildegarde to think she was still afraid of her.

Well, mostly, anyway.

To prove that she was genuinely sorry that she'd lost track of the time, she began quickly fumbling with the ties of her apron. Sister Hildegarde grunted impatiently as she went to help her, pulling the apron off as Anaxandra yanked the kerchief off her head. Off came the gloves she'd been wearing as well, and she tossed them onto the table as she scurried out of the kitchen with Sister Hildegarde on her tail.

"We had two scouts out this morning, as we usually do, and they told us that there were men heading north along the sea road," she said. "Keep vigilant for anyone approaching."

They were weaving their way through the narrow corridors of St. Margaret's, sometimes squeezing past other nuns, sometimes passing through doorways that were too low for

Anaxandra's height. She was quite tall for a woman, sturdy and healthy because that was the way the nuns at St. Margaret's liked to raise their foundlings. They were not abused or neglected like so many, but rather nurtured and well tended. They were also educated—not only in the usual subjects of reading and writing, all based on biblical teachings, but taught the ways of combat and warfare.

That particular educational domain belonged to the abbess, Mother Michael.

In fact, most of what St. Margaret's had become was based on the teachings of Mother Michael. She was only the fourth mother abbess since St. Margaret's had been founded, a woman who had been indoctrinated since birth to everything the order stood for. The nuns always chose the mother's successor very early, in infancy, and Mother Michael had been an orphan who had been chosen as a baby by her predecessor. All she'd ever known was the intense and sometimes isolated training that was required for her to take her position as head of the order.

And it was Mother Michael who had personally trained Anaxandra. They considered her one of their top warriors, a woman who could fight better than most. She'd seen battle, f a few times, in minor skirmishes for the local Douglas clan, who tithed a good deal to the abbey for the very purpose of using their might in exchange for the donations, and in all instances, she'd done splendidly. There were whispers that Mother Michael wanted Anaxandra to assume the role as mother abbess someday, but that rumor was cast with doubt because Anaxandra hadn't been chosen as an infant, as had been tradition. Currently, however, there was no chosen successor to Mother Michael, so the uncertain future of the order fueled those rumors.

All Anaxandra knew was that she didn't want the position. She wanted something else.

A life outside of the order.

But this was her life for the moment, and she went about her duties to the best of her ability. That included her shift as a sentry, and as she walked through the convent, it was with a destination in mind. They were heading for the armory. Sister Hildegarde was still behind her, and together they marched in silence.

The nuns, postulates, and wards of St. Margaret's did not wear the usual garb. There were no nun habits, no holy robes, no mantles of glory. Everyone wore the same thing—breeches made from wool, or sometimes linen, everything undyed and in their mostly natural state. Over that, they wore two tunics—one that was tight against the skin to keep things like breasts or rolls of skin from moving about and creating sensations of lust, as Mother Michael had told them, and a second, longer tunic made of the same material as their breeches, that fastened around the waist and hung to their knees.

Upon their feet, instead of slippers or shoes, were boots. Everyone wore sensible boots that were made from the flesh of the cows or sheep or pigs that had been slaughtered for food over the years. Boots were recycled from one nun to another, just as the clothing was. Dead nuns had no use for clothes or shoes, so they were passed on to younger women. The particular pair that Anaxandra wore had belonged to a nun who had died in a skirmish with Willem the Lion, so they were shoes that she held dear.

The spirit of battle was upon them.

So was the blood of the former owner.

Rather than be put off by it, Anaxandra drew strength from

it. Sister Eve, long ago, had been a strong and resourceful woman, and Anaxandra imagined she could feel the woman's spirit upon her as she wore her boots. But there was protection to wear when one was on sentry duty, so Anaxandra stopped briefly in the armory near the cloister entry and gathered a mail coat while Sister Hildegarde collected a crossbow and bolts. There was a sense of urgency because the changing of the guard on the wall of St. Margaret's was something that was taken very seriously. Unlike any other abbey in England or Scotland, St. Margaret's of Loch Doom was a military installation, and instead of a traditional church and cloister, it was configured like a castle because, in fact, it had *been* a castle very long ago.

It had been the home of Lady Agnes Herries, then known as Whiteside Castle because of the white moss that grew upon the gray stones. The long-established legend was that Lady Agnes had been widowed when her husband was killed in battle, and, despondent, she prayed for forty days and forty nights before St. Margaret appeared before her and told her to find a fighting order of nuns in her name. Revenge for her husband's death was the motive for the fighting. Whether it was a fever dream or a genuine vision was still something of a debate within the church itself, but Lady Agnes turned the property over to the local diocese, became a beguine herself, and began recruiting other widows and unmarried young women for her holy female army.

That was only the beginning.

More widows joined, bringing their children. Other children, foundlings, were given over to the order to nurture, and, as an order strictly of women and mothers, sentient creatures who were, by nature, protective over the children they bore, the order became less holy and more military. It really wasn't even a holy order any longer. Women took up arms to protect those children, and each other, and those in need. If an abused woman came to the order seeking protection, they would be most happy protect her, and if the husband came looking for her… well, suffice it to say that more than one husband went missing if he came around, seeking his wife.

The odd and fearsome reputation of St. Margaret's formed.

It was purely by chance that it sat upon the banks of Loch Doom, which, many years ago, had actually been Loch Duine, but over the years, the "N" became an "M" because it suited the abbey more. The locals began to call them *Na Ban-Teamplairean*, or the Lady Templars, and their name and reputation spread. As Anaxandra finished dressing, she couldn't help but think about all of the women who came before her because the evidence of their lives was in this very room. So many shields that the Templar nuns had taken into battle. So many weapons they'd used to defend the weak. So many souls in this very room that reminded Anaxandra every day of how fortunate she was to serve with women who were fierce and brave. Even Sister Hildegarde, a woman who had been one of the fiercest until a skin cancer on her right hand took away the use of that hand, but no one would acknowledge that, least of all Sister Hildegarde. The cancer was trying very hard to spread up her arm and kill her, but she wasn't going to go down without a fight. She pretended that her world was still normal.

Anaxandra pretended right along with her.

Such was the courage of every woman at St. Margaret's.

"Come," Sister Hildegarde said as Anaxandra finished donning the mail coat. "You must mount the wall. Hurry, now. There is no time to waste."

Jolted from her reflections, Anaxandra slung the crossbow over her shoulder but didn't take the bolts because she was braiding her long blonde hair into a single braid to keep it out of her face. Still, she followed Sister Hildegarde to the narrow spiral stairs wedged into a three-story turret, stairs that led to the wall walk. That was where Sister Hildegarde came to a halt, handing over the bolts when Anaxandra finished braiding her hair. The bolts went in a quiver strung across her back and she swiftly mounted the steps up to the wall.

On the narrow wall walk, she could see that the previous sentry was still there, still vigilant as the afternoon waned. Usually, there were two of them on the wall at any given time, and as the previous sentry, having caught sight of her, disappeared down another turret, she could see another sentry on the opposite side of the complex, watching the north.

With that observation, Anaxandra took up position near the gatehouse entry. It wasn't a big gatehouse as far as gatehouses went, but it did have two levels, many windows to watch the countryside, and many murder holes in the floor by which to rain down terror upon any attackers.

Anaxandra settled down at her post in the gatehouse, watching the countryside, the hills, and, to the south, the glint of the sea beyond. Dark clouds were quickly approaching from the east and she could smell a storm upon the wind, the same wind that brought whiffs of sea and salt. Usually, sentry duty was a simple thing because no one in their right mind would attack or even approach St. Margaret's, but with news of a group of men traveling on the road that was just over the hill, Anaxandra would remain vigilant.

That vigilance was about to pay off.

St. Margaret's was ready for what was to come.

CHAPTER THREE

THE WOMAN WAS starting to regain consciousness.

They could all hear her making noise draped over Mateo's lap. Grunting and groaning, mostly. She moved a little, too, but not much. Not enough. She was in terrible shape, so there was no real chance of her fighting off five powerful men, and no one was really sure if she was trying, but she was definitely semiconscious. Mateo had to put his hand on her back to keep her from sliding off one way or the other as they thundered down a small road, heading east.

Behind them, the clouds were beginning to thunder.

Rain would soon be upon them. Estevan was in the lead of their group as they galloped down the road. They crested the rise of a hill, entering a small valley, made flat by the water runoff into the sea to the south, but there were rocks and trees and a gravelly, sandy road to travel upon. The road led down into the valley, and in little time, they could see a gray-stoned fortress about a mile away. The last of the sun gleamed off the bastion before the clouds covered up the rays, one by one, until there was no more sun and only the darkness of an approaching storm.

The rain was coming in fast.

Knowing this, Estevan spurred his horse faster, covering the ground to the fortress at a swift speed. He wanted to announce their arrival and ask for help for the woman, wondering if the Templar nuns were really as aggressive as he'd heard. Men tended to exaggerate, and he could only hope this was the case with St. Margaret's. He'd never been to this place, but he knew it was St. Margaret's simply because his family had a castle in the Lowlands called Ashkirk, and in the solar of that castle lay many maps of the area. He knew that because a short time ago, he'd studied the roads before he headed northward, refreshing his memory, and this was the location all of the maps showed St. Margaret's of Loch Doom.

As he drew near, he could hear a distant shout. He wasn't sure where it came from, but he looked to the walls of the castle-like abbey, hoping to see someone he could talk to. He hoped to gain their attention, to show he was no threat. He'd slowed his horse to a walk, heading for what looked like the gatehouse, when a big, nasty-looking bolt slammed into the ground a few feet in front of him.

Startled, he yanked his horse to a halt and the animal reared up, frightened by the violence of the bolt. He tried to back up, but another bolt landed behind him, this one too close for comfort. Clearly, whoever was firing the bolts didn't want him to go anywhere. More than that, they were quite skilled with the weapon. Pulling his horse to a complete halt, he raised one hand while holding the reins with the other.

"I am not bearing arms against ye," he called out, his deep voice echoing off the walls. "I come seeking help. Why do ye fire bolts at me?"

There was no answer, at least not immediately. His gaze was

on the gatehouse and he saw, clearly, when a figure moved inside. It was positioned between the windows facing west, keeping itself concealed. But he also saw when the figure stepped sideways, partially into the light, and he observed the crossbow that was once again loaded and pointed at him.

"Who are you?" a decidedly female voice called to him. "What do you want here?"

"I told ye," he replied. "I am seeking help."

"We have no help to give you," she said. "Move along."

Estevan shook his head. "Ye misunderstand," he said. "My brother and cousins and I found a woman on the riverbank, nearly drowned. She's still alive, but she needs tending. Ye must have someone that can help her."

By this time, Kaladin and Mateo and Titan and Rodion were catching up to him, with Mateo having an obvious body slung over his thighs. They saw the bolts both before Estevan and behind him and came to a quick stop, staying well out of range of the bolts that were evidently flying from the walls.

Overhead, the thunder rolled.

"You will stay there and not move," the woman said. "And those men with you—tell them to stay back."

"I will," Estevan said. "I've no desire tae have a bolt shoved through my chest on this day. Or any day. It would bring my mother tae yer door, and ye'd not be pleased tae see her."

There was no reply, but he could see more figures in the gatehouse now, looking down at him. There was whispering going on. Behind him, someone must have made a move that didn't please the nuns because another bolt came flying out, zinging past Estevan and landing between him and the group about twenty feet back. He turned around to see Titan slap Kaladin in the arm, moving him back because he'd drifted forward a few feet.

That wasn't to be tolerated by the nuns.

"Ye've no reason tae fire those bolts at us," Estevan said, trying not to sound angry. "We'll obey yer wishes, but if ye hit one of us with those bolts, I'll bring my entire family down here and we'll burn this bloody place tae the ground, and ye with it. Do ye understand me?"

"Who are you?"

This was a different voice. Estevan now found himself looking at a woman with white hair and a thin, pale face, dressed in some kind of tunic from the waist up. That was all he could see from the window she was leaning out of. Her voice was low, almost mournful.

But deadly serious.

"Well?" she said again, before he could reply. "Who are you?"

"My name is Estevan dun Tarh," he said without hesitation. "My father is Lares dun Tarh, the Earl of Torridon. Behind me is my brother, Kaladin, and my cousins Titan de Wolfe, Mateo de Wolfe, and Rodion de Velt. If ye dunna know those family names, then ye should. They are the biggest houses on the border."

The woman seemed to be looking them all over. "I know those names," she said. "I know de Wolfe. And all the world fears de Velt. And dun Tarh… your father is Lucifer."

Lucifer's Legion.

Truthfully, Estevan wasn't surprised that even the Templar nuns had heard of his father, because Lucifer's Legion was what the sons of Lares dun Tarh were called. As one of the most unique clans in the Highlands, the dun Tarh name was known all over the country. Even down here in the Lowlands, and most especially among the religious orders. Anyone who made a pledge to the devil, as rumor had it that Lares had done, was known to those who feared the fires of hell.

Estevan was well aware of it all.

And he could play it to his advantage.

"He is, indeed," he said. "If ye know our families as ye say ye do, then ye know we are men of our word. We mean ye no harm, at least not at the moment, but that could change if ye fire another bolt at us. As I explained tae the other lass, we found this woman on the riverbank and she needs help. We're happy tae deliver her tae yer gate and then leave ye in peace."

More thunder rolled overhead, and the sky picked that moment to let loose. A deluge of rain and wind descended, complete with lightning rippling across the sky. The horses startled, shifting around nervously as the weather quickly grew intolerable. The woman with the white hair took a step back, away from the windowsill, so the driving rain wouldn't soak her.

"We are not a healing order," she said, now shouting over the elements.

Estevan cocked an eyebrow. "As someone said tae me, if ye fight as rumor says ye do, then ye have someone tae heal those wounded in battle," he said. But his patience was at an end. "Christ, woman, we've not come tae rob or molest ye. We found this woman on the riverbank. She's very ill. We've brought her tae ye for tending and that is all. Will ye not help her?"

Just as he finished speaking, a lightning bolt hit the top of a tree about a quarter of a mile down the road. The tree exploded, sending shards of wood flying into the air. The noise was so loud that even Estevan jumped, startled.

"Christ," he muttered to himself. "We're going tae be killed where we stand."

The woman with white hair must have thought the same thing, because the next Estevan realized, the enormous gates were rolling open and a dozen armed women appeared, half of them with crossbows pointing right at Estevan and his kin. Above the open gates, the white-haired woman was waving her hand from the window.

"Enter," she said. "Hurry, now. Come in and be sheltered."

More lightning flashed across the sky, and unless they wanted to be killed, shelter was necessary. Estevan spurred his horse forward, followed by the rest of them. All five of them moved into the gatehouse, which had a low ceiling. So low, in fact, that the men were forced to dismount or risk smacking heads on the stone ceiling.

Back in the pack, Titan had dismounted and made his way over to Mateo, taking the woman from him so the man could dismount his horse. With a limp, wet woman slung across both arms, Titan made his way to the front, where Estevan was being corralled by the same gang of women who'd opened the gates.

A rather fearsome gang of women.

"Where shall we put her?" Estevan asked.

He wasn't sure whom he was addressing because there were several of them, all armed, all staring him down as if expecting him to start trouble. They were all poised as if waiting to pounce. Truthfully, he'd never seen anything like it. But the white-haired woman moved into their midst, putting herself between the men and the armed women.

"To the sanctuary," she said, pointing to the north, where an enormous hall stood. "We shall tend her there."

More thunder shook the very ground and the rain was coming in sheets. The white-haired woman turned to the group behind her, snapping commands, and the woman with the crossbow, the one who had fired on them from the gatehouse, motioned for them to follow her. As they stepped out into the hammering rain, heads down as they headed for the sanctuary, the armed gang of women closed ranks behind them and followed them not only to the sanctuary, but inside as well.

Once they were in the dark, cool interior, the world was strangely silent.

The thick walls of the sanctuary drowned out the sound of the rain for the most part. The thunder could still be heard, though distantly. Estevan and the others found themselves looking at what had evidently once been a great hall, with a soaring ceiling, hard-packed earthen floors, and ventilation windows cut high on the walls. On the northern end, an altar had been built, but a massive firepit, original to the hall, remained in the middle of vast chamber. The supports that held up the roof had been painted with bright colors, once, but those colors had long since faded.

The sanctuary seemed old, dark, and dull.

Someone went over to the firepit and began to put fuel in it as the five men, with the limp woman, stood back by the entry. Frankly, they were afraid to move, afraid that one of those grim-looking women would put a sword through them if they so much as breathed in the wrong direction.

As they stood there in an uncertain bunch, other women began bringing in blankets and pieces of wood and canvas that ended up being a bed once they put it together. They moved the bed to the wall across from the firepit, which was just starting to flame. They put the blankets upon it, and the pillow. The woman with the crossbow, who had been standing a few feet away from them, motioned to the bed.

"You may put her down," she said.

Mateo carried the woman over to the bed, carefully laying her down. Estevan was beside him, assisting him by swinging her legs up onto the bed, but the moment they laid her down, she suddenly twitched. An arm flailed upward, striking Mateo in the face. As he stumbled back, surprised by the blow, the woman suddenly came alive.

"*Låt mig vara!*" she said in a raspy voice. "*Lämna mig!*"

No one had any idea what language she was speaking. Having no knowledge of where she was, or whom she was with, the woman pitched herself off the bed and ended up landing heavily on her backside. All flailing arms and scrambling legs, she ended up pressed against the stone wall, gazing at those around her with utter terror in her expression.

"Vem är du?" she cried. "Var är jag?"

Estevan was the closest to her. Seeing how frightened she was, he crouched down several feet away, tossing back his cloak and holding out his hands to show he had no weapons.

"Be at ease, lady," he said steadily. "No one will hurt ye, I promise."

The woman didn't understand him. She was sick and injured, and her eyes had a wild look about them. He remained still, unmoving, but behind him, Kaladin took a step out from behind Titan to gain a better look and the woman started shrieking again.

"Låt mig vara!"

Estevan glanced over his shoulder, enough to see Kaladin looking guilty and Titan grabbing him by the arm, pulling him back.

"*Stop,*" Estevan commanded softly. "Any movement has the woman in a panic, so stop moving."

That was true, and everyone seemed to still themselves, frozen. At least, the men were. Titan had a viselike grip on Kaladin to keep the young warrior from doing what he did best—disobeying commands. Therefore, they were all rooted to the spot.

But the women were moving.

The woman with the white hair slowly approached the frightened woman, extending the cross that was draped around her neck. It was wooden, and simple, but there was no mistaking what it represented.

"Be at ease, lady," she said soothingly. "We will help you. Come—get back to your bed. Come, now."

She kept holding her cross in front of her, making sure the woman could see it. The woman did, and perhaps that eased her a bit, enough to allow the woman with the white hair to gently grasp her by the arm. Another woman rushed forward, taking hold of the other arm, and together they managed to get the injured woman back onto her bed.

Estevan remained crouched where he was, afraid to move because it might set the injured woman off again, but the woman with the white hair caught his eye.

"You and your men will back away," she said quietly. "Back to the entry. And stay there."

Estevan obeyed. He moved away carefully, not making any sudden moves, with Titan and Mateo and Rodion and Kaladin following. The five of them headed to the other side of the sanctuary, taking their bags and weapons with them.

They made for an uneasy group. They'd only intended to leave the woman at the abbey and continue on to Dumfries, but the storm outside was rough. No one wanted to be out in it. Therefore, they were at the mercy of the sisters, who seemed to want to follow them around with weapons pointed right at their bellies. They were still lingering on the fringes of the sanctuary, undoubtedly waiting for one of them to make a wrong move.

But there were no wrong moves to make.

If they wanted to stay dry, and alive, then they would have to be compliant.

"Kal," Estevan finally said, "see tae the horses. Make sure they have shelter and food for the night."

Kaladin looked at him with surprise. "We're staying here?"

"Would ye rather be out in this storm?" Estevan said. "Think, Bully. We need shelter, and here we have it."

He had a point. As if to emphasize it, thunder rolled overhead and shook the very walls. However, Kaladin wasn't entirely in agreement. He wanted to be on the road to The Butcher's, but he had to admit that the storm was fierce. With no other recourse, he started to move on his brother's order. Unfortunately, that movement brought some of those armed women out of the shadows. They came toward him with weapons raised and Kaladin came to a halt. With frustration, he pointed to the door.

"I must see tae the horses," he told them. "Will someone show me where I can bed them?"

The woman with the crossbow was by the door. She stepped forward, pushing her way through the group of women, facing the very tall, and very big, Scotsman.

"They are safe at the gatehouse," she said, eyeing him as if both fearful and defiant at the same time. "When the rain stops, you may go to them."

Kaladin was trying to be both polite and patient. "We dunna know when the rain will stop," he said. "Those horses have been running since early this morning. They need food and proper rest, not simply standing at the gatehouse as we wait for the rain tae stop. Please let me tend tae them."

The woman was hesitant. She was about to refuse again when Estevan put himself between the lady and his brother, his intense gaze fixed on the woman with the crossbow.

"Lady," he said, his patience brittle, "those are expensive horses and they're like members of the family, so ye'll understand our need tae have them tended. If ye have an aversion tae my brother, then I'll go. Ye can escort me. I want nothing more than tae bed them properly and give them some food. I'll pay for the food, I swear it."

The woman with the crossbow was gazing at him with big, blue eyes, slightly tilted upward at the outer corners. Her blonde hair was very long, and very straight, braided, but there were tendrils around her face. He got a better look at her here, in the weak light of the sanctuary, and he had to admit that she was a pretty thing. She was almost delicate looking, like she should be sitting in a palace somewhere with glass slippers on her feet and rubies in her hair. She didn't look like a fearsome Templar nun, but he knew she could use that crossbow with skill he'd only seen in seasoned knights.

Perhaps if she had a warrior's soul, she had a warrior's compassion.

"Please?" he pressed. "I'll leave all of my weapons here. I just want tae see tae our horses."

She sighed sharply, lifting the wisps of hair around her mouth. "Very well," she said. "Come with me."

Estevan did. He followed her out of the sanctuary and into the driving rain, only they weren't alone. There were at least six women following him, their swords and crossbows pointing right at his back. He was a big man, and strong, with enormous hands and power, but even he thought having all of these woman following him was a little ridiculous. Normally, he didn't mind women following him, but this was different.

It was a different world altogether.

They found the horses in the gatehouse entry where they had left them. All of the animals were warhorses, seasoned and strong. Titan's horse didn't let anyone touch him but his master, but he was so exhausted that even he let Estevan gather his reins without a fuss. Estevan managed to gather three of them but struggled with the fourth. That had the woman with the crossbow stepping in to collect the last two. She began to lead them away from the gatehouse, out into the rainy bailey.

Estevan followed.

The stable for the abbey wasn't very large. In fact, part of it was in an old outbuilding, and then a shelter with a sloping roof was attached to it. A cow, a calf, some goats, and several chickens were in a corner of the outbuilding portion, trying to stay warm, and the woman with the crossbow brought the two horses she was leading straight into the outbuilding. That unnerved the cow and the goats a little, and they pressed further into a corner as all five horses were finally brought in, crowded, but that couldn't be helped. Once they were tied off, Estevan began removing the gear and saddles.

All the while, the woman with the crossbow watched. She watched him carefully remove the saddle of Rodion's steed and set everything down against the wall of the stable before moving on to the next one. He was working methodically, quickly, but the horses were tired and hungry and restless, so she finally slung the crossbow over her shoulder and moved to the horse closest to her. Deftly, she untied the cinch and pulled the very heavy saddle off. Mimicking what Estevan was doing, she put it neatly against the wall before moving to the next horse.

Soon enough, all five horses were free of their saddles, but Estevan took the saddle blanket from his own horse and began rubbing the animals down. The woman with the crossbow abruptly departed, leaving him wondering why she'd left him alone when she was so suspicious of his movements, but he soon found out. When she returned, it was with a few other women carrying buckets of water and oats. Lots of oats, filled to the brim of the buckets. Soon enough, all of the horses were slurping water and munching on the grain.

"That is almost all the oats we have," the woman with the crossbow said. "You will have to find us more, since your horses are eating our supply."

Estevan was standing at the head of his own horse, watching the animal blow out puffs of oats and dust with his head shoved into the bucket like it was.

"We'll go intae Dumfries in the morning and buy twice what ye've given us," he said. "What else do ye need?"

She looked at him, puzzled. "What do you mean?"

He came away from the horse's head. "Just what I said," he said. "What more do ye need? Food? Meat? Drink? My mother will take a stick tae me if she knows I ate yer food and dinna replace it and then some. Therefore, tell me what more ye need and I'll purchase it tomorrow."

She regarded him a moment. Truthfully, Estevan found himself looking at her also. They were both studying one another, not quite suspiciously, more out of curiosity. Estevan was quite curious about her, actually. His initial observation about her beauty was not wrong. Beneath the dirt, messy hair, and mannish clothing, she was exquisite. She was also tall, with long arms and legs. A little slender for his liking, but he was certain every ounce of her was strong from the way she'd handled that crossbow.

A unique woman, indeed.

"I will have to ask Mother Michael if we need anything more," she finally said. "Your offer is generous."

He shook his head. "I dunna think it is generous enough," he said. "Ye're giving us shelter from the storm. Ye dinna have tae, but ye showed mercy. We appreciate it."

"We could not very well turn you away once the lightning threatened," she said. "Are you finished with your horses now?"

He looked at the five snorting, crunching horses. "I think so," he said. "But I'll need tae check on them once they've finished eating tae make sure they're settling down for the night."

"Then mayhap you should remain here until they are done."

He nodded. "That would be a good idea," he said. "If ye'll allow it."

She nodded her silent reply, but she stepped outside where the gang of women and weapons were still gathered. A couple of them had helped bring in the oats and water, but for the most part, they were still armed, still waiting for him to make a wrong move.

He wasn't going to give them the satisfaction.

With the women hissing at each other outside the door, he went to check on his own horse, bending over to feel a fetlock, but in reality, he was listening to what the women were saying. It was clear that they were very nervous having men in the compound, and several of them were advocating to chase the men back out into the storm. But the woman with the crossbow held firm, wielding the name of Mother Michael like a weapon.

It shut the other women up fairly quickly. Soon enough, the group disbanded except for a couple of them still lingering by the stable door.

"You can bed down here for the night with the horses," the woman with the crossbow said as she entered the stable. "Your friends will remain in the cathedral."

He nodded, giving his horse a pat on the hindquarters. "As ye wish," he said. "Or we can all sleep in the stable with the horses. There's plenty of dried grass tae lie on."

"I think it is better if you stay where you are."

He cocked his head, looking at her curiously as he leaned on the back of his horse. "What are ye so afraid of?" he asked. "We told ye that we meant ye no harm. We've not shown any aggression since we arrived, yet ye still treat us as if we've done something wrong."

Her expression remained hard. "You are men," she said simply. "Men are not to be trusted."

He nodded. "I see," he said. "And ye've known enough men that ye can make this judgment?"

A ripple of confusion crossed her brow. "Nay," she said. "But the world is a terrible state right now because men do not trust one another. Why should I trust them if they cannot trust each other? Why should I trust you?"

"Because I'm not making war upon ye," he said softly. "I'm an honorable man, lass. All of the men with me are honorable. Such a thing does exist, I assure ye."

Her hard expression was wavering. "It… it is better if we do not trust you," she said. "Trust is a weakness, and we will not show weakness."

He smiled faintly. "Trust is stronger than the mightiest army," he said. "It can move mountains. Do ye consider yer friends weak?"

He was motioning to the women outside the stable. He could just see the tops of their heads from this angle. The woman turned slightly, catching sight of them, before returning her focus to Estevan.

"Of course not," she said. "None of us are weak."

"But ye trust them."

"With my life."

"Using yer logic, does that not make ye weak?"

He was using her words against her and she didn't like that. "I said that it is better if we do not trust *you*," she said. "I never said anything about not trusting my friends."

He grunted. "Then what applies tae men does not apply tae women."

"That is a fair statement."

His gaze lingered on her for a moment. "My name is Estevan," he said. "I know it's not a usual name for a Scotsman, but my family descends from the Spaniards who came with the Romans. It's tradition in my family for the children tae have names that come from Asturias or Castille or Aragon. May I ask yer name, lass?"

"You may not."

He chuckled. He couldn't help it. He started laughing and turned away from her, back to his horse, bending over again to check the animal's legs and purge thoughts of that stubborn woman from his mind. No matter how pretty she was, it didn't overcome that bullish manner. But his laughter eventually faded and he resorted to ignoring her. If she wasn't going to at least be polite, he didn't need to bother himself over her.

So he didn't.

It made for a long, cold night.

CHAPTER FOUR

G OD, HE WAS handsome when he smiled.

She hadn't been expecting that.

Anaxandra's heart did a strange leap when the man who had introduced himself as Estevan laughed at her response when he asked for her name. For a woman who had spent zero time around men in general, and had hardly even had any contact with them her entire life, the introduction of five very big, very strong warriors into her midst was a bit overwhelming.

And intimidating.

She was trying not to lose her head about it.

She was curious about men in general. How they spoke, how they acted, how they ate, how they fought. Aye, even how they fought. Since she'd been trained since birth as a warrior, she wanted to know everything she could about it. It was her vocation, her trade. It was all she knew. But the truth was that she'd only been surrounded by women her entire life, women who knew how to fight, but women nonetheless.

Unfortunately, she had been taught to both fear and shun men. That was how the order functioned. Since it was founded by a widow, and not a nun or a saint, it had a different set of rules. Of course, they prayed every day, on the liturgical schedule. And that was to keep the church happy so they could continue to benefit from the rules that applied to the Catholic Church. But beyond that, things got a little different.

It wasn't so much that they were taught chastity and abstinence, more that they were simply taught that men were vile creatures not to be trusted. Killing wasn't discouraged, not even really between each other, so the whole of the abbey functioned like some kind of weird civilization where the women traveled in packs.

That was the dark truth of it.

Anyone coming to visit, such as a visiting nun or even a priest, were discouraged to dig deeper than what they saw on the surface because of the feral way in which the order tended to function. Anaxandra was part of the Bow Pack, a group of women who had been primarily trained in the crossbow. There was the Foot Pack and the Animal Pack, to name a couple others. All of the packs would pray together and attend mass together, but when it came to actually functioning outside of the sanctuary, they tended to stick to one another.

Mother Michael did not discourage it.

In fact, she would use the packs against one another for training purposes, as she would call it. Anaxandra thought that maybe it was because she enjoyed watching women fight one another more than they were actually training, and sometimes people did become badly injured. When the warriors had brought the wounded woman to their doorstep with the logic that if they were a fighting order, then they had healers within, they had not been wrong. The order did indeed have women whose sole purpose was healing.

And those were the women who wielded the most power.

In the midst of all of this, they actually did have a few legitimate nuns, and those women basically ran the abbey. Sister Hildegarde was one of them. They tended the foundlings and delivered the education, cooked, sewed, and did any number of other odd jobs. Those women were usually the kindest of the bunch, surprisingly, and tended to stay neutral in any given conflict. But the workings of St. Margaret's of Loch Doom were much more than the outside world knew.

And that wasn't necessarily a good thing.

Therefore, when they had strangers in their midst, as they did now, everyone seemed to be on high alert. Suspicion was the order of the day, especially if those strangers were male. All Anaxandra knew was that she was both curious and fearful of the visitors. Curious because it was her nature, fearful because she'd been told to be. The truth was that she wanted to speak to the man in the stables. She was wildly curious about the outside world, the world he lived in, and wanted to know about it. She wanted to ask him where he had been, where he was from, and anything else that came to mind. More than almost anyone at St. Margaret's, Anaxandra was very curious about the Outworld. That was what they called it here.

The Outworld.

They had men from another world in their midst.

But she was behaving the way she was taught to behave toward them. It wasn't the way she *wanted* to behave. As she stood by the door, listening to the rain pound, she watched him as he tended one of the horses. She assumed it was his. Behind her, in the part of the stable that was more exposed to the elements, the two women with crossbows that had been left behind had fanned out to find better shelter from the rain. They were still close by if she needed them, but they'd settled into the shadows for the night.

Cautiously, she stepped back into the stable.

He was still bent over his horse, his hand on the front-left fetlock. He seemed to be feeling for something because he kept going back and forth between the front legs, comparing one against the other. She watched for a moment, opening her mouth to speak at one point but then quickly clamping it shut again.

But her hesitation didn't last long.

"What's wrong with him?" she asked.

Estevan's head came up and he looked at her. "I'm not sure there's anything wrong with him," he said. "His left leg feels hot tae the touch, but I canna be sure."

"Do you require a poultice?"

He shook his head. "I dunna think so," he said, looking back at the horse. "Give it some time. If it still feels hot in a little while, then mayhap ye'll be kind enough tae help. Clay mud will do, if ye have any around here."

She shook her head. "Not clay," she said. "But these grounds used to be a moor. The mud is rich with compost."

He nodded. "Thank ye for telling me," he said. "If I need the mud, I can gather it outside."

She nodded in return but didn't reply. His gaze lingered on her for a moment before returning to his horse. Anaxandra found herself wrestling against the urge to speak to him more than she already had, knowing she shouldn't but too curious for her own good. She wasn't entirely sure he would even speak to her, given their interaction from the moment she'd fired bolts to stop him to this very moment. She hadn't exactly been a welcoming conversationalist. Arching her neck, just a little, to make sure the other women guards were far enough away so that they couldn't hear any discussion, she stepped over next to the wall, leaning against it.

"Anaxandra," she said softly.

He didn't react for a moment. But then he realized there was no one else in the stable but the two of them, so he looked at her curiously.

"Did ye say something?" he said.

She nodded. "I said that my name was Anaxandra," she said. Then she shrugged. "You asked, after all."

Something in his pale eyes seemed to warm a little. "I did," he said. "Anax…?"

"Anaxandra."

"An unusual name," he said. "Are ye named for someone?"

She shook her head. "I do not know," she said. "I came to St. Margaret's as an infant, a foundling. I do not know where the name comes from, but it means 'defender of the people.'"

He smiled faintly. "Is that what ye were told?"

"It is."

"My name means 'crown.'"

"Does that mean you are royal, then?"

He snorted softly. "Nay," he said. "Not even close."

"But you said your father was the Earl of Torridon."

"That does not make him royal," Estevan said. "But he does have old bloodlines. We all do."

"We?"

"My brothers and sisters."

"How many?"

"Seven brothers, two sisters."

Her eyes widened. "Such a big family?"

He nodded. "There are ten of us," he said. Then he threw a thumb in the direction of the sanctuary. "My younger brother is with me. Kaladin. Ye almost killed him with yer bolts. Ye almost killed me, too."

She shook her head. "Untrue," she said. "If I had wanted to kill you, I would have. I simply prevented you from approaching the gatehouse too closely."

"Why?"

She seemed surprised by the question. "Because you do not belong here," she said. "We discourage any visitors. Especially male visitors."

"But we aren't visitors," he said. "We brought a sick woman we found by the river. In fact, were it not for the weather, we would be in Dumfries now, cozy in a gambling room, losing all of our money. So, I suppose I should be thankful for the weather."

Anaxandra pondered his statement curiously. "Gambling room," she repeated. "What is that?"

"Where men go tae gamble."

"What is gamble?"

He thought she might be teasing him, but from the expression on her face, he could tell that she was serious. He had to remind himself that the woman had grown up in an abbey. He was fairly certain that the subject of gambling had not been part of her upbringing.

"Well," he said, stepping away from the horse and reaching down to pick up two sprigs of dried grass. He extended one to her. "Let's say this is a gold coin and it belongs tae ye. Take it."

Hesitantly, she did. "What do I do with it?"

He held up the other sprig. "This is my gold coin," he said. "Now, let's say ye feel strongly that it is going tae stop raining by the time ye count tae five."

She cocked an eyebrow. "It is *not* going to stop raining by the time I count to five."

He held up a hand, begging for patience. "I know," he said. "But for the sake of argument, let's say ye feel strongly about it. Now, I tell ye that it is *not* going tae stop raining by the time ye count tae five. Ye believe so strongly that ye're right that ye tell me if ye're wrong, ye'll give me yer cold coin."

She was following him closely, realizing he was speaking of the dried grass in her hand. "This?" she said, holding it up. "I'll give you this if I'm wrong?"

"Aye," he said. "I accept yer wager and tell ye that if ye win, I'll give ye *my* gold coin. But if not, ye give me yers. One of us will have two coins in the end. That is a gamble."

She had to think about what he'd just said. After a moment, her brow furrowed. "Why should men want to do that?"

"Because it can make ye rich."

"Gambling can?"

He nodded. "Rich if ye win, poor if ye dunna."

She was still frowning. "And you do it for the money?"

He shrugged, smiling lazily. "For money," he said. "Or for whatever a man is willing tae wager. Food, horses, wine—a man can bet anything he wants in a game of chance."

The concept was quite foreign. Anaxandra was standing there, pondering a game that made no sense to her, when they both heard shouting. The women outside the stable made a break for the muddy bailey beyond, crossbows lifted. But there was still more shouting going on and there seemed to be a good deal of frantic women rushing about, some with clubs.

Puzzled, and startled, Anaxandra dashed out of the stable.

Estevan followed.

As the rain pounded, they ended up in the bailey. Visibility was difficult with the mist, even with some of the women bearing fat-burning torches, but Estevan could see clearly enough that he saw Kaladin outside of the sanctuary. He was the one shouting, telling the women to back away, but the moment he caught sight of his brother, he began to rush in his direction.

That was when Estevan realized the man had a bolt sticking out of his upper arm.

"Do ye see what they did tae me?" Kaladin was shouting to him, outraged. "They shot me!"

Estevan reached out to steady him. "Ye knew they would," he said incredulously. "They've been threatening tae fire at us since we arrived. Why did ye provoke them?"

Kaladin was furious. "Because ye went away and dinna return," he said. "For all I knew, they were holding ye captive somewhere. I demanded tae know where ye'd gone, but no one could tell me. So I came looking for ye and they shot me."

Now, Estevan was furious. Furious at his brother, furious at these foolish, nervous females. Anaxandra was next to him, looking at Kaladin with some concern, and he whirled on her.

"Is this what ye do?" he demanded, indicating his brother. "Ye shoot a bolt intae an unarmed man? Are the lot of ye truly so stupid and panicky that ye'd do this when all he wanted tae do was know where I'd gone?"

Surprisingly, she didn't rise to his anger. The truth was that she didn't know how to respond, so she simply reached out and grasped Kaladin by the arm.

"Come along," she said steadily. "We must go back to the sanctuary. We can remove the bolt there."

Estevan was livid, but he did as she suggested. With him on one side of Kaladin and Anaxandra on the other, they managed to get him back into the sanctuary, where Titan, Mateo, and

Rodion were waiting. They grabbed Kaladin, taking him from Estevan and pulling him back into the vast hall. That left Estevan to deal with the nervous nuns who had fired on his brother.

But he quickly saw that he didn't have to.

Anaxandra was already interrogating the group that had been left behind, angrily gesturing toward Kaladin. Mostly, she was met with quiet resistance, as if no one wanted to incriminate themselves, but one woman evidently spoke up and admitted it. The next thing Estevan realized, Anaxandra slapped the woman across the face so hard that she stumbled backward and tripped over her feet. As she fell to one knee, Anaxandra stood over her, scolding her, grabbing her by the hair and pulling it.

That made Estevan back off.

He'd never seen a woman behave like that. Anaxandra was clearly in charge, clearly respected by the other women, but he also took a moment to look at the others. Each one of them wore the same tunic, the same breeches, bearing weapons and looking as far from feminine figures as possible. And what Anaxandra was doing was something a trainer or a commander would do. She was dispensing discipline in a way that would teach the offender a lesson. A painful lesson, but a lesson nonetheless. He'd never, in his life, seen a woman strike another woman like that. His mother and her spanking didn't count. This was far more of a disciplinary blow.

It was rather fascinating.

But also very strange.

What kind of place is *this?* he thought.

Behind him, an unearthly howl rose and he turned in time to see Titan ripping the bolt from Kaladin's shoulder. It was really his upper arm, but the moment he did it, Rodion slapped a rag over it, something he'd had in his saddlebags, to stanch the blood flow. He went over to his brother, kneeling down beside him as Rodion and Mateo were trying to stem the blood.

"It's not serious," Titan told him. "They caught him in the meat of the arm, but we should rinse it with wine or ale to keep the poison away."

Estevan was relieved to hear that. He raked his fingers through his dark hair wearily. "Good," he said. "I dunna want tae spend any more time here than necessary. As soon as this rain stops, we depart. Wound or no wound."

Titan couldn't disagree. "There is something odd about this place," he muttered. "These women… they are not nuns, Es. But the woman we brought here—she's speaking a language I've heard before."

Estevan looked at him. "Where have ye heard it?"

"North," Titan said. "You have heard it, too. It's the language of the Northmen."

Estevan frowned. "Are ye sure?"

Titan nodded. "Aye," he said. "Rodion has heard it, too."

Rodion was focused on the bloody rag he was holding against Kaladin's arm. "I heard it," he said. "You know that language, Es. The princes of the isles are all around your father's earldom. Or, at least, they used to be. Did you not recognize what she said?"

Estevan shook his head. "I admit, I wasna listening closely," he said. "It sounded like…"

"*Låt mig vara*," Rodion said. "Think—do you know those words?"

Estevan thought hard. It was true that the language of the Northmen wasn't a stranger to the Highlands, and when he'd been very young, he'd had a friend who spoke the language a little because his parents were exiles from the Northman lands.

Låt mig vara.

"Leave me?" he finally said. "I think that's part of what she said, but I dunna know the rest. It has been a very long time since I've heard that language spoken."

"I do not know if the mother abbess knows," Rodion said. "She's been with the woman since you left, trying to calm her, but she does not seem to know her words."

Estevan looked across the sanctuary, where the white-haired woman was indeed bent over the cot of the injured lady. The woman seemed to be listless because he could see that she was squirming about, lifting a hand every so often.

"Should I offer tae communicate with her?" he said. "I dunna know how much good I'll be, but I can try."

"Mayhap you should," Rodion said, looking over to the injured woman also. "It might help establish some trust here. And mayhap they'll be willing to provide us with a little food."

He had a point. They'd been traveling all day and were hungry. With a nod, Estevan stood up and went over to the area where the injured woman was now lying with her hand over her eyes. The white-haired woman and a couple of other women were in a huddle, whispering amongst themselves. But that all ended when they caught sight of Estevan.

"I dunna mean tae intrude," he said when he saw that he had their attention. "But I think I may know her language."

The white-haired woman looked at him in surprise. "You do?" she said. "Why did you not say so before?"

Estevan shook his head. "Truthfully, I wasn't sure," he said. "She was speaking quickly and I simply dinna recognize what she was saying. I can try tae communicate with her if ye want me tae."

The white-haired woman looked at the woman on the makeshift bed. She had settled down now and was sleeping fitfully, so after some deliberation, the woman with the white hair shook her head.

"Let her sleep," she said. "If you are here in the morning, mayhap we can try to communicate with her then. But for now, she needs sleep."

"As ye wish."

"What language is it?"

"The language of the Northmen."

That seemed to bring the woman pause. She eyed him dubiously for a moment, deliberating as to whether he was right. She didn't seem to think so, but she wasn't going to outright disagree with him.

"I suppose we shall find out on the morrow," she said. "Return to your men. We shall speak upon the morning."

Estevan nodded, but he didn't leave. "As ye wish," he said. "But we've not eaten all day. Can we pay for a meal?"

The woman hesitated a moment before reluctantly nodding. "Aye," she said. "It will not be fancy."

"As long as it's filling."

She waved a hand in the direction of the men on the other side of the sanctuary. "Go, now," she said. "I will have food brought to you."

"Thank ye," he said. "May I ask what we should call ye?"

"I am Mother Michael."

"Thank ye, Yer Grace."

"Nay," she said, shaking her head. "Simply Mother Michael will do."

Estevan nodded, finally heading back to the men in the corner. The bleeding had stopped on Kaladin's shoulder and

Rodion was trying to see how bad the injury was as Estevan walked up.

"Well?" Titan said. "What did she say?"

Estevan watched Rodion work. "She'll send us food," he said. "But we are tae stay right here until morning unless we want any more bolts launched at us."

No one really wanted that. It was still raining furiously outside and the lightning was still bursting through the sky, illuminating the windows of the sanctuary from time to time. It was nearing sunset, so there was no reason to try to make it to Dumfries that night.

So much for The Butcher's.

True to Mother Michael's word, food was brought about a half-hour later, including ale that tasted like dirt, but it was better than nothing. The food consisted of a rich, savory stew of pork and beans with carrots and turnips, and Estevan was quite surprised that it was so delicious. The five of them ate until they could hold no more and drank the ale that gave them a strong buzz. It was enough to put all of them to sleep quickly.

It had been a long day.

As the storm raged and the sanctuary settled down into cold, still darkness, the snoring of the warriors could be heard. But they weren't alone. Anaxandra watched them, vigilantly, all night.

And one of them in particular.

CHAPTER FIVE

THEY FOUND THE remains of the boat.

Traveling in their vessel, smeared with mud and lines of charcoal above the waterline that was meant to make it blend in with the fog, the boat had traveled along the current for several weeks.

Following.

They knew that if they followed the currents, they would find her.

Drottningen.

The queen.

She had escaped them. At first, they'd kept her tightly locked in a cold, crumbling pele tower to ensure she would remain safe for always, a treasure to be proud of. For certain, it had taken years of missives, skirmishes, and negotiations with the men who lived on the outer isles, not terribly far from those who lived on the island known as Mann. The Manx lived there, descendants of the Northman raiders who still controlled some of the smaller islands and waterways on the west coast of Scotland.

But these men weren't Manx.

They were different.

In fact, they were hardly men at all.

They lived on the northern tip of the island, amongst the scrubby forests, the dead and broken trees, down in the vales that had been carved away by the sea over the centuries. They lived in rock cottages, half dug into the ground, and used branches and foliage as cover. Dirt cloaked their skin, mud masked their hair, and they spoke a language that no one could understand. The decent folk of the isle wouldn't go to the northern tip where these men lived, fearful of being cursed by their very existence. Everyone feared the Ormsfolk.

The Serpent People.

The same people who had followed the *Drottningen*.

And they were going to find her.

But that had been a difficult task. In spite of the reclusive and odd ways of the Ormsfolk, part of their culture was fishing. They had boats that they'd fashioned from wood from their forests and took to the seas easily. It had been one of those boats that the queen had taken in the dead of night, under a full moon, and sailed away on the current, for she knew how to sail a ship. She knew how to use currents. She was from a culture that lived on the sea, so the water was to her as land was to most men.

She thrived on it.

But the Serpent People knew the currents, too. They simply followed the tides by day, stopping only at night to search for signs of the queen. They were going on the assumption that the queen was a weak woman and would understandably need to stop at night to sleep. That had been their logic, anyway. Therefore, they'd stopped often, searching for the woman, stealing what they could to survive, killing those who got in their way. After almost two months of following the sea current through the Solway Firth and stopping every night to search for signs of her, they'd finally found evidence of the boat.

It was broken to pieces, and protruding out of the silt, but they recognized it. The queen had come ashore here. It was the mouth of a great river, flowing north into Scotland, which gave the Serpent People pause. Northern England was full of farmers and peasants, with a few great houses along the Scots border, but given that they were able to navigate by the stars, as their ancestors did, they knew they were in Scotland.

Venturing into clan territory was another matter because the Scots were fiercely protective of their lands. But the queen was here, and the fact that the boat wasn't completely covered by silt meant the tides hadn't a chance to bury it. That told them the queen had only just arrived, meaning she could not have gotten far.

Not far enough.

There were forty-six of them, spread out among five boats. They were heavily armed, with spears smeared with human feces and short swords that had been in poison brewed from the death cap mushroom. Perhaps they weren't great in number like the clans tended to be, but they could do damage simply by nicking the skin. But that didn't have to happen if they could find their queen before some Scots clan took her in.

They had to find her, and quickly.

As the sun began to set and a storm rolled in from the east, a group of them headed north, along the river. The search for their queen had begun.

God help the Scots if they wouldn't give her up.

CHAPTER SIX

St. Margaret's of Loch Doom

"**S**IR ESTEVAN. *ESTEVAN!*"

Someone kicked his foot, and Estevan found himself on his feet before he even realized he'd awoken. He found himself towering over Anaxandra and, woozy because he'd jumped up so fast, nearly falling onto her. She had to reach out to steady him.

"Are you well?" she asked.

He rubbed his eyes, finally standing without assistance. "Aye," he said. "I stood up too fast, I suppose."

"My apologies," Anaxandra said, looking at him with concern. "Are you sure you are well?"

"I am."

"Then Mother Michael needs you," Anaxandra said. "Come with me."

He did. A glance over his shoulder showed his brother and cousins all sleeping still. He was the only one awake. It was still dark, though he thought he could see a hint of dawn coming in through the ventilation windows high in the sanctuary.

Everything felt cold and damp, as the fire was down to the embers now, and a layer of blue smoke hovered about six feet off the ground. He was walking right through it.

"What's amiss?" he asked. "Why does Mother Michael wish tae see me?"

Anaxandra glanced at him. "The ill woman has awakened," he said. "She keeps drawing something in the dirt and speaking words we do not understand. Mother Michael hopes you can communicate with her."

Estevan wasn't so sure. Maybe he'd been ambitious thinking he could, since he knew the language so long ago. Scratching the back of his head, he was doubtful, but kept silent as they reached Mother Michael and the other nuns who had been assisting the ill woman. As he drew near, he could smell cloves strongly, something they were using in their medicaments. The injured woman had a paste on her wounds, which he assumed the clove smell was coming from.

But they could also hear her coughing.

The ill woman was also out of her cot and sitting on the ground, coughing and sniffling. It was clear that she was sick. The nuns were standing around her, puzzled, as she used a stick to draw in the hard-packed earth of the sanctuary. When Mother Michael noticed Estevan, she pointed to the drawings.

"Mayhap you can help us," she said. "She has been trying to tell us something, but we know not what. We cannot convince her to get back into bed because these drawings seem most urgent. Can you ask her, please?"

Estevan was still a little groggy as he dutifully leaned over the sick woman to see what she'd drawn in the dirt. He couldn't quite tell what it was, and the light was bad, so he turned to Anaxandra, who was standing behind him.

"Wake my brother, please," he told her. "I'll need his help."

Anaxandra rushed off. He watched her return to the sleeping warriors in the corner before returning his attention to the woman sitting on the ground. She had been looking at the drawings she'd made in the dirt, but when she heard his voice, she looked up at him. Yesterday, she'd had a good deal of fear in her expression when he came near, but this morning, the fear was diminished somewhat. Now, it was replaced by a feverish countenance, but as Estevan looked at her, he could see that she realized he and his brother and fellow knights had brought her to safety. They were not her enemy. When their eyes met, she pointed at the scribble in the dirt.

"Hjälp mig," she whispered urgently.

Mig. Estevan knew that meant "me," but the other word sounded suspiciously like "help." Was it possible she was asking for help? Or thanking him for help? He tried to think back to those days when he knew the language somewhat, thinking of what to say to her. He did remember the word for name because, long ago, the lads he used to play with had asked him what his name was in their language.

He pointed at her.

"Namn?" he asked.

Her eyes widened a little when he spoke a word she understood. That seemed to excite her.

"Leonore," she said. "Leonore Callia."

"What did you ask her?" Mother Michael asked.

Estevan turned his head in her direction. "Her name," he said. "It is Leonore Callia."

A sigh of satisfaction went on among the nuns who were standing around, including Mother Michael. Now they were getting somewhere.

"God be praised," she said softly. "We have her name. *Leonore*. A beautiful name. Will you ask her where she comes from?"

Estevan wasn't sure how to do that. He crouched down, a few feet away from Leonore as she watched him anxiously. The first thing he did was put his hand on his chest.

"Estevan," he said. "*Estevan*."

Leonore stared at him a moment in confusion before realizing what he was telling her. "Leonore," she said, hand on her own chest. "Mitt namn är Leonore."

"Mitt namn är Estevan."

That short exchange brought some delight. Leonore's face lit up and she laughed, probably with relief that she was getting somewhere with the language barrier. As Estevan smiled politely at her, Mother Michael patted him on the head, as if he were a dutiful child.

"Ask her where she comes from," Mother Michael said eagerly. "More importantly, ask her where she belongs. We must send her home."

Estevan sighed heavily. "I'm not sure I'm skilled enough tae ask her that," he said. "I dunna know enough of the language tae be clear, I'm afraid."

"Let me try."

They both looked over to see Kaladin standing there. He was sleepy, but alert, rubbing his eyes as he gazed down at Leonore. But Estevan frowned.

"What makes ye think ye can do better than me?" he said. "Ye dunna know the language either."

Kaladin crouched down next to his brother. "I was home with Papa as he did business with the princes of the isles while ye were fostering in England," he said. "Ye only played with some of those children when ye were very young. How much can ye know?"

Estevan pursed his lips with annoyance. "Fine," he said. "Ye try tae communicate with her. Let's see ye ask her where she's from."

Kaladin was determined to show up his brother. He looked at the woman and gestured to himself. "Kaladin," he said. "Jag är Kaladin."

Leonore's features brightened again, the same way they had with Estevan. "Kaladin," she repeated. "Kan du hjälpa mig?"

"Aye." Kaladin nodded. "Ditt hem?"

He had only asked her where her home was. It should have been an equally short answer. But Leonore's reply was long, painful, and complicated. No one, even Kaladin and Estevan, knew what she was talking about. She was gesturing north and south and then waving her hands about. She was also becoming more upset as she spoke, and by the time she finished, she was weeping. Kaladin and Estevan looked at each other in confusion, and concern, realizing they really couldn't communicate with her well at all. Not well enough to truly understand her.

"Ye dunna know what she said?" Estevan asked his brother.

Kaladin was loath to admit he'd failed. "Just a few words," he said. "I know the word for 'home,' and she asked about help, but beyond that… I'm afraid I only understood very few words."

"What did she say?"

"Something about her home being in the north and she'd been brought here."

"Brought *where*?"

"I dunna know."

Estevan realized they'd bitten off more than they could chew. As Kaladin continued to try to communicate with the women, Estevan stood up and faced Mother Michael.

"I fear we only understand just a few words," he said. "We know her name is Leonore and we believe she's asked for help, but beyond that, we dunna know anything more."

Mother Michael accepted his explanation, and her sense of concern returned. "We must communicate with her," she said. Then she cocked her head thoughtfully. "Mayhap we do not understand her language, but she may speak another."

Estevan wasn't sure what she meant, but Mother Michael pushed past him, kneeling down near Leonore. She fixed on the woman, who continued to cough and sputter.

"*Intellegisne me*?" she asked softly.

Leonore's eyes widened. After a moment's shock, she nodded firmly. "Ita facio," she said.

As Mother Michael smiled, Estevan understood what the woman had said. "The language of the church," he said. "If the woman attends church, then she knows it."

Mother Michael nodded. "With the Northmen, one can never tell," she said. "Sometimes they worship their pagan gods, but it seems Lady Leonore knows something of Latin. I should have thought of it earlier."

Estevan stood up stiffly from his crouched position near Leonore. "I thought my brother and I would be able tae help more," he said. "'Tis true that there are Northmen, still, in the north of Scotland. Not as much as there used tae be, but they're still there."

Mother Michael nodded in understanding. "Let us determine if we can find out more about her this way," she said, her focus still on Leonore. "Ubi est domus tua?"

Where is your home?

It was a simple question, or perhaps not so simple the way

Leonore began to speak again, gesturing with her hands. She went on and on, speaking haltingly in Latin, but enough so that Mother Michael and the rest of them began to understand her, just a little. Anyone who was part of the church, as Mother Michael and her fellow women were, would have known Latin because that was the language they prayed in. The language of all masses. And Estevan and his fellow warriors would have known it from their early education. It was, therefore, a universal language, and one that seemed to be telling a harrowing tale.

Lady Leonore was no lady.

She was a queen.

But that was as far as Estevan and Kaladin got. Titan suddenly appeared behind them, having been awakened at Estevan's request by Anaxandra.

"Mateo is ill," he said in a low voice.

Estevan and Kaladin turned to him. "Ill?" Estevan repeated, confused. "What do ye mean? He was perfectly fine last evening."

Titan started to speak, but Leonore suddenly burst out in a harsh coughing fit, covering her mouth with her hands in the process. That had Titan grunting with realization as he pointed to the injured, and now ill, woman.

"He must have caught it from her," he said. "He has a fever. The woman with the crossbow sent someone for food for him, but I do not think he can travel. Not in this weather."

Estevan and Kaladin, followed by Titan, made their way over to Mateo, who was lying flat on his back against the stone wall. His eyes were closed, but he was rattling as he breathed. When he coughed, it sounded as if his lungs were full of mucus.

Estevan knelt down beside him.

"Matty?" he said. "How do ye feel?"

Mateo's eyes rolled open. "I've been better," he admitted. "Strange… strange how it came on so suddenly. I did not feel ill yesterday."

Across the sanctuary, Leonore was coughing up a storm. They could all hear her. Estevan sighed heavily.

"I think we know who made ye ill," he said. "Titan says ye shouldna travel today. He's probably right—'tis still raining."

Mateo cleared his throat quietly, trying to cough up some of the mess in his lungs. "I suppose I could do with a day of rest," he said. "But if the nuns want us removed, then I shall have no choice but to comply."

Rodion, who had been at Mateo's feet, motioned to the men standing around. He stepped away from Mateo and they followed, eventually huddling in a concerned group.

"He cannot travel," Rodion said seriously. "He started breathing heavily only a few hours ago and has deteriorated quickly."

Estevan was looking over at Mateo, lying flat on his back, breathing loudly. "The woman he carried from the river is also ill," he said. "Whatever she has, she gave it tae him."

Rodion looked at Titan. "You know that Matty has always had weakened lungs," he said. "He has since he was a child. Any chill he caught went to his chest, and I can remember Aunt Amabella using hot water and mint and rosemary to help him breathe. Remember how we could not play with him in the winter?"

Titan nodded. "Aye," he said. "If there was an illness around, Matty would catch it."

"Then I need things to help him," Rodion said. "If we do not, I fear this may grow worse, and I cannot explain to Uncle

Markus and Aunt Ama how I let their son die on the cold floor of a nunnery."

He had a point. Even though Markus de Wolfe and his wife, Amabella—Mateo's parents—weren't actually Rodion's aunt and uncle, the families were so close that the familial distinction was simply accepted. Affectionate terms of address were used by all, regardless of bloodlines.

"He'll not die here if I can help it," Estevan said. He gestured between Rodion and Kaladin. "The two of ye decide what needs tae be done tae help him and what medicaments ye need. I'll speak tae the mother abbess and ask if we can stay here until Mateo is well enough tae travel. Titan, ye come with me. I may need yer skills of persuasion."

Titan nodded, and he and Estevan headed back over to the opposite side of the sanctuary, where Mother Michael was still trying to glean information from Leonore. They seemed to be having quite a conversation as Estevan and Titan walked up, but Leonore's chattering ended in a coughing fit, sounding much like Mateo had. Listening to that cough, Mother Michael shook her head.

"The poor lass is ill," she said to Estevan. "To be truthful, I'm surprised she is not dead, given what she has been through."

"Oh?" Estevan said. "Ye've learned more about her?"

Mother Michael nodded. "Aye," she said. "According to her, she's a queen to her people, from a place called *Södra öarna*. She says that is the name of her home."

"That's one of the southern isles," Estevan said. "I've heard of it."

"Are you certain?"

Estevan nodded. "Ye must remember that my father is the

Earl of Torridon, far tae the north, so he must deal with the lords of the isles frequently," he said. "We know the names of many of the isles they rule."

"Is he peaceable with them?"

"For the most part," Estevan said. "He does not bother them and they dunna bother him."

Mother Michael nodded in understanding, her focus moving to Leonore as the woman continued to cough. "She says that she was given or sold to men to the west," she said. "A hostage for an alliance, I believe. It is difficult to know what she means, but however she came to live with them, she has escaped them. She was trying to go home when her boat went ashore and she nearly drowned."

"And that is when we found her," Estevan said.

"Aye, you did," Mother Michael agreed. However, she kept her focus on Leonore. "She keeps drawing something in the dirt and speaks of *aleam*."

Estevan frowned. "Hazard?" he said, translating the Latin word. "Does she mean peril?"

Mother Michael nodded. "She could be speaking of her journey and how dangerous it was," she said. "Certainly, it must have been terrible."

"What is she drawing in the dirt, mother?" Titan asked. "May I see it?"

Mother Michael nodded, leading Titan over to Leonore, who was now being helped back to her cot by a couple of the other nuns. The light was growing in the sanctuary now that dawn had arrived and a few of the candle banks were being lit. Titan could see the scribbling and knelt down, peering closely at the dirt. Mother Michael stood with him for a few moments until one of the nuns helping Leonore called to her. She left

Titan crouched on the ground with Estevan standing over him.

"What is it?" Estevan said. "Do ye see something?"

Titan didn't say anything for a moment. He was staring at one of the drawings in particular. As he pointed at it, Estevan bent over his shoulder, giving the drawing a closer look.

"What do ye see?" he said. "It looks like water tae me. She's drawn the waves."

But Titan shook his head. "Those are not waves," he said. "Waves do not usually have a head on them. See it?"

It took Estevan several moments to see what he meant. There was, indeed, a head on one of wavy lines. He knelt down next to Titan, his brow furrowed.

"A serpent?" he said, fishing for answers. He looked at Titan. "Think about this, now. She says she was sold, or given, tae men in the west."

Titan was following his line of thought. "West of us is Ireland," he said. "But southwest is the Isle of Mann."

Estevan was on to something. That was clear in his expression, the way his eyes moved back to the drawing. He finally put his finger on it, literally. His finger was in the dirt.

"Who lives on the Isle of Mann, Titan?" he asked.

Titan didn't even have to think about it. He knew. "Jesus," he muttered. "*They* do. Ormsfolk."

"The Serpent People."

That realization was deeply concerning. Estevan stood up, and Titan with him, and they made their way over to Leonore, who had just lain down. But Estevan spoke to Mother Michael first.

"I think we may know what her drawings mean," Estevan said. "May I ask her?"

"Please," Mother Michael said, indicating the woman.

"Please ask her."

Estevan turned to the woman. "Domina mea," he said. "Estne periculum homines vermium?"

My lady, is the danger the worm people?

That brought Leonore off the bed. "Ita!" she cried. "Me invenient!"

Aye! And they will kill us all!

Estevan looked at Titan as their concerns were confirmed. Mother Michael, who had been listening closely, gently pushed Leonore back onto the mattress before turning to the men.

"Worm people?" she said. "Who are the worm people?"

Estevan sighed heavily. "Ormsfolk," he said grimly. "They are better known as the Serpent People. They are a clan that lives on the northern tip of the Isle of Mann. Ye've not heard of them?"

Mother Michael frowned as she thought on the question. "I do not know," she said. "We do not get many travelers here. Information does not come easily."

Estevan wasn't sure how to delicately phrase what he had to tell her. "These aren't ordinary men," he said. "They're more beast than man. They live in holes and breed eels in great ponds in their domain. That's why they're called Serpent People. But they are extremely territorial, and extremely violent, and if that woman belonged tae them, then they will come for her."

Mother Michael was listening seriously. "I see," she said. "We shall fight them when they come, then. As you have seen, we can defend ourselves."

Estevan cast Titan a long glance. When he didn't answer, Titan spoke up. "They do not fight like normal men, mother," he said. "They fight like mad dogs. They are known for hacking their enemies to pieces and then feeding those pieces to their eels. The woman is right—they are quite dangerous."

Mother Michael nodded patiently, a gesture that suggested she didn't take the threat seriously in spite of the rather grisly information. "We can easily defend ourselves," she said. "But you should go before they come. There is no reason for you to risk yourselves."

Titan almost laughed at the suggestion that they shouldn't expose themselves to the danger. "Unfortunately, we cannot leave at the moment," he said. "One of our companions is quite ill, something he must have contracted from the lady we found. He has a fever and is coughing the same as she is. We require shelter until he is well enough to travel."

Mother Michael didn't answer. She simply walked over to Mateo as he lay on the ground. She studied him a moment, listening to his breathing, before bending over to put a hand on his face.

"Ah," she said, pulling away. "He is indeed feverish. You may leave him here while you continue on your way."

Both Estevan and Titan shook their heads. "We'll not leave him behind," Estevan said quietly. "We simply require food and shelter until he is well enough tae travel. A few days should do. And we can move intae the stable so yer sanctuary will be clear for yer women."

"We can amply protect him. You do not need to remain."

"We are not leaving him, mother. Ye may as well accept that."

Mother Michael wasn't pleased. They weren't being disrespectful, simply firm. There was loyalty in that unwavering stance. But she still wasn't pleased about it, though deep down, she understood. She admired knights and their camaraderie. She'd studied it for years, envious of the bonds men shared in battle. Truth be told, perhaps there was a little envy for them now, even as they faced her down. She didn't like men, and she didn't want them at St. Margaret's, but this was an unprecedented situation.

"Very well," she said. "But you do not sleep inside the walls. You will sleep outside of the walls. There is a stream for water and game for food. You may tend to him in the daytime, but we will tend him at night."

Titan looked at Estevan to see the man's reaction, and he thought the command was just this side of ridiculous. It was written all over his face.

"If the Serpent People come, I dunna wish tae be caught outside of the walls," he said. "Tae expect us tae do so would not only be unfair, it would be ungodly. I dunna believe Jesus would turn away those in need of shelter or food or the protection of a fortress."

Mother Michael started to open her mouth, but Titan intervened. "Mother, we respect the reputation of St. Margaret's," he said quietly. "Everyone knows, and respects, the Lady Templars. Your abilities as an army are well known. But look in front of you—there are five fully trained knights at your disposal should the Serpent People come. No offense to you or any other nun here, but the five of us have been in more battles, and have seen more conflict, than you could ever hope to see. We are knights. You are simply women who know how to fight. There is a very big difference if you face an enemy as formidable as the Serpent People."

He had been both insulting and complimentary, and Mother Michael couldn't decide how she felt about it. Nothing he said was untrue. He, and his fellow warriors, had seen more conflict than she had. She'd seen seven battles in her lifetime.

But the men before her had seen many times more than that.

She'd be a fool not to concede that fact.

"Mayhap you have experienced battle more than I," she said. "But we do not even know if the Serpent People, as you call them, will find Leonore here. How can they? She fled from them and the sea is vast, young lords. So is Scotland and England. For them to find her would take a miracle. Would you not agree?"

Titan nodded reluctantly while Estevan simply shook his head. "It would take a miracle, indeed, but miracles do happen," he said. "More than likely, they will never find her. But if they somehow follow her trail here, it would be better if ye had our protection. That is all Sir Titan is saying. May we please remain inside the walls?"

Mother Michael was hesitant still. This was a nunnery, after all. As she tried to come up with an answer that wouldn't anger them, one of the nuns who had been tending Leonore came to her and whispered in her ear. At nearly the same time, women with something steaming appeared in the sanctuary doorway and Anaxandra was there, still with women who were armed with crossbows, and indicated where the steaming bowls should go. They were delivered to Mateo on the ground, to Rodion, who was with him, to Kaladin, to Titan, and finally to Estevan.

He sniffed the contents.

"Stew?" he asked the abbess.

Mother Michael nodded. "Probably the remainder from last night's meal," she said. "But before you eat, may I ask—do you have any medicaments with you? Anything to tend fevers or cough?"

Both Estevan and Titan shook their heads. "Nay," Estevan said. "The most we travel with are things tae stanch a blood flow. But nothing for illness. Why?”

Mother Michael glanced over at Leonore, on the bed. “Because the lady seems to be worse,” she said. “Much like you, we are prepared for battle wounds, not illness. Sister Hildegarde has informed me that we need medicines for the lady’s fever and, I would also assume, your friend’s fever. If you do not carry anything for such events, then we must procure them.”

“Where?” Estevan asked.

“Dumfries,” Mother Michael said. “Can you read?”

“I can.”

“Then if I write down what we need, will you fetch it?”

Estevan nodded. “I shall,” he said. “But ye dunna have tae write it down. I’ll remember what ye tell me.”

Mother Michael looked at him dubiously. “It may be more than just one or two items.”

“I’ll remember however much ye tell me.”

She didn’t question him a second time. She simply nodded and turned back for the women tending Leonore. That left Estevan and Titan with steaming bowls still in their hands, now starting to eat because they were hungry.

“Seems I’ll go tae Dumfries after all,” Estevan said, mouth full. “Ye remain with Rodion and Matty. I’ll take Kal with me and we’ll be swift.”

Titan, too, was shoveling down the stew, but he paused long enough to look to the ceiling for a moment. “It is still raining,” he said. “I can hear it.”

Estevan nodded. “Aye, but not as bad as it was last night,” he said. “Ye must remain vigilant here. If I were ye, I’d try tae convince Mother Michael that she needs ye on the wall.”

Titan cocked his head curiously. “You are concerned about the Serpent People.”

Estevan shook his head. "Ye've heard about them as much as I have," he said. "Probably more. They're closer tae yer father's properties than they are tae mine, but even we know about them."

Titan couldn't disagree. "True, but Mother Michael is correct," he said. "It would take a miracle for them to find her."

"Not if they followed her trail."

"What do you mean?"

Estevan shrugged as he took another bite. "That woman arrived on the banks of the River Nith," he said. "Remember the remains of the boat that Kal found?"

Titan appeared stricken, so much so that he stopped chewing. "Damnation," he muttered. "I'd forgotten all about it."

Estevan eyed him grimly. "I never gave that boat a second thought until we realized she was fleeing the Serpent People," he said. "If she was their captive and stole one of their boats tae flee, they'll follow her. They'll use the currents like she did, because I'd be willing tae wager she dinna row herself across the sea."

"Nay, she did not."

"Then she followed the currents," Estevan said. "And so will they. That will bring them tae the boat."

Titan swallowed the bite in his mouth. "Then we must dispose of it," he said. "Leave me Kal. I'll take him down to the beach and we will remove the remains of that boat so the Serpent People do not find it. It never occurred to me to destroy it when we found it."

Estevan grunted. "Nor me," he said. "I dinna mention the boat tae Mother Michael because I dinna wish tae frighten her, but I think I should. It will not take a miracle for those beastly fools tae find their captive. It will take a boat."

"Like a damn beacon."

Estevan put the spoon aside and drank the last of his stew, wiping his lips with the back of his hand. "Then there is no time tae waste," he said. "I'll go intae Dumfries and collect whatever medicines the abbess wants, but ye must take Kal and destroy that boat. I'll tell the abbess, but ye must go now."

Titan agreed with him. He, too, tossed back what remained in his bowl and turned for the corner where Mateo, Kaladin, and Rodion were. As he went to explain the situation to those three, Estevan went to Mother Michael.

"May I have word with ye, mother?" he asked.

She had been speaking to the other nuns who were tending Leonore, but she nodded to his request. They moved a few feet away from the nuns, and the ill woman, before he spoke.

"When we found Leonore, we also found her boat," he said in a low voice. "It was smashed upon the sandy shore, indicative of the journey that has brought her tae this point in time."

Mother Michael was listening closely. "I see," she said. "And why do you speak of this now?"

"Because we dinna remove it," Estevan said with regret. "We had no reason tae do it, and with the storm swiftly approaching, we were only thinking of finding shelter for the injured woman. Mother, that means that if the Serpent People are following her, and I have no reason tae believe they're not, then they'll find that broken boat. They'll come inland and they'll come tae the abbey, looking for her."

Now she was beginning to understand. "Ah," she said softly. "Then we do not need a miracle for them to find her. She has left a trail."

"She has," Estevan said. "But I am sending Titan and my brother back tae the boat tae destroy it. Hopefully we'll be in time, but if not, ye must be prepared tae tell the Serpent People that their captive is not here and hope they dunna demand entrance tae see for themselves."

Mother Michael nodded. "Of course," she said. "That would be the simplest thing to do, to tell them we have not seen her. If they push, I have several women with crossbows who are quite skilled with them. They know how to discourage men on our doorstep."

Her eyes were twinkling at she looked at him, and he smiled weakly. "They do, indeed," he said. "But even so, we'll try tae prevent them from coming. We'll do our best. I fear we've brought trouble tae yer door, mother. That wasna our intention."

Mother Michael's smile was genuine. "Of course it was not," she said. "You brought an injured woman to us and we are glad to tend her. But she needs the medicines I indicated, if you would be so good as to fetch them. I will send you with an escort."

She was pointing to the entry, where Anaxandra was standing. He almost declined the escort but thought better of it when he saw whom she was pointing at. Since Anaxandra was the only one standing just inside the door, it could be no one else.

Maybe he *would* like an escort.

"Very well," he said. "But we should go immediately."

"Agreed. I shall inform your escort."

While Mother Michael did just that, Estevan went over to the wall where his things were stacked. He was wearing his long tunic and breeches, but he reached into his saddlebags and began to pull out a padded tunic, meant for warfare, and other pieces of protection. All the while, Rodion and Kaladin and Titan were watching him.

"Did you tell her about the boat?" Titan asked.

Estevan nodded as he stood up and donned his heavy, padded tunic. "Aye," he said. "She knows. I told her that ye and Kal were going tae destroy it."

Titan nodded firmly and motioned to Kaladin, who began to grab his possessions. "We'll go now," he said. "Are you going alone to Dumfries?"

Estevan shook his head. "Nay," he said, strapping on a belt with an assortment of daggers. "I am tae have an escort. The woman who tried tae kill me with bolts yesterday."

Titan grinned. "I wish you luck with that one."

Estevan cocked an eyebrow. "Trust me when I tell ye that I'm going tae need it."

With that comment, they all turned to look at the entry where Mother Michael was just finishing her conversation with Anaxandra, who promptly bolted from the door, out into the rain. That tall, long-legged creature who was able to fire a crossbow so easily. There was something strong and formidable about her.

They only hoped Estevan could survive it.

And her.

CHAPTER SEVEN

Dumfries, Scotland

IT WAS STILL raining when they arrived.

The village of Dumfries was a curious mixture of architecture. There were cottages with mud walls and sod roofs, other cottages that were of stone, and still other structures that were built from the red limestone that was so prevalent in the southern portion of Scotland. Then there were buildings built of wattle and daub. But no matter what it was built of, it was wet as Estevan and Anaxandra arrived at the southern end of the village. The road they had traveled upon had turned into a muddy sea in some places, slowing their journey considerably. But nothing could stop it entirely. Now that they'd arrived, they were on the hunt for the apothecary stall, which Mother Michael had told them was near the church.

Estevan would have thought that Anaxandra knew exactly where the church was, but he'd found out in a brief conversation during their journey that she had never been to the village of Dumfries, not in the entirety of her life, because Mother Michael would not allow any of her wards travel to locations that she deemed unsafe and debaucherous. That included a village full of people—men, in particular. It was her job to protect the women under her command, which, Estevan was coming to realize, seemed to mean that they lived like hermits.

Therefore, he kept stealing glances at Anaxandra as they entered the village proper. She was trying very hard not to seem overwhelmed by the whole thing, but he could just tell by the expression on her face that the situation was bewildering. Perhaps it was even frightening, although he couldn't imagine a woman like Anaxandra being frightened of anything. However, the lack of exposure to the world outside of the abbey was reflected on her face. She had no idea how to process it all.

He thought it was rather fascinating.

In fact, he thought *she* was rather fascinating.

But he had to admit that the ride north from St. Margaret's had been a strange one. There had been limited conversation, and Estevan thought it was because she was simply trying to keep a distance from him, but as they drew closer to the village, he realized it was because she was nervous about being outside of the walls of the abbey. Every sight, every sound, had her on edge. Estevan wasn't sure if he should try to alleviate that fear, because she might take it as an insult. From his conversation with her yesterday, he was coming to understand that he was dealing with a unique young woman. She was fearsome, and well trained, but whatever battles she had fought in had been tightly controlled, presumably by Mother Michael, which meant there had been no time to wander or see the world outside of the fight.

That made a journey like this intimidating for her.

Therefore, he didn't want to run the risk of offending her by acknowledging that she was edgy to be in an environment she wasn't familiar with. She was too proud for that. That meant he kept silent for the most part, and it was an uncomfortable sort of silence. He wasn't quite sure what else they would talk about, and she never made the effort, so they were stuck in a perpetually strange situation.

And he wasn't the only one who thought it was strange.

While Estevan was mulling over the silence, Anaxandra was in her own world of anxiety. That was the only way to describe it. Though she had been out of the walls of St. Margaret's several times, it was only in the local area surrounding the abbey. Forests and burns and meadows. She knew how to hunt and did so frequently, but coming into contact with a village the size of Dumfries was something she had no experience with at all. She knew that Mother Michael had recommended her for escort duty because of her skill with crossbow in case Estevan ran into trouble, so there was logic to that. But there was literally no logic in sending her into the village she knew nothing about.

She hoped *he* wouldn't figure that out.

St. Margaret's was built of red limestone that had a weather-worn look to it. She was used to those old walls. But Dumfries had a mix of architecture, types of buildings that she'd never seen before, and it took all of her strength not to stop and inspect them. She was curious about everything, even though she knew that this was not a trip for her discovery. This was a trip to the apothecary to collect medicaments for a fever, and, courtesy of Mother Michael, she knew that the apothecary was near the church.

Wherever the church was.

Looking around the village for the church had her also looking at the people. Women were walking in the street, going about their business, and she was quite curious about the garments they were wearing. No one was wearing what she had on, breeches and tunics instead of a skirt and kirtle. She was well aware that women were expected to wear surcoats and garments without the legs defined, but she had never worn that type of garment in her life. She wondered how comfortable it was.

She wondered how she would look in such a thing.

Vanity was something that was heavily discouraged by the nuns at St. Margaret's, so she felt guilty even thinking about how she would look in a garment like that. As she and Estevan headed west on the main road that went through the heart of Dumfries, she caught sight of a woman wearing a pale blue dress and a matching robe that was lined with fur. The woman was trying not to get the bottom of the dress dirty as a servant helped her on to a small palfrey. She was far better dressed than anyone else Anaxandra had seen so far, and, in fact, her dress was quite lovely. Anaxandra found herself staring at it and not even realizing it. Everything she'd seen to that point had been drab and practical. The pale blue dress was made of a shiny material, something that looked lovely and soft.

She wondered how *she* would look in that dress.

"Look," Estevan said, breaking into her train of thought. "There is the church. See it? With the bell tower on the roof?"

Anaxandra tore herself away from the woman in the pale blue dress, looking down the road, toward the west. She could see a short, squat structure, nothing spectacular in the grand scheme of things. But Estevan suddenly came to a halt, pointing to the building that the woman in the pale blue dress was in front of.

"The apothecary," he said. "There it is, right in front of us."

That was true. Anaxandra had been so caught up in the sight of the first beautiful dress she'd ever seen that she failed to notice the shop in front of her. It didn't look like anything more than a run-down cottage with a roof that leaned unsteadily like a drunkard, but the sign over the door, in faded paint, announced the business within:

Aromatarius

That was the Latin word for the apothecary, so Anaxandra and Estevan dismounted their steeds, tying them to the post in front of the business. Anaxandra simply stared at the storefront as if unsure what to do, so Estevan took the lead and headed inside.

She followed.

But she didn't make it past the door.

Anaxandra stood, wide eyed, as Estevan wandered into the heart of the shop, looking at the tables that contained various ingredients. There was one woman in there already, speaking to an older woman who wore a dirty wimple around her head. It was supposed to be made of white fabric, but it was mostly yellow and stained. Estevan assumed one of the women was the apothecary, so he waited patiently until the business was finished.

The woman with the dirty wimple left the shop.

That meant the remaining woman was the apothecary, or at least worked for the apothecary. She turned to see Estevan and her round face lit up. She was older, with graying hair that was pulled off her face and round cheeks. When she smiled, he could see missing teeth. But that didn't prevent her from greeting Estevan as she walked up to him and slapped him, hard, on the arm.

"M'laird," she said with pleasure. "Do ye know what ye want?"

The woman was standing a little too close to him and had the unsettling odor of burnt meat about her. More than that, her friendly slap on his left arm had bloody well hurt.

"Aye," he said, taking a step back. "I am seeking medicaments for a fever. What would ye recommend?"

"A few things, m'laird," the woman said loudly, taking a step toward him as he took another step back. "Is this for yer bairn?"

"Nay. A knight."

"English?"

"Aye."

She leaned forward with a twinkle in her eye. "Are ye sure ye simply dunna want tae let the fever run him down?"

She started laughing, and that appalling smell of burnt meat began to envelop him. But it was more than just the burnt smell. *Garlic,* he thought. He'd smelled it before.

The woman reeked of garlic.

"He's my kin, so I need something tae help him," he said, growing annoyed. "We also have a sick woman that needs tending."

"Kin, too?"

"A stranger," he said, his patience at an end. "Do ye have something or not?"

The woman was still laughing, oblivious to his annoyance with her. Even if she wasn't, she didn't seem to care. Before she could say another word, however, Anaxandra was suddenly between them, her pale eyes blazing.

"He's not come to converse with you or give you a handsome vision to look upon," she barked. "We need parsley, mustard seed, and any concoction you have that might take down a fever. We will also need a willow bark potion or powdered willow bark for the same purpose. *Move!*"

She boomed the last word, and the older woman stumbled back, looking at her in both shock and outrage.

"Who are ye, coming around and shouting like that?" she said angrily. "I'll give ye nothing at all if ye do that again!"

The lack of Anaxandra's social skills were on full display as she unslung the crossbow and pointed it right at the apothecary. "I am from St. Margaret's," she said. "I'll do anything I please to get what I need. If you do not produce those items, I'll simply take them, so it is your choice. Get them or die."

"'Tis not that bad, love," Estevan said soothingly, putting his hand on Anaxandra's shoulder and pulling her back. He had been so stunned at her aggressiveness that it had taken a moment for him to react. When she looked at him, rage in her expression, he simply smiled at her and forced her to lower the crossbow. "She'll get them for us. Ye needn't worry. I know of yer concern for the ill, but the woman meant no harm."

He was trying to convey to the apothecary that Anaxandra acted as she had because she was very concerned for those who were with fever. He hoped it would work, because the apothecary was a big woman, and loud, and he didn't want to create a ruckus. He simply wanted what he'd come for. His focus remained on Anaxandra as she finally began to lower the crossbow.

The apothecary also had her attention on Anaxandra, evidently in surprise, as she realized who the young woman was. Leggy and blonde and wearing clothing that suggested battle, she looked like a Valkyrie.

"Ye're a Lady Templar?" the apothecary said. Then she

grinned. "I've only seen yer lot once or twice, and I've lived here my entire life. Imagine—a Lady Templar in my stall!"

Anaxandra had no reply, but Estevan could see that she was tensing up for another round of shouting. "They keep tae themselves," he said, continuing his efforts to defuse the situation. "Most religious orders do. Can ye provide me with the things for a fever? Mustard seed and willow bark, if ye have it. Our friend is quite ill."

The woman was still grinning as she turned around and began rummaging through baskets on one of her tables. Estevan was torn between watching her curiously and making sure Anaxandra didn't try to kill the woman because she wasn't moving fast enough. He ended up holding the hand that was holding the crossbow, reasoning that she couldn't raise it if he had hold of her.

Hopefully.

He knew from experience how good she was with that crossbow.

Oblivious to Estevan's efforts to prevent a bloodbath, the apothecary continued to rummage through baskets before finding what she was looking for. She held up a bunch of something green, waving it around.

"Onion," she said. "If yer knight has a fever and sickness in his chest, ye'll want tae boil the onion until it's very soft and then strain the water. Add honey and have him drink it."

Before Estevan could reply, she returned to what she was doing, talking to herself as she went about finding what they needed. Since she was doing what had been asked of her, Estevan finally felt safe enough to take his hand off the crossbow.

"Return tae the door," he told her quietly.

Anaxandra looked at him. "Why?"

"Because ye need tae guard me while I accomplish this."

That was all he said, but it sounded logical to her, so she returned to her post by the entry door.

But that crossbow was at the ready.

After much rummaging and collecting what was needed, the apothecary finally returned to him with a dirty basket full of things. He peered at it, noticing that she'd put a small earthenware phial into the mix. He pointed to it.

"What is that?" he asked.

"A rotten brew," she told him. "Have ye not heard of it?"

Estevan shook his head. "Nay," he said. "What is it?"

The apothecary shrugged. "It's brewed from old bread," she said. "It can help fevers or wounds. Ye stir it with wine and drink it."

Estevan nodded. "I'm grateful," he said. He meant it. "How much for everything?"

The woman's gaze moved from Estevan to Anaxandra, her back to them as she watched the street beyond the door. "Is she truly a Lady Templar?"

Estevan glanced at Anaxandra before replying. "What do *ye* think?" he said, grinning.

The woman laughed. "I think she wanted tae kill me," she said. "The next time ye come back, dunna bring her."

Estevan continued to grin. "Never mind that," he said. "How much money for these things?"

The woman snorted. "A penny each," she said. "Ye've got six things in the basket. Give me six pence and return the basket tae me."

Digging in the purse on his belt, Estevan produced the required coinage and thanked the woman.

"Ye've been helpful," he said. "Thank ye for the suggestion of the onion water."

The apothecary slapped him affectionately on the arm again, nearly staggering him sideways. "Onion with honey," she confirmed. "That will help him recover. Will ye tell me something, lad?"

"If I can."

"Do ye have any brothers?"

Estevan chuckled. "Seven," he said. "The two older ones are already married, but I'll send the younger ones yer way."

He was jesting, but she took him seriously. "Will ye?" she said. "Lad, that's the grandest thing anyone has done for me. What's yer name?"

"Estevan. And yers?"

"Lorna McKee."

"Thanks tae ye, Lorna."

He was heading for the door now with Lorna following. "If yer knight hasna recovered by the time ye return the basket tae me, I'll give ye something else for him," she said. "Is he married?"

"Nay."

"Then send him my way, too."

Estevan started laughing. They reached the door and Anaxandra turned to see them behind her, but Estevan pointed to the horses before she could speak. He didn't want her around Lorna longer than she had to be, fearful she'd try to lodge a bolt in the woman again. Anaxandra obeyed, heading for her horse as Estevan moved to his.

"I promise I'll send ye any man I can, Lorna," he said, though he didn't mean it. "Hopefully ye'll find a husband one day."

"What about ye?"

"What *about* me?"

"Are ye married?"

Estevan gestured in Anaxandra's direction. "Dunna ask that question in front of her," he whispered loudly. "Why do ye think she tried tae kill ye? She's the jealous type."

To her credit, Lorna seemed to accept that statement, bowing her head and casting Anaxandra a long side-eye to make sure the woman wasn't about to strike because she was protecting her property. Convinced that Lorna had finally gotten the message that he wasn't interested in whatever romance she had in mind, Estevan put his foot in the stirrup to lift himself into the saddle. But a big hand slapped him on the arse before he could make it.

He could hear Lorna laughing all the way back into her stall.

CHAPTER EIGHT

"WE'RE NEVER GOING tae reach The Butcher's," Kaladin said glumly.

He and Titan were nearing the mouth of the River Nith as it joined with the Solway Firth, heading toward the area where the ruins of the small boat was found yesterday. The rain had let up, but only for the moment. They were in a patch of blue sky, and all around them were clouds and rain. But for now, that spot of blue sky allowed sunbeams to shine upon the shore banks of the river.

It wasn't particularly sandy, but very silty. The land around the river was lush and full of greenery, so the riverbank was rocky and dirty this far south. Kaladin knew right where he'd seen the boat, but his mention of The Butcher's was more for the fact that they were heading in the opposite direction of the establishment.

That wasn't the way he wanted to go.

Titan was aware of this. He felt much the same way, but unlike youthful Kaladin, he kept his feelings to himself.

"If not this time, there will be another time, I'm sure," he said steadily. "Now, where, exactly, did you see the boat yesterday?"

Kaladin directed his distinctive black-and-white horse all the way to the river's edge. He looked around, orienting himself, until he pointed southward.

"Down there," he said. "In fact, I think I can see it."

Titan strained to see what Kaladin was seeing, even as Kaladin took off in that direction. He followed, but as they approached what looked like a pile of broken wood, the landscape leveled out and they could see something else.

More boats.

"Stop," Titan commanded. "Kal, stop here."

Kaladin obeyed, reining his horse to a halt with Titan alongside him. They could both see that there were five more boats on the shore, not far from the wreckage. Concerned, Titan began to look around.

"I do not see anyone else," he said. "Do you?"

Kaladin stood up in his stirrups, searching for another living soul. "Nay," he said. "There's no one."

Titan didn't say anything, but he didn't like what he was seeing. In fact, he had a bad feeling about the entire situation. Dismounting his steed, he began to make his way over to the wreckage. Kaladin wasn't far behind him when Titan came to a sudden halt.

"Look at all of the footprints," Titan said, pointing. "They're all around the wreckage of that boat."

Kaladin was starting to catch on. "It's what Estevan was talking about," he said. "The Ormsfolk. The Serpent People. God's Bones, do ye think it's them?"

Titan couldn't think of who else it would be. Slowly, he backed up, stepping only where he'd stepped before.

"Find something to wipe away our tracks," he told Kaladin.

"I do not want anyone knowing we've been here."

Kaladin turned to their mounts, several yards back, munching on seagrass. "What about the horses?" he said with concern. "They'll see their hooves in the dirt."

"Nay," Titan said, shaking his head. "They're still on the grass for the most part. They may notice a little, but we cannot worry about that now. I need to get a better look at that boat."

Kaladin rushed into the grass about ten feet away, going to the nearest sapling, growing crooked against the constant sea breeze, and broke off two good-sized branches with leaves on them. He returned to Titan, handing him one, and the men began to erase their footsteps from the silty shore.

"If the rain comes, it will wash any evidence of us away completely," Titan said. "And it has been raining all night, which leads me to believe these men have arrived within the past couple of hours."

Like everyone else, Kaladin had heard stories about the Serpent People and the way they fought. That was common knowledge for most people on the west coast of Scotland. He'd heard that there had been a time, long ago, when the Serpent People raided the southern coast, Galloway and the surrounding area, but they evidently hadn't done that for a while. Still, the fact that they were facing the very real possibility that the Serpent People had indeed come after their captive had him edgy.

"If that is true, then where are they?" he said, looking toward the east. "They found the boat and they've gone off... but where?"

Titan shrugged. "They'll walk to the first settlement they come to," he said. "Caerlaverock Castle is not far from here. It's possible they've gone there first."

"Where is it?"

Titan pointed northeast. "That way," he said. "It's a Clan Maxwell property, fortified. I suspect that if the Serpent People go there, they will not gain entrance, but it has only been a couple of hours at most. They are probably still there."

"How far is St. Margaret's from Caerlaverock?"

Titan shrugged. "Not far," he said. "That might be their next stop."

Which meant they had to return to the abbey immediately. But they needed to try to identify the other boats first, to confirm their suspicions, so they made haste down to the boats, neatly beached in a row. They inspected them, all the while dragging the branches behind them to try to blot out their footsteps without disturbing the prints that were already there. The boats smelled of piss and were cluttered with rubbish and dried fish, indicative of a sea journey. As Titan rounded the third boat they'd come to, he suddenly came to a halt.

"There," he said, pointing to something on the side of the bow. "See it?"

Kaladin peered closely. Something was scratched into the side of the boat, faded. He could barely make it out.

"It looks like a shape," he said. "What is it?"

Titan sighed heavily. "I've seen it before," he said. "Do not forget that Mateo's great-grandfather was a Nordic prince. All of the de Wolfe sons were schooled in their culture and teachings because it is part of our heritage and our alliance."

"*What* is it, then?"

"An othala."

"What is that?"

"It represents the letter 'O' in the language of the Northmen."

Kaladin stared at it for a moment. "Ormsfolk."

"Indeed."

No more words were spoken between them at that point. There was no need. After covering their tracks back to their horses, they took off as fast as the steeds would take them.

It would seem that a serpent was on their doorstep.

CHAPTER NINE

THERE IT WAS.

The Butcher's.

Estevan could see the gambling den in full sight, tucked in between a tavern called The Sheep Pile and a cottage that was used by the tavern for paying guests. Truthfully, The Butcher's was artfully camouflaged to make it look like it was part of The Sheep Pile.

But it wasn't.

Sadly, for him, the gambling den seemed to be quite busy. He could see men standing outside of it, talking and drinking, and there were more people going in and out of the tavern. It was midmorning, nearing noon, so he could only assume the gamblers had just awoken and were now ready to wager away their money, whereas those visiting the tavern were ready to start in on their daily drink. Whatever the case, the establishments appeared to be busy.

Much to his disappointment.

"What is that place?"

The question came from Anaxandra on his right. Silent Anaxandra. A woman who couldn't even speak to him on their journey north, but now, she'd evidently found her tongue. He looked to see what she was pointing at.

"That place right there?" he said.

She nodded. "There are many people there."

"That's because it is a tavern," he said. Then he pulled his horse to a stop. "They make a drink from apples and oats and honey. I've had it before. It's quite strong."

She looked at him curiously. "And you want some?"

He shook his head. "Nay," he said. "But Mateo might. If the man has a sore throat or cough, it could help him."

"But that is why we have the onions and things from the apothecary."

Estevan shrugged. "It canna hurt."

He headed over toward the tavern, but there was a livery across the street. In truth, it was simply an outbuilding with a corral for horses, but Estevan remembered it from the last time he was here, nearly three years ago. It didn't look any different than it had then. As he approached it and dismounted, Anaxandra pulled in behind him.

"*What* are you doing?" she said. "We must return immediately."

He looked up at her. "I'm going tae find Matty some of that drink," he said. "Mayhap it'll help the woman, too. Do ye want tae come with me or will ye wait here?"

She looked as if she didn't understand the question. Her features took on a kind of blank expression, and then she looked over at the tavern, watching the people milling around the entry. There weren't many, just a handful really, but there were enough. And they were men. The more she looked at the tavern, the more apprehension she began to feel.

"I… I do not know," she finally said. "I have never seen a

place like that. What's it for?"

He looked over at the tavern too. "Drinking," he said. "Eating. Sleeping if ye've no where else tae go for the night. M'lady, I'm coming tae think ye simply dunna know about life outside of St. Margaret's. Ye told me that ye've never been tae Dumfries, but have ye been anywhere at all? Ever?"

Anaxandra shook her head. "Nay," she reluctantly admitted. She seemed hesitant to continue, but her frustration got the better of her. "Mother Michael does not allow us to go anywhere. When she told me to escort you to this village, it is simply because I am skilled with my weapon. I could help you in a fight. It is not because I know the road or the land or the town. I do not know anything, and I feel like—"

She suddenly stopped, embarrassed at her outburst. For Estevan, she was simply confirming everything he had suspected, so he leaned on his saddle, gazing up at her.

"What do ye feel like, lass?" he said softly. "This is all very new. If I were ye, I'd feel overwhelmed and possibly even afraid. This is a good deal tae manage for someone who has hardly been out of St. Margaret's."

His patient tone nearly undid her. She wasn't used to such things, and most especially not from a man. "I feel as if I'm in another world," she said. "I will admit something to you. I do not want to be a nun. I have a wandering soul, as Mother Michael says. I think about things in the Outworld."

"Outworld?"

"Here," she said, gesturing to the street, to the buildings. "Mother Michael calls this the Outworld. She says it is wicked, with wicked people, and that we are only safe living within the walls of St. Margaret's. She does not like that I think on the Outworld and wonder about it."

Estevan had a gentle expression on his face, one of patience and understanding. Coming around his horse, he held up a hand to her.

"Come with me," he said quietly.

Anaxandra didn't know why he was holding a hand out to her. She didn't need his help dismounting, so she slid off her horse and collected her crossbow.

"Where are we going?" she asked.

With a lazy smile on his face, Estevan winked at her before calling to the man who was in charge of the livery. He asked the man to tend the horses, but he also handed the fellow the basket with the medicines in it for safekeeping. After giving the man a coin, Estevan turned to Anaxander and took her hand in his.

"Come," he said.

Like a fool, she simply followed him. She followed him toward the tavern, but to the west of the tavern was a merchant stall, the first in a line of such stalls, and the fabrics billowing from the entry door caught her attention. When she hesitated a little, Estevan turned to see why. Then he saw what had her attention.

"Do ye want tae look in the stall?" he asked.

She shook her head quickly, as if fearful of such a thing. "Nay," she said. "I... I've simply never seen anything like that."

The smile never left Estevan's lips as he pulled her over to the stall. It was like towing a barge. She didn't want to go, but she wanted to go, but she didn't want him to *know* she wanted to go. Estevan tugged on her, pulling her up to a table that was underneath an awning of sorts.

"Look at this," he said, picking up a piece of fabric that was as fine as angel's wings. "That is a beautiful piece. My mother would love it. So would my sisters. Zora would fight my mother for it."

Anaxandra was looking at the fabric in awe. "Zora is your sister?"

"One of them," Estevan said. "I have two. Zora is the baby. A tall, red-haired pest of a baby. There are times when I'd like tae put her in a basket and send her out tae sea."

That brought a grin from Anaxandra. "She's young, then?"

"She will have seen seventeen years this winter," he said. "She has every man in the Highlands pining for her, and even some from England. The lass needs tae pick a suitor and become their problem."

His annoyed manner was exaggerated as he said it, leading Anaxandra to understand that he was jesting. "A suitor?" she said. "I do not know this word."

He looked at her with some disbelief. "A suitor," he repeated. "Someone that comes tae court a woman. Do ye know about that?"

Anaxandra was suddenly embarrassed. He spoke as if she should know, and that made her defensive. "I have been raised in an abbey," she said, putting the fabric down. "Just how much do you think I know about your world?"

She started to march away, but he grabbed her by the wrist. "Easy, lass," he said in his deep, soothing tone. He had the ability to sound quite calm and, frankly, quite seductive if he wanted to. "No need tae fret. I simply asked a question."

"You delivered judgment."

He shook his head. "Nay, I dinna," he said firmly. "If ye dunna know, I'll tell ye. Would ye like me tae tell ye about suitors and courting?"

He could see her features tightening. Her breathing began to come more rapidly. "What does it matter?" she said, her voice hoarse with emotion. "I will never have a suitor and no one will ever court me, so it does not matter. I do not want to go with you any longer. We must return immediately."

With that, she turned away from him, but not before he saw tears in her eyes. She was storming back in the direction of the livery and he caught up to her, grabbing her by the arm, which was the wrong thing to do. She balled a fist and swung on him, but he threw both of his arms around her to hold her fast, preventing her from striking him.

It was the only thing he could think of in the moment.

"Easy, lass, easy," he murmured, his mouth against the side of her head. "I wasna trying tae offend ye. Ye said ye dinna know about such things and I simply offered tae tell ye. If ye want tae know about the world outside the walls of the abbey, I'll tell ye. Ye dunna have tae become angry with me."

She was struggling in his embrace. "Release me," she growled. "Release me or you will regret it."

That only made him tighten his grip. "Nay," he said. "I'll not release ye, because if I do, ye'll try tae beat me again and I'll not lct ye. Stop yer slruggles."

She wouldn't, but she wasn't fighting like she had been before. It was enough of a lull to cause Estevan to realize just how good she felt in his arms. She was soft and warm. He had blonde hair in his mouth and didn't regret it.

He could have held her like that all day.

"Are ye calm now?" he asked, though he really didn't care if she was or not. He was hoping that, maybe, she wasn't. At least for a little while longer. "Well? Can I let ye go without losing teeth?"

By this time, she'd stopped fighting him completely. "I will not strike you," she said.

Instantly, he let her go, but her hair was caught up in the

neckline of his tunic, so he had to disengage it. It felt rather soft in his fingers. Like silk. He couldn't help but notice how flushed she was.

Mayhap she liked it too, he thought.

"Come back tae the tavern with me," he said, not giving her time to think or speak. "I must retrieve the drink for Matty. Come in and see what a tavern looks like."

Once again, he grabbed her by the wrist and pulled her with him. Anaxandra let him, though by her expression, she was displeased. He didn't care as long as she wasn't trying to throw a punch. They were about ten feet from the tavern door when he suddenly veered over to the merchant stall again, back to the table with the fabric. He picked up one of pale blue and held it up to her.

"This is the color of yer eyes," he said. "For yer trouble in escorting me tae Dumfries, I'd like tae buy it for ye."

Anaxandra looked at him in shock. "Me?" she said incredulously. "I… Nay, you mustn't!"

He wouldn't listen to her. "It's my money and I can spend it how I please," he said. He was still holding her wrist as he pulled her into the stall. "Let's see what else I can buy ye."

Anaxandra was beside herself. Now, in the middle of the stall that was packed with goods, the unfamiliar smells of faraway places and faraway things filled her nostrils. She could smell cinnamon and sandalwood and other spicy scents. The merchant, a small man with a receding hairline, came out to meet Estevan, who proceeded to tell him that he wanted something pretty for the lady—a necklace of gold, if he had it. As the man directed him toward his vault with jewelry, the man's wife came out from the rear of the stall and descended on Anaxandra.

"Ah!" she said with delight, flashing her big, yellowed teeth. "What a lovely lady we have! But where is yer fine clothing, lass? What are ye wearing?"

Estevan heard her and came away from the merchant, putting himself between Anaxandra and the loud-mouthed wife. "There is nothing wrong with what she's wearing," he said. "This is what she chooses tae wear, as she's a woman of great skill and training."

The merchant's wife looked at him fearfully, but also with confusion. "I meant nothing by it, m'laird," she said. "I simply meant… that she's a lovely woman. A lovely woman deserves lovely things."

Estevan turned to look at Anaxandra, who was flushing a deep red color. *She's embarrassed,* he thought. Perhaps coming into the merchant stall had been a mistake. He certainly hadn't meant to embarrass her.

"M'laird," the merchant said, catching his attention, "something like this would be quite nice for the lady."

He held up a gold chain, delicate, with a gorgeous cross pendant on the end of it. The cross was inlaid with small, slender garnets, giving it a rather "bloody cross" look, but it was a stunning piece. Momentarily forgetting Anaxandra's embarrassment, Estevan took the cross and held it up to the light.

"How much do ye want for it?" he asked.

The merchant didn't want to blow the sale with a big price, so he was hesitant to answer at first. "It is of great quality," he said. "I purchased it in London from a man who brought it all the way from Rome. If the lady likes it, I will give ye a good price."

"I like it. How much?"

"Two pounds?"

"Sold."

It happened so fast. Estevan gave the man his money and immediately turned to Anaxandra, putting the necklace around her neck. Before she knew it, he was pulling her out of the shop and into the tavern next door. Anaxandra was trying to look at the necklace, so much so that she didn't watch where she was going. She plowed into a man near the tavern entry and ended up splashing his ale all over his chest.

"Clumsy chit!" the man shouted, cuffing her on the shoulder. "Watch where ye're going!"

Anaxandra didn't have a chance to respond. Estevan was there and the man went flying, out into the road and landing heavily. He was out cold, and whatever remained of his drink spilled in the mud, mixing with it. Anaxandra stood rooted to the ground, eyes wide, as Estevan went after the man, grabbed him around the neck, and tossed him out into the street for a wagon or a horse to run over.

Only then did he turn back to Anaxandra.

"Come," he said politely, as if nothing violent had just happened. "I'll find ye something hot tae drink on this damp day."

Anaxandra's mouth was hanging open. He took her by the wrist again and pulled her into the tavern, which was low-ceilinged and dark. There was a fire in the hearth, a few tapers around the common room, but the windows were covered against the rain. Estevan led Anaxandra around the corner from the door to where there was a small alcove, shielded from the common room.

Unfortunately, it was occupied.

"Get out," Estevan growled.

The lone man sitting at the table bolted up and fled. That

left the cozy little alcove empty, and Estevan indicated for Anaxandra to take a seat. She looked nervous, her eyes darting about, but sat down as requested. When Estevan tried to help her remove the crossbow from her back, she wouldn't let him. She didn't want to remove it. He finally gave up and sat down next to her.

"Although we had something tae eat before we left St. Margaret's, I find that I'm famished," he said. "Will ye eat something with me?"

Anaxandra didn't answer at first. She was still looking around, craning her neck to peer into the common room. "We cannot take the time to sit and eat," she said. "We should not even be here. You know we must return to the abbey."

He nodded. "I know," he said. "But it will take some time for them tae bring the special drink I'll order, so we may as well eat whilst we wait."

"Eat what?"

"Whatever they have."

As if on cue, a serving wench walked by, a tray with cups in her hands, but Estevan grabbed her before she could get away.

"The lady and I require food," he told her. "And I need some *öl*. Does old Bartha still make it?"

He was referring to the owner of the tavern, the same man who was involved in The Butcher's next door. At least, he had been involved the last time Estevan was here. Things might have changed. But the woman nodded to his question.

"Aye," she said. "He still makes it. Let me take these cups tae the lads over there and I'll return tae ye."

Estevan let her go, watching her cross the common room, which wasn't packed in spite of the people milling around outside in the damp weather. True to her word, the woman returned to him, wiping her hands off on the stained apron she wore.

"So ye require food, do ye?" she said. "'Tis a weak man who eats during the day, lad."

She chuckled as he grinned. "True," he said. "But ye have good food here. What's ready?"

The woman put her hand on his shoulder, something close to an affectionate gesture. "Something tae please ye," she said, all but ignoring Anaxandra. "Stewed beef with onion and carrots and peas. I can bring it and plenty of bread."

"Then do it," Estevan said. "And bring me a bladder of *ól*. I've a sick friend in need of it."

The wench winked at him and headed back to the kitchen. Estevan returned his focus to Anaxandra, who was watching him closely.

"What?" he said. "What's amiss?"

She didn't answer him right away. She looked around, at the common room, before she was able to reply.

"This," she said. "All of this."

"What about it?"

"Why did you buy me that necklace?"

"Because I wanted tae."

Her hands flew to her neck and she unfastened it, putting it on the table in front of him. "I cannot keep it."

"Why not?"

"Because… because I cannot."

"Ye'll have tae give me a better reason than that."

She frowned. "Because no one has anything like that at St. Margaret's," she said. "It is jewelry. That is only for the vain, and I am not vain."

Her words may have been of refusal, but she moved her

gaze to the necklace, staring at it rather longingly. Estevan watched her carefully.

"It is not for vanity," he told her. "A cross upon yer neck is a symbol of yer devotion tae God. He would be pleased if ye wore it."

His words had some impact, but she didn't waver much. "You have not told me why you bought it for me."

"I told ye. Tae show my gratitude for yer escort tae Dumfries."

She shook her head. "I cannot accept," she said. "Mother Michael would be very disappointed if I did. She would probably take it from me. And… and the other women would think less of me."

"Why?"

She shrugged. "Because a man gave it to me."

"What's wrong with men?" Estevan said. "I know that St. Margaret's is a nunnery, but ye're not a nun. Ye dunna want tae be."

"Nay, I do not."

"Then what do ye plan tae be?"

Her features tightened, hard and stubborn as she considered his question. "That is no concern of yours."

He gazed at her for a moment. He'd spent their entire journey trying to be kind to her. His words had been polite, his gestures generous, but still… still, she hadn't softened. If anything, buying the necklace had made it worse. Now she was acting as if he'd done something horribly offensive, and when he tried to get to know her a little, she'd shut him down.

Well, she had.

He *was* shutting down.

"Ye're right," he said after a moment. "It's not. In fact, nothing about ye is my business, so forgive me for trying tae show ye some kindness. Forgive me for trying tae gift ye with something lovely because I thought ye might like it. I should have known ye have no sense of gratitude in ye."

She stiffened. "I did not ask you to buy me anything."

He rolled his eyes. "That is the whole point of a gift, lass," he said, offended by her attitude. "But I suppose ye wouldna know that. I dunna know what yer Mother Michael has been teaching ye at St. Margaret's, but she certainly hasn't taught ye manners. She hasn't taught ye tae be polite or gentle. But I'm going tae wager that ye dunna even know what I'm talking of, so let's leave it at that."

With that, he stood up and began yelling at the nearest serving wench, who came to a startled halt as she listened to him yell. He wanted the *ól* and he wanted it at that very moment, and the woman went running for it. He was a big man with a big voice, so much so that a man came out from the kitchens in the rear to find out why he was yelling. He didn't seem to have a reason other than they'd not brought him the drink he wanted fast enough, so when the wench came running for him from the rear of the establishment, holding a sealed bladder for him, he grabbed it from her, gave her a coin, and headed for the door.

"Come," he barked at Anaxandra. "We're leaving."

Anaxandra grabbed the necklace and jumped up, following him out into the rain, which was starting to let up a little. The sun was beginning to peek out from behind the clouds. But Estevan didn't notice. He was marching across the road, back to the livery where their horses were standing just inside the shelter. Their fat horse arses were facing him.

The livery man was nearby and, seeing them return, went to

meet them with the basket of medicines that Estevan had given him for safekeeping. Estevan swung himself onto his horse first, tied off the bladder of drink, and then took the basket. Then he reined his horse out of the livery. He didn't even look to see if Anaxandra was with him. At that moment, he didn't much care.

He wasn't exactly sure why he was so angry at her, to be honest. He'd never met anyone like her, so perhaps there was part of him that wanted to break through that shell she seemed to keep around herself. She was humorless and stiff in everything she did, but she was also focused and, he suspected, deadly in any given situation. In a sense, she behaved like a woman who had never been trusted and had never possessed a reason to trust. There was something so guarded about her, and he realized there was part of him that wanted to know why.

Why was she so guarded?

Had she suffered a trauma that made her the way she was? Or was it something that had been taught to her? Ever since he'd come to St. Margaret's, he knew there was something odd about the place. He knew there was something odd about the women there. They were all guarded, just like Anaxandra was, with all of them having the same suspicious expression and the same unfriendly attitude. He didn't know why he had expected more from her.

She'd tried to kill him once, after all.

Perhaps this was just a situation that he was going to have to give up on. He wasn't exactly trying to make a friend out of her, but he would have at least liked to have made a pleasant acquaintance. Truth be told, he forgave her for shooting at him. Given the situation, he understood. But he was rather sad that he couldn't break through whatever walls she had. She didn't seem to want him to break through.

He thought he had seen signs that told him differently.

But he hadn't.

That woman who seemed so bewildered by the outside world, yet so fascinated by it, didn't want, or need, his help. Maybe he had hoped to open up that world to her so she could understand something beyond the walls of St. Margaret's. Perhaps it all boiled down to the fact that he was simply offended that she hadn't fallen for his manly charms. He'd used a technique on her that he'd used on other women, and they'd been slaves to his allure. But not Anaxandra.

She was too smart for him.

Lost in thought, he headed for the road south, out of town. It was the same road they had used before. More of the sun was peeking out now from behind the clouds, illuminating the sodden landscape. Gulls were flying overhead, riding the drafts as the sunrays warmed the earth and the heat began to rise. Estevan could feel that warmth on his face, and for a moment, he turned his face upward and closed his eyes, taking a minute to enjoy it. He'd spent the past night in the cold damp, so the rays of the sun were most delightful. But he caught sight of Anaxandra riding beside him, and that took him back to the subject at hand, which was his failure to captivate her.

Perhaps he was simply losing his touch.

Just as they reached the road, they could see a man running toward them. He was beaten and bloodied, enough so that Estevan looked at the man with concern. He appeared positively battered. The man was crying and gasping, staggering as he reached Estevan and Anaxandra, who had to stop their horses so they wouldn't run him over. As they watched, the man collapsed in the mud in front of them.

"Help me," he gasped. "Please! Help me!"

Estevan looked down at the man. "What ails ye?" he said. "Do ye need a physic?"

The man sobbed. "They're dead." He began to weep. "All of them, dead."

Estevan handed the basket over to Anaxandra so he could dismount. Holding his reins, he pulled the man to his feet. "*Who* is dead?" he asked. "Do ye need a physic, man?"

The traumatized man clung to Estevan. "They killed my wife," he wept. "My son. They killed my chickens and bit their heads off, eating them. They ate their heads!"

Estevan wasn't getting anything useful out of the man, so he gave him a good shake. "I canna help ye if ye dunna start making sense," he said sternly. "Who killed yer family? Tell me what happened so I can understand."

The shake had startled the man, bringing him around a little. He stared at Estevan as if seeing him for the first time. He blinked, forcing himself to form a coherent thought.

"They came from the river," he said, his swollen face full of terror. "There were many of them. They spoke a language I dinna understand. I dunna know what they wanted because I couldna understand, and when I dinna do as they wanted, they took a dagger and cut my wife's throat."

By this time, Anaxandra was off her horse, listening to the man's tale. "Where do you live?" she asked.

The man pointed south. "Whinny," he said. "I have a farm."

"Whinny?" Anaxandra repeated, looking at Estevan. "Where is that?"

He was still looking at the man. "It's a settlement near the sea," he said. "We passed it on our journey north, before we found the woman on the banks."

"Raiders, then?"

Estevan suddenly had a bad feeling about the situation. It was something the man had said that had his attention. They were attracting a bit of a crowd as people saw him supporting a bloodied, beaten man. People were starting to stand around, asking questions. But Estevan was focused on the man in his grip.

"Ye said they spoke a language ye dinna understand?" he asked the farmer.

"Aye," the man said. "I've not heard it before."

"And they came from the sea?"

The farmer shook his head. "I dunna know."

"Did they speak something like this—*Mitt namn är Estevan. En kvinna?*"

The man nearly panicked. "Aye!" he cried. "It sounds like that!"

He started weeping again, terrified, and Estevan let him go. As the man began to wander away, into the crowd that had gathered, Estevan turned to Anaxandra.

"We must return tae St. Margaret's," he muttered grimly. "Now."

She could sense the apprehension. It was bleeding from him like a geyser. "Why?" she said. "What has happened?"

He looked at her, knowing she hadn't been privy to the conversations he'd had with Titan and his brother about the Ormsfolk coming after Leonore. He didn't want to frighten her, but something told him she wasn't easily frightened when it came to danger. She was a trained warrior, after all.

For her own safety, she had to know.

"The woman we found on the riverbank," he said. "Did ye hear us speaking of her?"

Anaxandra shook her head. "Nay," she said. "I was not close

enough last night or this morning to hear what you were saying. I just know that Mother Michael needed help translating the woman's language."

That was probably true. She hadn't really involved herself in his interactions with Mother Michael, but rather stayed by the door as a guard. "Then I'll make this brief," he said. "The woman we brought tae St. Margaret's escaped from a clan known as Ormsfolk. They're also called the Serpent People. They're not like normal men, Anaxandra. Ye heard the farmer describe his attackers as killing his chickens by biting their heads off and eating them."

Her brow was furrowed with concern. "Ormsfolk," she repeated. "I've never heard of them."

"That's good," he said. "Because ye dunna want tae meet them in battle. We suspected they might be following the woman we brought tae St. Margaret's, but I fear that farmer may have confirmed our suspicions. We must return tae the abbey before the Ormsfolk figure out that their captive is within the walls."

He was already mounting up. Anaxandra followed after him, still holding the basket of medicines, which she handed to him once he was in the saddle. "But why should we worry so much?" she asked. "Mother Michael will not admit them. We can defend ourselves."

Estevan took the basket from her. "That is what Mother Michael said," he muttered. "I dunna have time tae tell ye the terrible tales of these men, so ye simply must trust me. Ye think ye can defend yerselves because ye've never faced them in battle."

He seemed edgy and brusque. That wasn't something Anaxandra had ever seen from him since they'd met, so she simply mounted her horse and began to follow him down the road. He'd moved on without her, so she had to pick up the pace to catch up with him. Mud splattered on her feet from the horse, but she wasn't paying attention to that. She was watching Estevan as he surveyed the countryside like a cat surveying a mouse. When he finally headed off the road and into the trees because he didn't want to run into the Serpent People if they were taking the road north, she followed. By the time they reached St. Margaret's some time later, he was in already in battle mode.

A storm was coming.

She could feel it.

CHAPTER TEN

Dumfries

THEY'D COME OFF a smaller road from the south because traveling the more popular road would bring their numbers to the attention of people who could possibly run home and summon men to stand against them. Therefore, it was better that they not be seen if they were to achieve their objective.

They had already started with one farm.

The farm had been close to where they'd located the queen's boat, so it stood to reason that she would have gone to the farm for assistance. Even though they had turned the place inside out and killed the occupants, they hadn't come across the queen or any signs of her. Even so, the farm didn't escape unscathed. They stole what they could, killed what they could, and burned the place behind them.

Now, they had arrived at a large village.

Since there were so many of them, it was better if just a few entered the village at first. Too many strangers would attract attention. Therefore, only four of them ventured into the village, leaving the rest of them back in a copse of trees on the village perimeter. One man in particular was the leader of the Serpent People.

His name was Bastijn.

"She could be anywhere."

A man with a yellowed beard and piercing black eyes spoke in a guttural tone, in a language used by the Northmen. His name was Willem and he was Bastijn's commander. They were on the edge of the village, scoping out a business that might be the central location for news or gossip. They wanted information and they didn't want to go hunting for it. The only place they could think of would be the church. The priest would surely know of any distressed people who needed help. Priests usually knew everything. When Willem pointed out the squat, sturdy building to Bastijn, they both nodded as if, indeed, they were thinking the same thing.

A church was the perfect place to find out what they needed to know.

The rain had stopped for the most part, leaving dark, puffy clouds blowing across the sky as the wind picked up. The road was very muddy and people were trying to navigate it as they went about their business. Bastijn and Willem were focused on the church, but also curious about their surroundings. Where they came from, there were no big villages, only scattered settlements, so an organized village was something they didn't see often. Willem was just getting a look at a shop with the word *Aromatarius* painted over the door when a round woman suddenly stepped outside, nearly crashing into him.

She yelped.

"Apologies, lad," she said, reaching out to slap him on the arm. "I should have looked where I was going. Did I hurt ye?"

Willem, as well as Bastijn and several other men of their clan, knew the language that the English and Scots spoke. With the trading across the sea that sometimes happened, they had to know a few words of it in order to buy, or possibly sell, goods. Therefore, they understood what the woman was saying. But Willem didn't like the fact that she'd slapped him and was preparing to wrap his hands around her neck until Bastijn saw what he intended and put his hand on the man's wrist to still him.

He smiled weakly at the old woman.

"No harm," he said. "We should be more careful."

The woman was very friendly. "No need," she said. "Ye can run intae me any time. I dunna mind!"

She laughed loudly, again slapping Willem, who grimaced and rolled his eyes. Bastijn still had his hand on the man's wrist, making sure he didn't try to slap her in return.

"You are understanding," he said in his slightly stilted speech, since it wasn't his native tongue. "We go now."

"Where?" the woman said. "Ye should come in my stall. See what I have. Do ye need anything? Medicines? Roots? Mysterious potions?"

Bastijn lifted a dark eyebrow. "What is mysterious potions?"

Her smile faded somewhat. "Love potions," she said. "Or mayhap a potion tae strengthen yer spirit. Any kind of potion. Do ye understand that?"

Bastijn nodded. "*Ja,*" he said. He made drinking motions. "Like this."

The woman nodded. "Like that," she confirmed with her own motions. Then she peered at him and his companions. "Ye're not from around here, are ye?"

Bastijn shook his head. "Inga," he said, using the word in

his language for "no." "Nay, not here."

"The isles tae the west?"

Bastijn motioned westward. "Ja," he said. "West."

She was back to smiling again. "Welcome," she said, slapping Bastijn, this time on the arm. "We dunna get many strangers here, and now I've seen two in one day. A nun from St. Margaret's came in earlier. Can ye believe that? A Templar nun!"

Bastijn had no idea what she was talking about, so he nodded. "Ja," he said. "A nun from St. Margaret's."

The old woman was clearly thinking back to the encounter. "Aye," she said. "Tall lass. Blonde hair. She tried tae fight me, ye know, pulled out her sword and everything, but I fought her and I won. I beat a Templar nun!"

Bastijn glanced at Willem, and he could see that the man's patience was gone. Unless he wanted a scene, and probably a dead woman at his feet, then they were going to have to move on to the church.

"Tack," he said, which was an expression of gratitude in his language. "My thanks."

"For what?" she said. When he tried to move on, she grasped his arm. "Dunna be in such a hurry. Come inside. I told ye that I have whatever ye might want. Do ye have sores on yer skin? A sour stomach? Do ye feel ill? The nun that came in this morning had a lad with her. They needed something for a fever. They had a woman with them that had a sickness. A stranger, he said. I gave him something tae cure it."

Willem, having had enough of the overbearing woman, pushed onward with the other two men behind him, but Bastijn grabbed him before he could get away. That bold apothecary running off at the mouth had told him something that sparked his interest.

A woman was ill at St. Margaret's.

A stranger.

That, most definitely, had his attention.

"A stranger?" he said. "Did he say more?"

The woman shook her head, but she was pleased that she had his attention. "Nay," she said. "But mayhap all strangers coming tae the village are ill. How good it would be for my business!"

She started laughing, grasping him by the arm and trying to pull him into her shop. Bastijn let her because he wanted to know more about the strange woman who was ill. "I'm seeking a woman," he said. "She would be a stranger here. My...*fru.* Wife."

The woman cocked her head in thought. "I've not seen any strange women other than the Templar nun," she said. "Come inside. Let me sell ye something."

"Where is St. Margaret's? Mayhap the nun has found my wife."

The woman managed to get him to her door. "Back down the road tae the south," she said. "Before ye reach the sea. But beware, because the nuns there know how tae fight, and they might take ye for an enemy."

He wasn't exactly sure what she meant by that. "Why?" he said. "Do we look like an enemy?"

The woman shrugged. "Yer men," she said simply. "They dunna like men, which is surprising, considering the one that came today had a man with her. And jealous was she when he spoke tae me!"

He wasn't sure what to say to that, so he nodded his head. "We will go now," he said. "Farväl. Farewell."

"Wait!" the woman said, grasping at him again. "If ye dunna find yer wife there, come back tae me. I'd make a good wife, and I willna run off."

She was cackling again, and he forced a grin, shaking his head. "One wife is enough," he said. "Thank you for your talk. We go now."

He and his men moved off before she could grab him again. In fact, they seemed to be moving rather swiftly toward the road that led south, to the sea. St. Margaret's was well off that road, so they'd have to be sharp about it, but the woman wasn't going to tell them so. She'd already given them too much help in finding a wife she hoped they'd never find. Perhaps that would lead them back to her.

She could only hope.

Lorna McKee wouldn't realize until much later, after she heard what happened to St. Margaret's, that she'd cheated death that day.

CHAPTER ELEVEN

"SEND WORD TAE Tristan de Wolfe at Blackpool Castle. He can be here in five days or less."

The suggestion came from Estevan. He, Titan, Kaladin, Rodion, and even Mateo were standing in a huddle in the sanctuary of St. Margaret's, trying to make a decision on how to reinforce the abbey. Given what Estevan and Anaxandra had seen in Dumfries, coupled with what Titan and Kaladin had seen on the silty banks of the River Nith, it was clear that the Serpent People had indeed followed their captive to Scotland.

And they were here.

"Why send for help?" Mateo asked, his voice hoarse from coughing. "We should simply leave. We've no loyalty to these women."

Estevan frowned. "These women provided ye with shelter in the midst of a storm," he said. "Moreover, they're in danger because of the woman *we* brought them. This is of our doing, Matty. I'll not abandon them now."

Mateo simply shrugged and turned away. Coughing, he went to lie back down again on a cot that Mother Michael had brought in for him when everyone was out on their errands. As he fell back on the bed, sputtering, Titan shook his head.

"He does not sound well," he said. "He is not usually so cruel. The fever must be affecting his mood."

Estevan watched the big man lie there and struggle to breathe. "Ye know he'll get off his deathbed and fight if the Serpent People come," he said quietly. "I'm concerned that they're already here, Titan. De Wolfe may arrive in four days or less, but that may not do us any good. It may be too late."

"Can we summon the Douglas clan?" Titan said. "These are their lands, after all. Threave Castle is not far from here."

Both Estevan and Kaladin shook their heads. "They're not allies," Estevan said. "They'd sooner spit in my eye than support a dun Tarh. Our best hope is an English army at this point, though they'll be crossing clan lands tae get here. Armstrong and Maxwell lands."

"If they tell the clans why they're crossing, they should let them pass," Kaladin said. "We should send word tae Carlisle Castle. Tate de Lara has the largest army on the west coast. He'll come tae our aid."

Estevan nodded thoughtfully. "He will," he said. "He's been an ally for many years with de Wolfe and de Velt. But taking his army intae Scotland will be risky for him."

"Why?"

"Because it's one thing for de Wolfe tae cross intae clan lands," he said. "They have ties tae Clan Scott and Clan Kerr. There would be no concerns. But de Lara has no such ties, and he has a very big army. They're likely tae take that as a sign of aggression, and the man could get himself intae trouble with the border lords."

Kaladin wasn't happy with that response. "Then *who* do we send for?"

Estevan looked at him. "Darien."

Kaladin's eyes widened. "Of course," he said. "Why dinna I think of our brother? Wigton House is very close!"

"Wigton?" Titan repeated. "Isn't that in Cumbria?"

"Aye," Estevan said. "It's Darien's demesne. Wigton House used tae belong tae my mother, her family's home, but she gave it tae him as a wedding gift. It's a big manor house with a decent army."

"How many men does your brother carry?"

"Two hundred, the last I heard," Estevan said. "It's a smaller army, but very well appointed. My brother spends money on his men. Most importantly, they can be here in two days at the most. Since they are smaller, they can travel more swiftly."

Before Titan could reply, Rodion spoke up. "You *do* realize that all of this will go away if we do one simple thing, don't you?"

Everyone turned to him. "What is that?" Estevan asked.

Rodion lifted his hands as if it were the easiest solution in the world. "If the Ormsfolk come looking for Leonore, all we have to do is deny that she is here and they'll move on to the next target," he said, looking at the men around him. "We are assuming that St. Margaret's is going to be attacked. We can solve this issue by simply denying the woman they're looking for is here."

Estevan cocked an eyebrow. "I know it *seems* simple, Rody, but it isn't," he said. "The last time I mentioned this situation tae Mother Michael, she was convinced that her women could protect this place from anyone who attacked it, including the Ormsfolk. I think her arrogance alone will compel her tae tell the truth, and then we'll have a wild bunch of animals trying tae scale the walls. And they willna stop. My da tells stories of the

Serpent People attacking in waves, for months on end, until hardly anyone was left alive."

Beside him, Kaladin was nodding his head. "And they poison their weapons," he said. "Take care that ye're not nicked by a blade, because they rub poison on them. If the wound does not kill ye, the poison will."

Rodion could see how serious they were, so his argument was a losing battle. "God help us," he muttered. "Is the mother abbess really that stupid?"

"Not stupid, but proud," Estevan said. "Ye've been around enough proud men tae know that their arrogance outshines their common sense at times. 'Tis the same with the abbess, I think. If they ask, I fear she'll tell them the truth."

"If that is your genuine fear, are you going to tell her to keep her mouth shut?" Rodion said. "Even if she does not want to lie about the woman in her care, are you going to tell her that if she does not, she'll be in a battle she cannot win?"

"Of course I am," Estevan said. "But in the event she doesn't listen, we will need reinforcements badly. We need tae send for Darien because I'm not entirely sure that forty or fifty women, plus the five of us, can hold off the Ormsfolk if they are determined enough tae get in. Do ye want tae die at their hands, Rody? Because I dunna. I'll not let that proud woman end my life because she thinks she can hold them off."

That summed up the situation, and Rodion was compelled to concede the point. "Then I suggest we send a messenger immediately," he said. "If this is as dire as you think it will be, there is no time to waste."

"I'll go," Kaladin said, watching everyone turn to him. He shrugged. "I have the fastest horse. I can make the journey tae Darien in a day."

Estevan sighed at the announcement of his younger brother, so bold and so daring. All of life was a big adventure for him. "Ye do have a fast horse," he admitted. "But if ye get yerself killed, Baby Bull, Mabel will have my hide."

"I do not think we have much of a choice," Titan said quietly. "We cannot send one of the women to deliver the message. They would not know where to go. *I* would not know where to go. I'm afraid you or Kaladin are the obvious choice for this, since you know exactly how to reach Wigton House."

"I said I'll go," Kaladin said in a tone that discouraged argument. "The sooner I leave, the better."

Estevan was forced to give in. But he looked at his brother for a moment longer, hoping he was making the right choice. "Very well," he said. "Collect yer horse. We'll speak tae Mother Michael about the situation."

With a quick nod, Kaladin left the sanctuary, throwing open the big, heavy wooden door open to the light and air outside. And he left it ajar. Estevan had to smile because it reminded him of when they were young, how Kaladin left every single door open, enough that his mother would shout at him to stop being so inconsiderate. Chamber doors, entry doors, stable doors, wardrobe doors… it didn't matter to Kaladin. Doors were not meant to be closed, in his opinion.

Even sanctuary doors at an abbey.

"I'll ensure he departs with a clear head," Rodion said, moving past Estevan. "He'll need to think clearly, you know. He cannot stop at The Butcher's and he cannot stop at every tavern he sees. He'll need to ride until he reaches Wigton and not stop for anything."

Estevan waved toward the door. "Then ye tell him," he said. "He never did listen tae me."

With a smirk, Rodion headed out, following Kaladin's trail, leaving Titan and Estevan alone. Over against the wall, Mateo was snoring again, that heavy snore that was the result of congestion. Estevan had given him the onion water with honey almost as soon as he and Anaxandra returned to the abbey, and it seemed to be helping a little, as he slept heavily. Estevan's focus lingered on him for a moment before he turned to Titan.

"We must tell Mother Michael about all of this," he said. "She wasna in the sanctuary when Anaxandra and I returned, and my priority was Matty at the time, but now that he's settled and we have a plan, we must speak with her. I suspect she'll be none too happy about us sending for reinforcements."

Titan waggled his eyebrows. "Anaxandra, is it?"

He was focusing on something that was not the subject of the discussion. It took Estevan a moment to realize what he'd said, and when he did, all he could do was roll his eyes. "Good Christ," he muttered. "I traveled with the woman. Of course I'm going tae ask her name."

Titan fought off a grin. "I did not say a word about it."

"It was yer tone."

"What tone?"

Estevan looked at the man with such exasperation that Titan burst out laughing. He slapped him on the arm.

"I jest with you, Es," he said. "Since when are you so sensitive?"

Estevan wanted desperately off the subject. "I am *not* sensitive," he said. "'Tis simply ridiculous tae suggest anything improper."

Titan threw up his hands. "Who said anything about improper?" he said. "But methinks you protest too much. Is there something going on I should know about?"

Estevan growled. "I despise and loathe ye," he said, turning away. "We must seek Mother Michael."

Titan snorted the entire way.

Mother Michael was not easy to locate. Every time Estevan tried to ask one of the women he came in contact with, she would shake her head and run away. Mother Michael didn't exactly ban the men from going to any other part of the abbey, though she had tried to keep them sequestered in the abbey, but this was a special exception. If Estevan couldn't find someone to fetch the woman, then he would have to fetch her himself.

First, they checked the outdoor spaces before proceeding into the cloisters, which he wasn't particularly eager to do. The cloisters were part of the original castle that had been built so long ago. There were outbuildings and an old keep that had been linked over the years by covered walkways or poorly built corridors. The whole complex was rather odd that way. As they crossed the bailey, passing the living quarters and heading toward the kitchens and the stables, they ran across chickens and dogs and, on occasion, a child. The abbey was famous for being a foundling home, but Estevan realized that the entire time they'd been there, they hadn't seen any children at all. Not that it was unusual, because children didn't normally roam freely in a place like this, but he was curious where the children were being kept.

He found out soon enough.

He also found Anaxandra.

To the east of what was formerly the keep was a section of the bailey that had been transformed into vegetable gardens. Most castles wouldn't plant their food source outside of the walls if they could help it, because food could be stolen, and the same school of thought seemed to apply to the abbey. There were neat rows of greenery, and he could see several children and adults working the garden. It was quite muddy from all of the rain, so everyone was covered from wrist to elbow with dark mud. Anaxandra was at the end of the garden, taking baskets from the children who had picked the vegetables and then dumping those vegetables into a small cart.

Estevan paused a moment just to watch her work. He had only ever seen the woman with the crossbow in her hands, tough and unwavering, so he was coming to associate her with a soldierlike mentality. Certainly, she'd had that mentality with him ever since they'd been introduced. After the scene in Dumfries left him frustrated when he tried to get to know her a little, he had to admit that he was surprised to see her in peasant clothing, working alongside the children. More surprising still, she was actually smiling. It was the most relaxed he'd ever seen her.

In his opinion, how a person behaved toward animals and children told a lot about their character. He could see that she was quite patient with the little ones and instructing them in a kind but firm manner. The more he watched, the more impressed he became. He had genuinely been afraid that she had no idea how to be kind or generous, but he could see that wasn't the case. He began to feel guilty about getting angry with her.

Perhaps he needed to apologize.

"Es? Did you hear me?"

Titan was talking to him. No, he hadn't heard him. He'd been too swept up in the sight of Anaxandra. Quickly, perhaps *too* quickly, he answered.

"Aye, I heard ye," he said. "I dunna see Mother Michael here, but I can ask Anaxandra where she is. Hopefully she willna run from me, too."

Titan could see the young woman with the long blonde braids and the face of an angel, helping with the garden. Realizing that was what Estevan had been looking at, he chuckled low in his throat.

"I said that there seems to be a small chapel to the left," he said, pointing to what appeared to be oriel windows built into the northern wall of the garden. "I suggested we look there, but you can just as easily ask Anaxandra. I'll wait for you here."

Estevan was struggling not to be embarrassed. Casting the man a threatening glare as Titan continued to chuckle, he headed in Anaxandra's direction, skirting the muddy garden until he came within range of her. She was just dumping another basket of carrots into the wagon, and, frankly, he could feel himself becoming interested in her far more than he should have. He thought she was a lovely lass, beautiful in fact, and he was curious about her, but he thought he had curbed it. Any tasks they'd completed together had been all business. When he'd try to pry into her life in Dumfries, she'd shut him down. But that only made him more curious about her, and that could be a dangerous game with a Lady Templar involved.

God help him, he knew that.

But he didn't care.

❧

SHE COULD SEE him coming.

Anaxandra had spent the past hour thinking about the journey to Dumfries. It wasn't necessarily the apothecary that she was thinking about, that vulgar woman who seemed quite interested in Estevan, but more the interaction between her and Estevan at the tavern.

The necklace he'd purchased for her was around her neck, tucked down deep into her tunic. She was terrified of losing it or having somebody steal it, so even if she wasn't sure why he'd bought the thing, she didn't want anything to happen to it. She had to admit that it was quite beautiful, and perhaps that was the problem—she *liked* it. She'd never known anyone to be generous with her, and certainly not a man, so that had confused her. Confusion had made her guarded. She simply didn't know enough about men to know whether or not Estevan was toying with her or if he was sincere.

The truth was she didn't know anything at all.

Anaxandra didn't know how to talk to a man. She didn't know how to behave when he talked to her. She didn't even know how to react when he bought her a gift simply because he wanted to. All of those events, when it came to Estevan, had made her combative, and that certainly wasn't the reaction she should have given him. She'd spent her entire life being told that men were vile creatures who were only out to hurt women, but Estevan had not proven that point. At least, not so far. In fact, none of the men who were with him had shown anything other than concern and courtesy.

And then there was Mother Michael.

Anaxandra had watched Mother Michael interact with Estevan. She had not seemed defensive or frightened or any of the other emotions that were supposed to stir in a woman's soul when she was around a man. There was no hurt or fear. In fact, Mother Michael seemed to be quite tolerant of their presence and had even shown kindness to them, especially in the case of the sick knight. She seemed to show a good deal of concern for him.

That was most definitely *not* what Mother Michael had

been teaching all of these years.

Anaxandra had never had any reason to doubt the teachings of Mother Michael, as they were teachings that had come down from previous abbesses. It was all of the opinions of Lady Agnes Herries, a well-known man hater. Anaxandra had never considered that the standards by which they all lived to be a farce, but with the introduction of five polite men, it was possible that Lady Agnes had been wrong.

Anaxandra simply didn't know what to think anymore.

One thing was for certain, however. As difficult as it was for her to even consider that everything she'd been taught was a lie, she suspected that she needed to apologize to Estevan after being so unfriendly with him in Dumfries. After he'd bought her an expensive gift, no less. The truth was that she didn't know anything about the man who had bought her the gift. She didn't know his heart or his character. But she did regret the incident in Dumfries.

She simply didn't know how to tell him.

On this day, it was her turn to work with the children in the garden, making a late summer harvest of some of their vegetables. Members of her Bow Pack were working there as well. The foundlings—all eleven of them—were in the garden, pulling vegetables under the watchful eye of Sister Hildegarde, who was snapping at them one moment and praising them the next. Anaxandra had to grin when the woman broke up a fight between two little brothers. She thought the woman was at her best when she was dealing with young children. Like she was a natural mother. Perhaps they were instincts, or perhaps learned behavior, but as Anaxandra watched Sister Hildegarde, she wondered how good of a mother she herself would be. *If* she ever had children. The truth was that she hoped to, someday.

But not if she didn't learn how to behave around a man.

Speaking of children...

Anaxandra caught sight of Estevan and another knight as they entered the garden area. She pretended to be busy, still going about her duties, but she was keeping an eye on them. When Estevan broke away from the other man and headed in her direction, she could feel her heart begin to race. Was it fear? Or was it something else? She truly didn't know.

All she knew was that the sight of him was making her breathless.

"What are you doing here?" she asked as he came near. "Did you come to help?"

She didn't know why she asked him that. It was just something to say, nervous chatter. But he took it as a joke.

"I'll help if ye need it," he said, smiling. "But it looks as if ye have plenty of help. They're doing a fine job."

He had a beautiful smile. Anaxandra's heart began to race a little faster and, instinctively, she smiled in return. It was the first time she'd ever smiled at him. It came as something of a shock when she realized she'd done it, but that didn't stop her from continuing. The smile remained.

It felt rather natural.

"They always do a fine job," she agreed. "This will be our late summer harvest, and everyone is very excited because our cook will prepare honeyed carrots and everyone loves them."

Estevan peered into the wagon full of vegetables that seemed surprisingly organized. "Me too," he said. "So ye keep bees?"

Anaxandra nodded. "We do," she said. "In the forest to the east."

"And no one steals yer honey?"

"Dogs guard the hives," she said. "Moreover, who is going to steal from the Lady Templars?"

He snorted. "Only fools."

"Only fools, indeed," she said, dumping in the last basket of carrots and handing it back to the brown-haired child. She seemed to sober, eyeing him as if considering what to say next. "Did your friend enjoy his drink? The one you got in Dumfries?"

Estevan nodded. "It has soothed his throat," he said. "But I think he'll be down for a couple of days at least. Whatever illness infects Leonore is infecting him all the same."

"Leonore. That is the woman you brought to us."

"Aye."

The conversation lagged, but it wasn't uncomfortable. Still, Anaxandra knew she should say something about Dumfries and the way they had left it. He didn't seem angry now, but that didn't mean he wasn't harboring ill feelings toward her.

She really didn't want that.

"If… if I was offensive to you in Dumfries, I did not mean it," she said quietly. "I know you were only trying to be kind. But I must return the necklace to you because we are not permitted to keep personal possessions like that."

He regarded her a moment, his pale eyes drifting over her. "I overstepped myself," he said simply. "I dinna mean tae. Ye must remember I'm not used tae having interaction with nuns. Or with ladies who live in a convent. I forgot myself and I apologize."

That was easier than she had expected, given the man's bold nature. Anaxandra found herself staring at him in return, noting the square jaw, the straight nose, and the way his cropped hair seemed to go in all directions, like an unruly child's. But she didn't mind.

She rather liked it.

"It was not your fault," she said. "I think we were both in a situation we have never been in before. It was… overwhelming for me."

"Ye dunna think ye'd like tae return tae Dumfries someday?"

She nodded quickly. "I would," she said. "I did not mean I wanted to stay away forever. I simply meant that I'd never been there before. There were a lot of people. A lot of things to see."

"And a pushy Highlander forcing ye tae accept gifts and eat in a tavern," he said, his eyes twinkling. "Ye're not tae blame, lass. I should have been more thoughtful."

She looked at him for a moment. "The fact that you would say such a thing is generous," she said. "And you tried to be kind about educating me on the Outworld. About courting and such. The truth is that I would like to know. I have lived in a world of only women, only knowing things about women, and only knowing men as living beings to be avoided and nothing more. You are a great mystery to me."

He snorted softly. "Not much of a mystery, I promise," he said. "And I'll tell ye anything ye wish tae know."

She smiled, her cheeks flushing red. "That is kind, but you probably will not be here long enough to tell me anything I should know," she said. "You asked me what I planned to do if I did not become a nun. I became angry with you because the truth is embarrassing."

"Will ye tell me?"

She took a deep breath, throwing caution to the wind. "I want to marry and have children," she said. "But a dream like that in a place like this is forbidden. Please do not tell Mother

Michael I have told you."

He grew serious. "I would never betray what ye told me in confidence," he said, moving closer to the cart. "But I do have a question."

"What is that?"

"How do ye plan tae find a man tae marry if ye never leave the abbey?"

Her cheeks flushed further as she lowered her gaze. "That *is* the question, isn't it?" she said. "The answer is that I do not know. I am not bound here, you know. I have taken no vows. But they did raise me from infancy, so I owe them my very life. I should like to find a wealthy husband who would donate a goodly sum of money to St. Margaret's in payment for what they've done for me. I would like to see St. Margaret's thrive and become more of a charity order."

His brow furrowed. "What kind of charity?"

She shrugged, looking at the children who were carefully navigating the garden. "We need a patron," she said softly. "There are many children in need. Many women in need. St. Margaret's was originally founded by a widow who wanted to provide a place for safety for widows and orphans. But when the church became involved, as a patron, that is when it became religious. But it is also a military place to protect the women and children, with violence if necessary. This is not a pleasant place sometimes."

He leaned against the side of the wagon. "It looks calm enough tae me."

She shook her head. "What you see is a coexistence," she said. "There are groups of us who live and work together. One group does not mingle with another group. I am part of the Bow Pack. There are other packs, like the Animal Pack, the

Flame Pack, and the Moon Pack."

He thought that was a curious thing. "Packs?" he repeated. "Like dogs?"

She nodded. "Like dogs."

"But what do these packs do?"

She thought on the question. "The Bow Pack are the women who are trained in the crossbow, like me," she said. "The Animal Pack tends the stables and yard, the Moon Pack is the night watch, and the Flame Pack tends the armories and weapons."

"Interesting," he said. "Ye function as several groups in one place."

"We do."

"What happens when ye're required tae fight a battle?"

"That's a simple thing," she said. "It is the only time we come together as a whole, but even then, each group fights together in spite of the fact that we are under one command."

"Mother Michael?"

She nodded. "Mother Michael was trained for her position since she was old enough to walk," she said. "That is how this order picks their leaders—from birth."

"I see," he said, interested. "Who will succeed Mother Michael?"

Anaxandra shrugged. "That is another question right now," she said. "No one has been selected yet. I've heard whispers that Mother Michael wishes me to succeed her, but that is not what *I* want."

"Ye want marriage and children."

Anaxandra nodded firmly on a subject she was passionate about. "Aye," she said. "But I am worried."

"What about?"

"That a husband would find my ability with the crossbow off-putting," she said. "One time, an old widow came to lodge here and she said that men like women to wear fine things and be docile, not warriors. Is this true?"

He fought off a grin. "Some men, mayhap," he said. "Not all. Some men might actually be proud of yer skill."

That came as a surprise. "Truly?" she said. "Where could I find such a man? In London, mayhap? I hear that weaker men live in London and would be willing to accept a wife's flaws."

He rubbed at his chin, trying to rub away the smile he couldn't seem to keep off his lips. "I dunna think that is entirely true," he said. "A man who would be proud of yer skills could be anywhere. In London. In Nottingham. In Berwick. In Edinburgh. Even in the Highlands. It's the heart of the man that defines his character and what he will accept, not where he lives."

That was new information to her. "I understand," she said, mulling over what he'd said. "Then I suppose in order to meet such a man, I would have to leave the abbey and search for him."

She clearly didn't understand how it all worked, courtship and marriage, which was incredibly sad, in Estevan's view. The fact that Mother Michael didn't see fit to explain even the most basic things about society, or men in general, was truly criminal. But maybe she didn't even know herself, trained in the abbey since birth as she was. Estevan had never seen anything like it in his life. But thinking on Mother Michael reminded him that he needed to find the woman.

But he was certain this conversation with Anaxandra wasn't over. Not in the least.

He had ideas.

"There's a little more tae it than that," he said. "I'd be happy tae speak with ye about it later, but the truth is that I came here for a reason. I am looking for Mother Michael. Do ye know where I might find her?"

Anaxandra nodded, pointing to the far side of the garden where the oriel window in the wall was located. "There," she said. "That is her chapel. Shall I tell her?"

"Would ye, please?"

Anaxandra nodded, stepping out from behind the cart and wiping her hands on her apron. She smiled at Estevan nervously as she went, and he watched her walk over to the old stone wall with the doorway and the windows built into it. He made his way back over to Titan as Anaxandra disappeared into the door in the wall.

"What was that all about?" Titan said.

Estevan kept his eye on the door. "I'll tell ye later," he said. "This place… it's strange, Titan. These women know nothing about the world. They call anything outside of these walls the Outworld. Did ye know that?"

Titan shook his head. "I'd not heard that," he said. "Where did that woman go?"

"To tell Mother Michael we wish tae speak with her."

Titan turned to look at the door as well. "What did she say to you that makes you think this place is so strange?"

Estevan shook his head. "Where tae start?" he said. "This place may have a religious name on it, and be referred to as an abbey, but these women aren't nuns. Not all of them, anyway. And the women eat and live in packs, like wolves. The packs dunna mix."

Titan looked at him, brow furrowed. "Is that so? Odd."

Estevan cast him a knowing look. "Indeed, it is," he said. "I suspect there's even more oddities than we know of."

Titan opened his mouth to reply, but Estevan caught sight of Anaxandra emerging from the chapel. She was waving them over.

That had the men moving for the door.

"Mother Michael is inside," Anaxandra said when they drew close. "She will receive you."

The men nodded politely. As Titan headed into the chapel, Estevan smiled at Anaxandra, who blushed and smiled in return. But he dutifully followed Titan a moment later, entering a low-ceilinged chamber that smelled of something strange. It was simply a chamber, with no hearth, but what looked like a makeshift altar at one end. On the altar were bowls of something that was smoldering, hence the smell.

Mother Michael, dressed in her dirty tunic and breeches, was standing by the altar.

"My lords," she said. "How may I be of service?"

Now they were going to get down to business. Thoughts of Anaxandra forgotten for the moment, Estevan replied.

"I'm afraid I bring gloomy tidings, mother," he said. "We've seen signs of the Ormsfolk. They have reached the shores of the mouth of the River Nith and they know of Leonore's boat. Titan has seen the footprints."

Mother Michael's attention turned to Titan as he nodded. "Aye," he said. "There were five boats and each boat can carry ten or twelve men. They were on the rocky shore and they made no attempt to conceal them, which means they do not care if we know they have arrived. I suspect they want us to know."

Estevan nodded too, cutting in on the conversation. "The point is that if they arrive here, looking for her, ye must tell them she's not here."

"But she is here," Mother Michael said.

Estevan nodded patiently. "I know, but ye mustn't tell them that," he said. "Mother, I realize ye dunna feel the need tae lie simply because ye're the Templar nuns and ye feel that ye can defend yerself adequately, but let me assure ye that the Ormsfolk dunna care who ye are. They'll not leave until they have her, until yer women are dead. They'll be relentless in ways ye've not seen before. Do ye understand me?"

Mother Michael seemed peeved. "I have told you before that we can defend ourselves," she said. "We have been here for many years, young lord. Clans call upon us for assistance when their armies are insufficient. I assure you that we can fight off a few dozen men."

"But these are not ordinary men, mother," Titan said, appalled at the woman's lack of understanding. "They fight like animals. They carry poisoned weapons. They will not stop until they have the woman they came for, but meanwhile, they will kill anyone who has resisted them simply for sport."

"They will not get inside these walls."

"And if they do?" Estevan said, having much the same reaction to her stubbornness as Titan was. "They'll kill anything that moves."

"You do not seem to understand," Mother Michael said, her patience wearing thin. "We can protect ourselves. Our order was founded on that premise, to protect women and children. We will not fail."

"And if ye do?" Estevan asked. "What about all of those children I saw harvesting vegetables? What of them? Are they expected tae fight for their lives, too? Because I can tell ye that the Ormsfolk will take them back tae Mann and either eat them, sell them, or treat them like slaves. Is that the life ye want for those children?"

Mother Michael looked at him with some horror. "*Eat them?*"

Estevan nodded. "They've been known tae eat children, so I've heard," he said. "And I'll remind ye that they tend tae hack up their enemies and feed the body parts tae the blood-eating eels they raise. I canna stress enough that this is not a normal enemy."

Mother Michael finally seemed to lose her smugness as the gravity of the situation was setting in. "That is not true," she said. "They do not eat children."

"I'm afraid that is the rumor."

"You are saying that simply to frighten me."

Estevan sighed heavily. "I dunna think anything frightens ye," he said. "I swear tae ye that this is all true. And if ye willna deny that the woman they're looking for us under yer roof, then ye must prepare yer women. They must be ready tae fight."

He'd rattled Mother Michael a little, and she looked away, pacing slowly across the chapel floor, which was stone. Dusty, old stone that had been walked upon by abbesses before her. They were in a private chapel, a chamber that had never changed in usage since the abbey was a castle. There were bodies under the stone of those who had originally built the castle.

Mother Michael paced over their bones, thinking.

"If you think this threat is so serious, then what do you suggest?" she finally asked.

Estevan was feeling hopeful that she might actually be listening. "I'm sending my brother tae summon the army of our older brother, who lives near Carlisle," he said. "We can have two hundred men here in three days or less. That should deter the Ormsfolk and keep them away from St. Margaret's."

"And if it does not?"

"If ye dunna tell them that the lady they seek is within these walls, then there shouldna be any worry."

He was essentially telling her not to answer any questions about the lady truthfully should the Serpent People come sniffing around. God, he hoped she listened to him. The woman didn't seem to understand that the world she didn't know about could be very cruel, indeed.

Brutal, even.

"Mother Michael," he said, lowering this voice, "ye've lived yer entire life here, taught by women who have also lived their entire lives here. Ye've built yerself a world that exists only within these walls. Believe me when I tell ye that the Outworld is a cruel place, with cruel people, and we are trying very hard tae keep ye safe. But we need yer cooperation. Ye *must* listen tae us when we tell ye that if the Serpent People discover the woman they seek is within these walls, yer lives are all in danger."

She regarded him from across the chamber, her dark eyes glittering. "Who told you about the Outworld?" she asked. "Anaxandra?"

He didn't deny it. "She was a good escort," he said. "She explained that she'd never been tae Dumfries and that everything outside of the walls is called the Outworld."

Mother Michael considered that for a moment. "I see," she said, though she didn't sound pleased. "What else did she tell you?"

"Nothing much more," he said, not wanting to get Anaxandra in trouble. "She said that she had come tae the abbey as an infant and that ye had raised her. She's very grateful."

Mother Michael snorted softly. "Did she also tell you that I mean for her to succeed me?" she said, watching him shake his head as if surprised by the question. "I do, you know, but I also know that she does not want to. She has a wanderer's soul, that one. I do not know what she thinks she will find beyond the walls, but it can only do her harm. She is better off with us, here. The world will not accept her kind."

"What do ye mean?" he asked. "What kind is she?"

Mother Michael sighed faintly, moving over to the oriel windows that overlooked the garden and part of the stable yard. "A bastard," she said quietly, catching sight of Anaxandra over by the wagon once more, helping with the vegetables. "She does not know the circumstances of her birth and I do not intend to tell her, but I will tell you because I have a feeling that your presence here has awoken that wandering spirit in her once again. She is not satisfied with life here and wants to leave us, but it will only come to tragedy for her."

Estevan's brow was furrowed. "Why?"

Mother Michael turned to look at him. "Anaxandra's full name is Anaxandra Tweed," she said. "That is her registered name. I was with Mother Gabriel, the woman who held this position before me, when Anaxandra was given over to us by a very nervous servant, who proceeded to tell us everything. She had just come from the House of de Longley, you see. They are the Earls of Teviot, of Northwood Castle, and it seems that the earl, James de Longley, had fathered Anaxandra with one of his wife's ladies-in-waiting. The servant proceeded to tell us that the wife tried to kill the infant, so the earl sent her to us, where she would always be protected. That is what we do here, young lord. We protect women and children. But Anaxandra knows nothing of the Outworld, or how to survive, and she would only come to harm. I know you do not wish to see that."

Estevan was stunned at the story. He knew the House of de Longley, as it was allied with his father. It was also a longtime ally of the House of de Wolfe, and with the heir to the de Wolfe empire listening to every word, he was certain that Titan was shocked also. He turned to Titan, in fact, to see how the man was handling the news.

The man was just as stunned as Estevan was.

"Her father is *Jamie* de Longley?" Titan said hesitantly.

Mother Michael nodded. "Aye," she said. "I do not know much of the family, of course. Only what the servant told us. But it would be best if you do not tell Anaxandra what I have told you. She has never asked and I've never spoken of it. It would be the best thing for all concerned if you do not mention it."

Estevan shook his head. "It is not of my affair," he said. But he looked at Titan before finally gesturing to the man. "But ye should know that Titan is the heir tae the House of de Wolfe. His father is the current Earl of Warrenton. Titan bears the title Viscount Kilham. His family is very close tae the House of de Longley, so this is something of a surprise, I'm sure. I'm confident he'll never speak of it, either."

Titan looked at Estevan before emitting a long, heavy sigh. "Nay, I would never speak of it," he said. "To anyone. Jamie de Longley has four sons and no daughters. The lads are all excellent knights and good men. Jamie is a good man, too. He is very much respected by all of his allies. His wife is from Aragon. It's tradition in the House of de Longley that the heir to the earldom marry from one of the noble Aragon families they are allied with. I think Jamie's great-grandfather started the tradition. Adam de Longley married an Aragon princess long ago. So did Jamie. Now that I think on it, I believe I heard my father mention that when Jamie married, his wife had brought all of her ladies with her from Aragon. The cathedral in Kelso was full of them when the marriage took place."

Mother Michael returned her attention to the window. "That explains her name," she said softly. "When she was given over to us, we were told that her name was Ana Alexandra Carlota Crisanta. A very big name for a very little girl. It was Mother Gabriel who changed it to Anaxandra. The first two names together to produce one."

"That makes sense," Estevan said. "I told her she had an unusual name and she said it means 'defender of the people.'"

Mother Michael nodded. "That is what we told her as she grew older," she said. "When a child comes to us as a foundling, we must make them feel wanted and important. Ana is our defender. She is the best archer we have. I'm sure you must realize that."

She meant when they first arrived and found a bolt driven between them and the abbey, and Estevan grinned weakly. "She is quite skilled," he agreed. But his smile soon faded. "My brother *is* going for help, mother. All of the skilled archers ye have may not be able tae hold off what is coming if they discover their woman is here. Will ye please promise me that ye'll not tell them that their woman is here?"

Mother Michael lingered by the window a moment longer before moving toward Estevan. Her expression was surprisingly soft as she looked at him.

"I am touched that you would be so concerned for us," she said. "I've never met a man who has the heart that you do. It is a pure heart, Estevan dun Tarh. I can see that in everything about you, and I appreciate it. You did not bring this burden down upon us, as St. Margaret's was established for just this purpose. To protect women. God will protect us. Mayhap he has already done that by causing your friend to be ill so that you will stay here and fight alongside us in our hour of need. *If* there is an hour of need. But I suppose we shall find out."

With that, she headed out of the chapel, out into the day beyond. Estevan and Titan stood there, watching her go, before turning to one another.

"What does *that* mean?" Estevan said, puzzled. "Will she do as I've asked? Or will she be truthful and suffer the consequences because she believes that St. Margaret's is strong enough tae stand against anything?"

Titan shook his head. "I cannot tell you," he said in exasperation. "I've got a very bad feeling that the woman's arrogance will get us all killed."

Estevan cocked his head. "But is it arrogance?" he said. "Or is it faith?"

"What do you mean?"

"She believes God will save St. Margaret's."

Titan shook his head again, heading for the door. "She believes *we* will save St. Margaret's," he muttered. "Come along, Es. We have a lot of planning to do."

Estevan couldn't argue with him because they surely did.

God help them, they did.

PART TWO

CHAPTER TWELVE

THE JOURNEY HAD been pleasant, so far.

Autumn was a particularly lovely season in the Lowlands of Scotland because the blooms from summer were just experiencing their last bits of life and the foliage was starting to turn color. The weather wasn't extreme at this point in the year, but rather mild by day and cold by night. Sometimes rainstorms blew in, as they had over the past few days, but for the most part, the weather remained calm.

That was what they had hoped for.

Lares and Mabel dun Tarh, the Earl and Countess of Torridon, were traveling from their summer home of Ashkirk Castle back to the Highlands of Scotland where their main family home was located. Castle Hydra was this structure and had been in Lares' family for hundreds of years, receiving its strange name from legends of serpents in the loch nearby. Lares was anxious to return because the Hydra was as much a part of his family as any of his children, all of whom had been born there. His blood flowed through those old stones and, in turn, those old stones fed his soul.

They were part of each other.

There wasn't anything about it he didn't miss when he was away from it, so returning to that legendary bastion was something he looked forward to.

Even if his wife didn't.

Mabel wasn't born there. She was English and preferred the more mild seasons from the land of her birth. Ashkirk Castle, which had been in the dun Tarh family for generations, was the closest she could get to what she had always been used to. She'd learned to love the moors that surrounded Ashkirk Castle, from the colors in the spring to the bucks in the fall. It wasn't exactly the vibrant greenery she was accustomed to in her native England, but it had its charm.

But mostly, she loved it for Lares' sake.

For many years, he had been her entire world. They had ten children together, eight boys and two girls, and they had shared the highs and lows that life sometimes brought. There was a devotion between them that was rare in married couples, something that suggested they drew the very breath of life from one another. They'd never spent any significant length of time apart and they never did anything without one another. Mabel mostly did what her husband wanted, and in this case, he wanted to go home early.

They had been scheduled to leave for the Highlands in another couple of weeks, but now they found themselves well on the road, trying to avoid Clan Douglas, and staying mostly to the coast. The lands they were traveling in were not terribly populated and the roads were not well maintained, so the rains from the past few days had managed to create vast lakes where a road should have been. That had made travel a little difficult, and considering Mabel and her daughter, Zora, were traveling in a fortified carriage, which was the only way her husband would allow her to accompany him on these long journeys, the pace was slowed considerably. Mabel and Zora would have to climb out of the carriage so her husband and about thirty soldiers could steer it up onto the soft shoulder so they could get it around the puddles in the road.

Zora duh Tarh, both Mabel's youngest child and her youngest daughter, was her companion these days because out of all of her children, Zora seemed to have the wildest streak of all, and Mabel kept her close. She had seen seventeen years, but as Mabel said, Zora was a young lass with the soul of an old woman because she more or less thought she knew everything about the world in general. Zora was not afraid to lie to her parents, nor was she afraid to go against their wishes. In fact, she thrived on it, which was part of the reason they were leaving Ashkirk early. Zora had struck up a friendship with a young blacksmith that had seemed to grow intense fairly quickly.

The only safe thing was to get her out of there.

Zora, in fact, had a penchant for attracting men of all ages and statuses. She was tall, with auburn hair and long legs, and a lovely face that perpetually seemed to smile. She would talk to anyone and was interested in everything. She could get around her father quite easily with a smile, but her mother was far more difficult. Mabel didn't fall for Zora's affections when she was in trouble or when she wanted something, which were sad times for Zora. She had spent the entire journey from Ashkirk trying to convince her mother to return to the castle because, surely, the weather was about to turn terrible and they would never make it alive to the Highlands. At least, that was the story when the rainstorms kicked up a couple of days ago. Zora had tried harder than ever to get her parents to turn around and go back to Ashkirk, but it was no use.

Lares and Mabel were headed for the Highlands, and Zora with them.

And that was that.

When the rain passed and the sun came out, Zora realized that she was destined for the Highlands whether or not she wanted to be. Therefore, she had been in a funk, pouting and unwilling to speak to her mother, who was clearly ruining her life. She was in love, she had confided in her mother, and she was desperate to return to the smithy she loved. Mabel had reminded her that it was a blacksmith today, but last month, it had been a knight from Pelinom Castle. Rodion de Velt had come to Ashkirk with a couple of his father's knights and Zora was positive that one of them, a big lad by the name of Brooks de Reyne, was to be the love of her life.

Zora hadn't been happy about the reminder.

It wasn't as if Mabel didn't understand a young woman's heart, because she had been a young woman once herself, too. She knew that Zora was just coming into her own and exploring the big emotions that she felt these days. Young women grew so quickly and seemed to mature so much faster than boys did, and Zora was simply caught up in the growth cycle. Mabel understood it completely, also because Zora had an older sister, Lilliana.

St. Lily, as Zora begrudgingly called her.

Mabel had watched Lilliana go through the same thing, though to a lesser degree, because Lilliana didn't have the gregarious personality that Zora had. Lilliana kept to herself and, in fact, the man she ended up marrying didn't even know that she was fond of him until their marriage. When Mabel thought of the extremes that her daughters displayed as far as their personalities, she thought that God might be playing a joke on her. She already thought He was playing a big enough joke on her when she married Lares dun Tarh, but her daughters seemed to be even a bigger joke than that.

Good thing she had a sense of humor.

"Mama?" Zora half spoke, half whined. "May I *please* get out and walk? Or ride a horse? This carriage is making me ill."

It was the first time Zora had spoken to her all day, and Mabel smiled faintly. "It's funny that you should say that," she said, focused on her sewing. "Long ago, I made the same request of my mother, once. We were traveling to collect your Uncle George because he'd injured himself and the road was terrible. It was making me ill."

"This road is making *me* ill!"

"Then summon your father and ask him for a horse to ride," Mabel said. "You'd better make that two. I'm not feeling so well myself."

Excited that she was going to break free of her prison, Zora climbed onto the bench next to her mother and tried to peer from the iron-barred opening. The carriage was fortified, meaning it could withstand an attack—and even an enemy trying to burn it—so the windows were small and mostly only for ventilation. Zora pressed her face against the bars in search of Lares, but only saw her brother, Caelus.

"Cae!" she shouted, sticking her hand out of the window. "Over here!"

If Kaladin was the Baby Bull of the family, Caelus was the Giant. Caelus dun Tarh was the tallest brother, long-limbed, muscular, and just plain big. He had enormous hands and a tremendous wingspan, which made him particularly formidable in a fight. He was also one of those old souls, a man who was simply born wise and mature, so when Estevan and Kaladin rode on ahead to Castle Hydra, Caelus had remained with his parents to command the escort. He was quite capable. Though he was fifth in the birth order, and the fourth son born, most people thought he was the eldest simply by his manner.

Caelus was a serious, unbreakable man.

To all but his little sister.

"Cae!" Zora said again as he came near. "Mama says we can ride. Can ye please bring us horses?"

Caelus lifted an eyebrow. "I hate tae say that I dunna trust ye, but I dunna trust ye," he said. Then he leaned down so he could look inside of the window and spied his mother. "Mae, is this true?"

The sons sometimes called their mother by her given name purely because they'd grown up with their father revering the name of his wife—*Mae*, the affectionate nickname. When Lares spoke it, it was like a prayer, so they'd grown up hearing their father call their mother by her name in the most respectful way possible, and in time, it came to supersede even the titles "Mother" or "Mama." Therefore, "Mae" and "Mama" were interchangeable and Mabel did not mind in the least. The name was spoken with love. She set down the sewing in her hands as Caelus asked the question.

"I'm afraid it is," she said, sighing. "The carriage ride is terribly rough. Find your sister and I horses, Caelus, before our heads are shaken right off our shoulders."

Caelus grinned. Sitting up straight, he reined his horse back toward the rear where horses to replace the ones pulling the wagons and the carriage were tethered. His brother, Lucan, was guarding the rear of the escort along with about fifty soldiers, and he came forward when he saw Caelus heading in his direction.

Lucan was one of two brothers in the family that had a shade of red hair. In Lucan's case, it was auburn and flowing, and, coupled with his pale hazel eyes, made him quite the handsome lad. He had Mabel's bold temperament and a stunning intellect. There wasn't much Lucan didn't know or couldn't figure out, and he had women chasing after him from one side of Scotland to the other.

He met his brother near one of the provision wagons.

"What's amiss?" Lucan asked.

Caelus threw his thumb back in the direction of the fortified carriage. "Mama and Zora are uncomfortable in the carriage," he said. "Pick a couple of horses and bring them forward. They want tae ride."

Lucan turned around and went to work. Soon enough, Mabel had an enormous, stocky horse to ride comfortably, while Zora had been given a younger mare who had a good deal of energy. Soon, Zora was galloping up and down the column, howling with pleasure, delirious with the freedom of being outside of the carriage. The men in the army were grinning at her as she rode up one way, singing and squealing, and then back down the other way doing the same thing.

She was having a marvelous time.

Mabel was riding in the front with her husband, plodding along companionably and watching their daughter ride around as if she'd lost her mind. Lares was smiling as he watched Zora, his baby, while Mabel thought that her daughter would sleep well tonight with all of the activity.

Sometimes, a girl just had to have a little fun.

"Should I stop her?" Lares asked, watching Zora charge across the road and down an incline, spraying mud as she went. "I dunna want the lass tae fall and hurt herself."

Just as he said that, the horse slipped and tossed Zora off into more muddy grass. She landed on her side, rolled to her belly, and slid ten or twelve feet down, laughing the entire time. Lucan went after the horse as Caelus, riding beside his mother, shook his head with disapproval.

"She acts like a child," he said. "Mae, ye need tae do something about her or no man will ever want tae marry her. Ye'll never be rid of her."

Mabel started to chuckle while Lares frowned. "What if I dunna want tae be rid of her?" he said. Then he pointed an imperious finger. "Go down there and help her. Dunna let her lie in the mud."

Rolling his eyes, Caelus did as he was told. As Mabel and Lares watched, Caelus reached a hand down to his sister, who was just picking herself up. She placed her hand in his and he lifted her onto his horse behind him, complaining because she was getting him muddy. That caused her to hug him tightly from behind, coating his entire back in the dark, rich mud. Greatly irritated, he spurred his horse up onto the road, taking off at a run as she screamed and held on tightly.

Mabel and Lares watched them go.

"He's trying to punish her," Mabel said. "If she falls off and hurts herself, Caelus and I will come to blows."

Lares growled. "I'll bloody well murder him," he said. "He shouldna be so rough."

"Lilliana was never like that," Mabel said, thinking on her eldest daughter, who was quiet and elegant. "We never had to worry about her."

"Nay, we did not. But Zora…"

"She's a lively one."

The parents could both agree on that. As they debated

whether or not to try to rein in Zora's wild nature, for Mabel was in favor of it and Lares wasn't, Caelus and Zora were thundering down the road as Zora squealed with delight. The road was still muddy from the rain and they probably shouldn't have been going as fast as they were, but Caelus trusted his mount. He was very sure-footed. However, after about a mile, he slowed down to a walk and Zora slid off the horse, rubbing her buttocks.

"That hurt," she grumbled. "Ye tried tae throw me off, Caelus."

Caelus fought off a grin. "If I were trying tae throw ye off, ye'd be lying on our back somewhere back on the road."

Zora frowned, but she didn't snap back at him. She could see the party from Ashkirk in the distance. It would be a while before they caught up to them. Still rubbing her arse, she began to walk with Caelus plodding alongside her.

"We're going back tae the Hydra rather early," she complained. "I was hoping tae stay at Ashkirk at least intae the autumn season."

Caelus knew why. "Ye're the daughter of an earl, Zee," he said quietly. "Ye canna marry a blacksmith."

Zora stopped rubbing and scowled at him. "I dinna say I wanted tae marry him."

"Dinna ye?"

"Nay!" she nearly shouted. "I simply found him interesting. He's English, ye know."

"I dinna know," Caelus said. "What's wrong with a good Scots lad?"

"Nothing," Zora said. "Except sometimes they're just so… *Scots.*"

He looked at her suspiciously. "What does *that* mean?"

She shrugged. Off to her left, blue flowers were growing on the side of the road and she went to pick them. "It means that most Scots lads never even leave their village," she said as she ripped flowers out of the ground. "They spend all of their time in Scotland. They dunna know anything else."

He was growing offended. "I spend all of my time in Scotland, ye know."

She waved him off, blue flowers clutched in the other hand as she resumed her walk. "But ye've been places," she said. "Ye trained in England, Cae. Ye've been tae London. Ye've even been tae Paris. Ye've fought in Flanders. Ye've seen the world a little. That gives ye a broader sense of life."

He wasn't so offended by the time she was finished. "So ye want a lad with a broader sense of the world?"

She nodded. "And the blacksmith that Papa and Mama are so opposed tae is an educated man," she said softly. "His grandfather was a cleric. He can recite poems from memory. He just happens tae be a smithy, and that's nothing tae be ashamed of."

She had a point. Caelus looked down at his little sister, a smile playing on his lips. "And so, my little Zee is growing intae a woman of substance," he murmured. "Just like that."

Zora looked up at him, seeing the warmth in his eyes, and she smiled. "I want the man I marry tae be a man of substance, too."

Caelus nodded, thinking about his father and how he was going to handle Zora being married at any time before she was fifty years of age. "Someday," he said. "When the time comes, we'll help ye find someone worthy."

"Will ye?" she said earnestly. "Well, ye and Darien and Aurelius, mayhap. Even Estevan. He's very smart. But *not* Cruz and *not* Kal. They'll simply beat on the man and I'll never be married."

Caelus started laughing, mostly because she wasn't wrong. Cruz had a temper, all fists at times, and Kaladin was simply big and frightening and liked throwing that around for the reactions he would receive.

"Dunna worry about them," he said. "When the time comes, we'll make sure they leave yer lad alone. We did it for Lily and we'll do it for ye."

"Thank ye."

"Ye're welcome," Caelus said. He started looking around, at the landscape around them, feeling the sun on his face. "Do ye want tae ride with me now? Mae will swat me if I let ye wear yerself out."

Zora saw more flowers on the side of the road, yellow this time, and ran to them. "In a moment," she said, tearing the yellow blooms out of the earth. "Where are we, anyway?"

Caelus had to think a moment. "We left Annan this morning and are taking a wide berth around Douglas lands," he said. "We'll run intae the mouth of the River Nith as it meets with the sea and then head north tae Dumfries."

"How long will it take?"

He shrugged. "We should be in Dumfries by nightfall."

"Are we going tae see Estevan and Kal?" she asked. "They left before us, but mayhap they dinna travel so fast."

Caelus paused before answering because the first thing that popped into his mind was the fact that The Butcher's was in Dumfries, and if his brothers had spent more than a couple of days there, then Mabel was sure to spy their horses and those two would be in for a row. There were two things going against Estevan and Kaladin right now—the fact that all of the dun

Tarh brothers knew about The Butcher's, and enjoyed gambling there, and the fact that hardly two days had passed after they'd departed Ashkirk that Mabel and Lares and the entire army had departed behind them. They weren't supposed to leave for weeks, but Lares was homesick and wanted to get back to the Hydra.

So… here they were.

Caelus had a mind to send Lucan up ahead to Dumfries to warn Estevan and Kaladin if they were, indeed, at The Butcher's. Caelus knew that was where he would be. The last thing they needed was for Mabel to bust into the place and drag them out by their ears.

Not a good look for a grown man.

As he was pondering that very scenario, something caught his eye down the road. It took him a moment to see that it was a rider, so he called over to Zora.

"Zee," he said quietly. "Come over tae me. Now."

Zora had finished pulling the yellow flowers but had spied some white ones. She heard her brother, looking up at him to see why he was giving her orders. He nodded his head in in the direction of the incoming rider and it took Zora all of a split second to realize what he meant. Flowers in hand, she darted across the road to him.

Caelus put a hand down, pulling her easily onto the back of his horse again. Since he'd trained as a warrior, his broadsword was already strapped to his saddle, ready and waiting. He didn't turn around and rush back to the escort, however. He simply paused, waiting, wondering why the rider was moving so swiftly. That indicated panic to him. As he watched, the vision became clearer. There was something about the horse that was recognizable to him, he thought. A big black horse with a white breast.

Kaladin had a horse like that.

"Christ," he muttered. "That's Kal."

"*What?*" Zora gasped. "How do ye—"

Caelus cut her off when he spurred his horse forward, rushing to meet Kaladin as the man raced down the road toward them. In little time, they came within close proximity of one another and Kaladin reined his excited horse to a halt, as did Caelus. The warhorses sensed something in the air, some kind of tension, and began to dance around and kick. That had Zora sliding off the back of Caelus' horse before she was thrown. She landed on her feet, fortunately, and with her flowers intact.

"Kal!" she cried. "What are ye doing here?"

"Me?" Kaladin said incredulously. "What are *ye* doing here? Both of ye?"

Caelus managed to calm his horse a little. "Mae and Papa are heading back tae the Hydra," he said, pointing down the road. "See?"

Kaladin could see the escort at a distance, but he was greatly puzzled. "Why?" he said. "They weren't supposed tae leave for the Hydra for another few weeks. What happened?"

Caelus shrugged. "Papa became homesick when ye and Estevan left," he said. "We left almost immediately after ye did. Where *is* Estevan, by the way? Why are ye racing down the road like a madman?"

Kaladin shook his head. "Papa needs tae hear this," he said. "And thank God ye're here. How many men does Papa have?"

"A few hundred," Caelus said, sensing his brother's urgency. "Why? Kal, what's wrong?"

Kaladin motioned to him. "Come," he said. "I'll tell ye."

He sprinted down the road, heading for the escort, while

Caelus was a bit slower because he had to carry Zora. He raced back down the muddy road, reaching the escort shortly behind Kaladin. Lares and Mabel were shocked to see one of their sons riding alone on the road, but they were also greatly concerned because Kaladin seemed quite excited. Lares shouted at the men behind him, holding up his hand, and the entire column ground to a halt.

Something was in the air.

"Kal?" Lares said as he returned his attention to his son. "What's amiss? Why are ye here?"

Kaladin told him. The entire story, from finding Leonore until that very moment. Everything that had happened over the past two days was now in the lap of Lares, who listened to the harrowing tale with increasing disquiet. What concerned him the most was hearing that the Serpent People, those ancient peoples that most western Highlanders feared, were in southern Scotland and, quite possibly, could be upon them at any moment, since Kaladin didn't know where they were. No one seemed to.

The entire story was baffling.

"This is madness," he hissed when Kaladin was finished. "Ormsfolk are here? And ye're sure of it?"

Kaladin nodded. "Titan and I saw their boats," he said. "We saw their footprints. They're looking for their captive, Papa, and they're going tae find her at St. Margaret's of Loch Doom."

Lares grunted. "And that's another thing," he said. "What on earth possessed ye tae take the woman tae the Templar nuns? Ye know they're a fighting order, not a healing order. Why'd ye do it?"

"Because we dinna want tae carry her all the way in tae Dumfries," Kaladin said, frustrated that his father didn't understand the logic. "She was injured, Papa. We thought it best tae take her tae the closest place where she might receive help."

Lares didn't like the sound of any of it, but he stopped short of calling his son foolish. Estevan wasn't foolish. Cruz was and Leandro was. Lucan used to be, but he'd grown out of it. Kaladin could be on any given day, but even Lares could see that his sons had been trying to do the right thing. But the fact that they'd taken the injured woman to St. Margaret's of Loch Doom was…

Ill advised.

Now, those reclusive nuns were involved in this.

"Ye did what ye thought best, I suppose," he finally said. "And now ye fear that the Ormsfolk are here?"

"Aye."

"But what makes ye think they'll end up at St. Margaret's?"

Kaladin lifted his shoulders. "Should we assume they willna?" he said. "I think it would be foolish not tae assume that, at some point, they will come. There's not much between the mouth of the River Nith and Dumfries, so if they head up the road and stop at every farm or church tae look for their captive, at some point, they'll come tae St. Margaret's."

"And ye simply tell them that the woman is not within the walls."

Kaladin shook his head. "That is the problem," he said. "The abbess at St. Margaret's is a woman named Mother Michael. Ye already know that St. Margaret's is a fighting order. They protect women and children. Mother Michael is convinced that she'll be able tae fight off the Serpent People and protect the injured woman, no matter what. Mother Michael's confidence in their fighting ability will compel her tae tell the

Serpent People that, indeed, the woman they seek is within the walls of the abbey. And they canna have her."

Lares sighed heavily, looking at Caelus, at Lucan, and finally his wife. He could see their grim faces. He certainly didn't want to drag his wife and daughter into a battle, but it sounded as if there may be little choice.

His attention returned to Kaladin.

"And ye were riding tae Darien for help?" he said.

Kaladin nodded. "Aye," he said. "I've been riding since yesterday. How close am I tae the border?"

"Close," Lares said. "But ye needn't summon Darien because I'm here. We'll go tae St. Margaret's with ye and reinforce the ranks. But I'm sending yer mother and sister back tae Annan first."

"You'll do no such thing," Mabel said, outraged. Before Lares could reply, she looked at Kaladin. "You said that Matty was ill?"

Kaladin nodded. "Aye," he said. "So is the injured woman. She passed on whatever is making her ill and now he has it, too. He was the one who carried her from the river. Estevan went intae Dumfries yesterday tae find medicine for him."

"Did he?"

"He brought something back for him."

Mabel sighed sharply. "I must see to him," she said. "His mother would never forgive me if I did not and tragedy befell him. I will tend him myself."

"I'm sure that's not necessary," Lares said as gently as he could. "I'm certain the nuns at St. Margaret's are seeing tae his needs well enough."

Mabel pursed her lips. "Rubbish," she said, turning for her horse. "Zora, find your mount. We are going to St. Margaret's of Loch Doom."

Zora moved swiftly because Mabel's orders were not meant to be ignored. "Can I help, Mama?" she asked.

"Of course you can help," Mabel said. "You will be a great help. Now, if your father would stop standing there with his mouth gaping and help me mount, we can be on our way."

Lares hadn't realized his mouth was open. But, then again, Mabel's bold decisions always had his mouth hanging open because he couldn't believe her at times. She'd heard all of the information about the situation, but still, she wanted to go.

"Mae," he said, moving over to her, "did ye not hear Kal? There may be a battle."

Mabel gestured for him to lift her up to her horse. "I heard," she said. "And if there is a battle, you'll need someone to tend the wounded. Zora and I will do it."

There was no talking her out of it. Lares knew that. They all knew that. With great regret, Lares lifted his wife onto her horse and then helped his daughter get settled. When he turned around, he could see his sons standing around, uncertain about what to do next, and he simply motioned to them to mount their steeds. That settled the question as to whether or not Lares was going to permit his wife and daughter to join them at St. Margaret's.

Evidently, it was going to be family affair.

Within minutes, the entire army was moving out.

Help, for the Templar nuns of St. Margaret's, was on its way.

CHAPTER THIRTEEN

St. Margaret's of Loch Doom

THERE WAS A good deal of coughing going on.

Lying on her cot, pushed over against the wall to keep it out of the draft, Leonore had been listening to the big knight on the other side of the sanctuary cough heavily for the last several minutes. He couldn't quite seem to catch his breath, so he lay there and hacked. Given that she was from the people who spent most of their time at sea in a chill climate, she had been around men who had their fair share of illnesses. But she knew this particular illness was her fault.

Her condition, however, wasn't nearly as bad as his. He had seemed to take the brunt of whatever she brought with her, and this was the third day of their illnesses. Leonore was holding her own while Mateo seemed to be getting worse. The truth was that she felt rather guilty about it, considering he was only ill because of her. Even now, she lay staring at the ceiling, listening to him cough and wondering if someone was going to help him. But he just kept at it. Finally, she turned her head enough to see that there wasn't anyone in the sanctuary other than her and the sick knight. It seemed as if the sanctuary had been full of women since she got there, but not at this moment.

She and her sick savior seemed to be on their own.

Quietly, Leonore set up in bed, coughing a few times herself before she was able to catch her breath. She was still dressed in the same clothing she'd been dressed in when she had been brought here, the very same clothing she had been wearing on her journey across the sea and even months before that. Because she had been a hostage, she didn't have any personal possessions, but what she was really missing was her shoes. She didn't have them anymore, so she could only imagine they were buried under the silt by now, somewhere near her boat. Therefore, she put her bare feet on the cold, packed floor of the sanctuary and carefully stood up.

The man's coughing was growing worse. He had rolled over onto his side to try to stop the cycle, but to no avail. He was sputtering and choking and when Leonore was halfway across the sanctuary floor, she noticed an earthen pitcher next to his bedside. She didn't know what was in it, but at this point, anything would help soothe that cough. As she reached his cot, she knelt down and picked up the pitcher, bringing it to her nose for a quick sniff. It smelled of onion. Reaching out, she put her hand on the man's shoulder and tried to encourage him to sit up.

"Sede, sede," she said softly. *Sit up, sit up.* "Oportet bibere." *You must drink.*

She was speaking Latin, the language of the church, because she assumed he would be able to understand her better. No one knew her native tongue, so she spoke Latin in the hopes of communicating adequately. Still coughing, the big man sat up and grabbed at the pitcher she was holding for him. Putting it to his lips, he sucked down the liquid, trying to quiet the cough.

It worked enough that he was able to catch his breath, but his eyes were red and his chest rattly. He took a few deep breaths before looking at her. She smiled at him and encouraged him to drink more.

"Bibere," she said softly.

Drink.

He did, again. He nearly drained the pitcher, wiping his mouth with the back of his hand. The cough had abated for the most part and it gave him a moment to rest, which he did gratefully.

The man was exhausted.

"Gratias," he finally said, realizing that a sick woman had gone out of her way to help him. "You have been helpful. I am appreciative."

He spoke Latin to her because, like all knights, he'd had to learn the language during his training. Since it was the official language of the Catholic Church, and knights were sworn to God by vocation, it was something they knew. He'd been fairly oblivious to what was going on around him over the past three days, mostly sleeping and trying to manage his illness, but he was more lucid now. He vaguely recalled the nuns attempts to speak with her, which was why he knew Latin was her language of choice.

"Mateo," he said, putting his hand on his chest. "My name is Mateo."

She smiled, a lovely gesture. "Leonore."

Mateo smiled in return. "Are you feeling better, Leonore?"

She nodded. "I will be well soon."

"Good," he said. "My apologies, but I have been sleeping much of the past few days. I did not hear how you came here.

Will you tell me? I am the one who carried you away from the river."

He was speaking simply, using simple words, and using his hands to emphasize his meaning. But she understood him well enough and her smile faded.

"I was a hostage of the Ormsfolk," she said. "I was given over to them by my father because there had been raids. People were killed. The Ormsfolk demanded satisfaction or they would kill my son, who had been captured during one of the raids."

Mateo's brow furrowed. "If he was captured, why were you a hostage?"

She shrugged. "Because my father valued my son more than me," she said. "I was traded for his safe return."

That was an unwelcome fate, but sadly, it was common. "I am sorry," he said. "For you, for your son, for your father. What of your husband?"

"He is dead."

"And your son is his heir?"

"He is."

"Did the Ormsfolk know he was the new king, with your husband dead?"

"They did not."

That made more sense now. "So your father gave you over to the Ormsfolk for the boy because he was more valuable," he said. "But how did you come here? To these shores?"

Leonore sighed heavily and sat back on her heels, her smile completely gone. "Because I was held in a cold stone tower, with no heat and hardly any food," she said. "Days and days of no hope, only desolation. I could no longer stand the torment, so I stole a boat and I left. The sea took me to these shores and my boat was broken on the rocks. And that is when you found me."

His smile faded as well. "So I did," he said. "I can only imagine that the Ormsfolk were terribly cruel to you. You have the right to survive."

She nodded. "I am going home," she said firmly. "My father is a man of his word, so he would not try to free me, but I was never told not to escape."

"And you did," Mateo said. "That was very brave."

"Do you know of someone who could help me return home?"

"Where is home?"

"Jura."

"Where is that?"

"An island to the north."

"Off Scotland?"

"Aye," she said. "It is to the west. Sometimes we will take a boat to Glasgow, which is closest."

He understood the general area. "We are going north, to the Highlands," he said. "Far to the north, past Invergarry, past Loch Ness. When we go, you can come with us, but I should tell you that we have seen signs of the Ormsfolk. They found your boat."

All of the color drained from her face. He could see it. Her breath caught in her throat and tears instantly filled her eyes. "Nay," she whispered. "Please… they have not. They *cannot*."

He could see the terror in her expression. "I am afraid they have," he said. "But you must not fear. The nuns here will protect you. And my friends… we are knights. We will help. We have sent for more men also."

Leonore's hands flew to her mouth in horror, perhaps in disbelief. When she blinked, tears spattered. Mateo reached out to take her hand.

"Do not fear," he said in a surprising show of compassion. "I promise, we will help."

"Please…" she whispered. Then, she swallowed hard and continued. "If I could only leave, I will go north. I do not need an escort. I did not mean for men to go to battle for me."

Mateo indicated the sanctuary. "Not only men will go to battle for you," he said. "This place is inhabited by warrior nuns and it is their duty to protect women. You are a woman, so they will protect you."

Leonore only seemed to grow more frantic. "They cannot," she said, standing up on quivering legs. "You do not understand. I have seen the Ormsfolk in battle."

"Leaving will not—"

She cut him off. "They have brought prisoners into their village," she said, growing agitated. "I have seen them cut off hands and feet and arms and toss them into the ponds where the eels eat them. They leave their prisoners alive and cut off pieces of them, a little at a time, and toss it to the eels. If they find me here, they will do the same thing to me!"

Mateo stood up, albeit slowly. He was feeling weak and woozy. But he towered over Leonore as he reached out to grasp her wrist, trying to keep her calm.

"No one is going to cut you into pieces," he said, his voice soft as he turned her around for her cot. "You will not worry. I will not let them take you prisoner again."

She was trembling and weeping. "You cannot stop them," she said. "If they want me, they will find me."

"I can stop them."

She dug her heels in, refusing to move, as she turned to face him. "Will you give me your word that you will not let them take me alive? You must put a sword in my belly before they can take me. Promise me."

Now, Mateo was the one starting to feel horror. "I will give you my word that I will not let them take you hostage again," he said. "You seem to have a poor opinion of my fighting skills."

She shook her head, grasping both of his hands tightly. "You have not seen what I have seen," she wept. "You have not listened to the cries of pain from prisoners left without feet, without hands. The Ormsfolk will cut something off and then leave them long enough to start healing and then cut off something more. The screams of men and women losing their legs haunt my dreams."

Mateo sighed heavily. "You are ill, my lady," he said. "Your mind is not thinking right. You must sleep."

He was trying to push her into bed again, but it was like trying to move a tree. She was rooted where she stood, unwilling to move.

"They brought one man to the village, a warlord from an isle in Scotland," she said. "I do not know what made him special, but they had a particular torture for him. Little by little, they cut off his limbs and threw them to the eels. When they cut off his legs, the big bones, they had fire waiting, and they burned his flesh to seal it as soon as they chopped his leg off so he would not bleed to death. The smell of burning flesh is something I cannot get out of my nose. When there was nothing more to cut off from him, they cut off his ears. I heard someone say that they cut off his manhood, too. Then they put him in a dirt hole to die, with only his head left. He sang for eight days in that hole. I know this because I marked the days."

Mateo couldn't keep the disgust off his face. "What did he sing?"

Leonore broke down in tears. "*Te Deum*," she whispered.

"He sang to the glory of God for eight days before he sang no more. Then they threw dirt over him and buried him."

As she wiped her face, Mateo envisioned a limbless man singing God's praises as he waited to die. It was horrific. But it explained why Leonore was so terrified.

And why the fear of the Ormsfolk was well founded.

"Get back to your bed," he told her, softly but firmly. "I must find the others. We will have a plan to repel the Ormsfolk, should they come. But you must sleep because if you are to help us fight back, you must be rested."

She was being pushed closer to her bed, but she was still resisting. "I do not want to sleep," she said. "I must leave before they come."

"You cannot," he said. "If you leave the safety of the walls, and they are nearby, they could capture you. That is not what you want."

She hadn't thought of that. After a moment's deliberation, she shook her head. "It is not," she said quietly.

"Then you must stay and let us protect you."

There wasn't much more she could say after that. She was shaken, exhausted, and ill. She let Mateo push her back to her bed, where she sat heavily before lying down.

Mateo stood back and watched.

When he was certain she wasn't going to get up again, he turned back for his own cot, thinking to take a quick lie-down before going out and finding his friends and cousins. Dawn was starting to break and a new day was upon them. Clearly, something was going on that he hadn't been part of, but he needed to be. If the Ormsfolk were as bad as Leonore said, then he definitely needed to be part of whatever was being planned. And he would be once he closed his eyes for a few moments.

Will you give me your word that you will not let them take me alive?

God help him… he hoped it didn't come to that.

CHAPTER FOURTEEN

THE DORMITORY OF St. Margaret's used to be the former storage vault of the castle before the order took over. It was sunk down into the ground, on a lower level, and it had arched ceilings of stone and floors of hard-packed earth. That meant in the winter, the cold would seep up through the ground and make it nearly impossible to stay warm. Not even the braziers could stave off the bone-numbing dampness.

Anaxandra's bed had a prime location against the wall so she could see the entire chamber. The dormitory was where everyone slept except for the nuns, who slept in their own chamber on the floor above. Mother Michael also slept in an alcove off her chapel, as was her right as the leader of the order, but Anaxandra was relegated to the dormitory where everyone else slept. There were a total of forty-seven women and children at St. Margaret's—eight nuns, sixteen children, and four mothers who were there with their children, leaving nineteen women who were either widows or simply women who had grown up as foundlings and become part of the army.

It made for a crowded dormitory sometimes.

Morning came before Anaxandra was ready for it. She was

warm and cozy when Sister Hildegarde shook her awake. It was before dawn and Anaxandra had a day ahead of her that included duties on the wall followed by fashioning more bolts for the crossbows. Her garden duties were over for the time being, as they weren't daily. Therefore, at Sister Hildegarde's urging, she was up and moving, stumbling out of bed as she headed for a corner of the chamber where the women washed. Water was already there, having been drawn in buckets by some of the younger members of the group, and she washed her face and used a community reed, frayed, to brush her teeth. That was how one lived in a commune and most especially with a religious order.

Personal possessions did not include things like combs and teeth-brushing tools.

Washed and brushed, her hair pulled into a tight ponytail at the top of her head, tied off with fabric strips, Anaxandra followed Sister Hildegarde out of the dormitory just as some of the other women began to awaken.

"I heard you went into Dumfries with one of the men who came," Sister Hildegarde said when they were on the ground level. "How was that?"

Anaxandra shrugged. "It was nothing," she said. "I rode escort so he could purchase medicines for his comrade."

"What's his name?"

"Who?"

"The man you escorted."

"Estevan."

"Your Estevan is wandering around the bailey," Sister Hildegarde said as they approached the door that led outside. "He looks like he's inspecting the compound, and I want to know why. Do you know?"

Anaxandra was fairly certain why. "There seems to be some concern about the injured woman in the sanctuary," she said. "They think she is in danger."

"What danger?"

They came to the door and Anaxandra paused, facing the old nun. "Estevan explained it to me yesterday," she said. "As we were leaving Dumfries with the medicine for his friend, we came across an old man who had been beaten. He said the men from the sea had killed his family and that they spoke a language he did not understand."

Sister Hildegarde wasn't following. "What does that mean?" she said. "What does that have to do with us?"

"Because the injured woman in the sanctuary was the hostage of a clan called the Ormsfolk," Anaxandra said quietly. "They spoke the language that the farmer identified because Estevan knows a little. He was able to speak a little to the old man, who told him that it was the same language his attackers had used. For that reason, Estevan feels that the strangers who beat the man are the Ormsfolk and they are looking for their hostage."

Now it was starting to make some sense for Sister Hildegarde. "But why would he think that?"

Anaxandra shrugged. "Because of what they did to the farmer," she said. "They were very brutal, something the Ormsfolk are known for."

"And he thinks they will come here?"

Anaxandra nodded. "Aye," she said. "They will look at all of the homes and farms and abbeys near where the woman was found. Especially an abbey—where else would a lost or injured person go? To seek help and comfort within God's holy sanctuary, of course. And if they ask Mother Michael if their hostage is here, you know what she will tell them.”

Sister Hildegarde did. Some of the hardness faded from her face, replaced by awareness of the situation. “Aye, I know,” she said with regret. “She will confirm that the woman is here. She believes in our ability to defend ourselves against anyone. That is the nature of our order.”

“Exactly,” Anaxandra said. “She will not deny it. Estevan says that the Ormsfolk are unlike any people we have faced. He thinks… he thinks they will breach the walls and kill us all.”

Sister Hildegarde pondered that. Unlike Mother Michael, she was pragmatic about life in general. She was older than Mother Margaret and had seen more fighting, more battles. She knew that even the strongest, sometimes, would fail. Especially if an opponent was determined enough.

“Then we are facing something dangerous,” she murmured.

“Estevan believes so.”

“It would be prudent to prepare.”

“How do you mean?”

Sister Hildegarde gestured to the building behind her. “You know I was a companion of Mother Gabriel,” she said. “She was our head before Mother Michael was. Mother Gabriel was a believer in preparing for all possibilities, so we should prepare for the prospect of our enemy breaching the complex. First, we must ensure that the children are safe.”

Anaxandra agreed. “We can put them in the dormitory,” she said. “The door is iron. It cannot be burned should our enemy manage to make it inside.”

Sister Hildegarde nodded. “I was thinking the same thing,” she said. “I will start moving food into the dormitory, discreetly. If Mother Michael sees, she will want to know why I am doing it and become angry with me when I tell her. I know her—she will feel that it is a lack of faith in our abilities."

"It is not a lack of faith," Anaxandra said. "It is simply being safe. The children cannot fight. They will need a place to go should St. Margaret's be attacked."

"Agreed," Sister Hildegarde said. Then she waved Anaxandra out of the door. "I will tell her. Go, now. You have duties to attend to. And so do I."

Anaxandra headed out into the early morning. Everything was cold and purple as the sun was just starting to rise. Her breath hung in the air in a cloudy vapor. She was halfway across the bailey when she noticed Estevan with two men, over near the gatehouse, and her heart did a strange little leap. She'd never experienced that before and she actually staggered to a halt, hand on her chest because she thought she was becoming ill. But when she looked at Estevan, it happened again.

The man made her twitch.

She had no idea what to make of it.

He was walking around the bailey with two of the four men he had arrived with. She didn't know their names, but she was coming to know their looks. Both of them were big and muscular, but one was blond and the other had dark hair, like Estevan. She also knew that his brother had departed the abbey yesterday, but she didn't know where he was going. She suspected it had something to do with the Ormsfolk.

Perhaps he'd ridden off to find them.

But perhaps not.

In any case, it seemed so strange to have men at St. Margaret's, walking the bailey in the early morning. Anaxandra had been here her entire life and never seen anything like it. Nor had the other women, and the anomaly had all of the packs talking together, which was something they didn't normally do.

Usually, the packs stayed to themselves, but in this case, there was a need for information sharing. Last night, before everyone went to bed, it was all they could talk about.

Since Anaxandra had gone into Dumfries with one of the men in question, everyone had questions for her. They wanted to know his name and what he was like. They wanted to know if he was married and to whom. They wanted to know where he was from. So many questions, and she finally couldn't answer them anymore, and then they started hypothesizing as to why the knights were still here. Of course, Anaxandra couldn't comment.

It was a wonder she'd gotten any sleep at all.

Now, she stood in the cold light of morning, watching men she didn't know plan for a battle that may or may not come. The thought of a fight didn't bother her in the least, but when she thought of Estevan fighting, it made her feel sick. The thought of him in danger turned her stomach. Certainly, she'd put his life in danger by firing on him on the day he arrived, but that was then. This was now.

She didn't like the thought of him facing danger at all.

Taking a deep breath and summoning her courage, she approached Estevan and his men.

"Is there something I may help with?" she asked.

They hadn't seen her coming. The three of them turned to her and Estevan smiled as their eyes met. Seeing his smile made Anaxandra want to smile, but she didn't want anyone to *see* that she was smiling at him, so she struggled not to smile.

It made her look like she was grimacing.

"Good morn tae ye, m'lady," Estevan said. "Did ye sleep well?"

God help her, but her cheeks flushed a dull red at the question. She stood here, proud and strong, prepared to be of assistance, but his smile and kind question had her melting like snow under the sun.

She was an idiot.

"Well enough," she managed to say. "May I help with what you're doing?"

Estevan nodded, a smile still on his lips. "I'm sure ye can," he said. "But let me introduce ye tae these men. I dunna think ye know them. Tae my right is Titan de Wolfe, who will one day be the Earl of Warenton. And the man on my left is Rodion de Velt, from the House of de Velt. Ye'll never meet more important men in yer life, m'lady. And they're not only my good friends, but also my kin. Good knights, this is Anaxandra. She's the best archer I've ever seen."

Anaxandra looked at the enormous, dark-haired man who was gazing back at her rather judgingly, though she had no idea why. She had no idea that he knew a little secret about her birth involving people he knew and was related to. But he nodded his head politely at her. She bobbed her head in return, nervously, before turning to the other man. He was fair, with dark blond hair and eyes that had green centers with darker outer rings. They were very unusual eyes. But the smile on his face was more genuine as he greeted her.

"You are a fine marksman, my lady," he said. "I saw it for myself."

Anaxandra was quickly falling into embarrassed ineptitude. She had no idea how to respond to a compliment, from a man, no less. Estevan and Rodion were smiling at her while Titan, the big one, was simply watching.

"I… I am well trained," she said. "It is my duty."

"And ye do it well," Estevan said. He could see from her

expression that she was uncomfortable and overwhelmed by the attention, so he took pity. "Ye can indeed be of assistance. Since ye know this place so well, in yer opinion, where are the weaknesses in the defense perimeter? May we discuss that with ye?"

He was diverting the conversation to something she would know about, something to take her mind off being in front of three men at once. As he'd hoped, she immediately turned to the wall and began heading toward the gatehouse. In fact, she seemed overly eager about it.

Perhaps to get away from all of those appraising male eyes.

"St. Margaret's was a castle many years ago, so it was built to withstand an attack," she said, pointing to the wall walk overhead. "Long ago, it was called Whiteside Castle. You'll note that the walk encompasses the entire wall. There are no blind spots or gaps."

She was on a subject she knew, so her confidence was apparent. Estevan, Rodion, and Titan followed her, looking up at the wall, which was in good condition considering only women lived here and probably didn't have much experience in repairing masonry.

"I seem tae remembering hearing that it was a castle once," Estevan said. "It certainly looks like one. The woman who lived here turned it intae a foundling home, did she?"

Anaxandra nodded. "Legend says that St. Margaret appeared to Lady Agnes Herries, the widow of Lord Herries, and told her to establish an order of fighting nuns in her name," she said. "Lady Herries turned her castle into what you see today, but I believe the point is that it was built to withstand an attack."

They had reached the gatehouse by that time. Titan and

Rodion went to inspect the portcullis, which was lowered. The gates were on the outside of the portcullis, to be closed in case of attack. Even if the gates were burned or destroyed, the portcullis would be there as a second layer of protection. Estevan could see Titan picking at the portcullis, testing it.

"Are there any other ways in or out?" Estevan asked.

Anaxandra nodded. "The postern gate," she said. "It is back by the garden, where we were yesterday."

"We'll need tae see it."

"As you wish," Anaxandra said. "I assure you that it is a strong gate."

He glanced at her. "I believe ye," he said. "But if we are tae help defend this place, then it's a good idea if we know as much as we can about the defenses."

Anaxandra watched him as he watched his friends inspect the portcullis. They were tugging on it now, trying to feel the strength of it.

"Do you truly think they are coming?" she asked softly. "We have watches in the countryside, you know. More will be sent out this morning. If they see something, they will come back and tell us."

Estevan puffed up his cheeks, blowing out a hissing breath as he considered what she'd just said. He was hesitant to say anything about a patrol because he suspected that was part of their normal routine, but he didn't think it was a good idea. Not at this time.

Not with an escaped queen in their sanctuary.

"Why do ye send out a watch?" he asked. "What are ye looking for?"

Anaxandra shrugged. "Anything that could be detrimental to us," she said. "Anything out of the ordinary. That is how we saw you and your men."

"Us?"

She nodded. "Our watch saw you on the road, so we knew you were in the area," she said. "It is good to have eyes around you, is it not?"

He looked at her, a smile creeping across his lips again. "It is."

"Then you approve?"

He burst into laughter. "Would it matter if I did not?" he said. "St. Margaret's has their own way of doing things that has worked well for them over the years. They dunna need my approval for anything. Except..."

"Except *what*?"

He sobered quickly. "Except if the Ormsfolk are truly out there, then ye shouldn't have women riding alone," he said. "Not even a pair of women. 'Tis not safe for them. In fact, the Ormsfolk could capture them tae bargain an exchange—them for the woman in the sanctuary."

Anaxandra grew serious as well. "I did not think of that," she said. "Mother Michael may not have, either. I must tell her."

She started to turn away but he stopped her. "Ye... ye aren't planning on going out on watch, are ye?"

She shook her head. "Nay," she said. "That is not one of my duties."

"Good."

"Why would you say that?"

The corner of his mouth twitched. "Because I would be worried for ye," he said, then quickly: "And dunna ask me more than that because I willna tell ye."

She cocked her head and fully faced him. "Tell me what?"

"I told ye not tae ask."

"Why not?"

He started to chuckle. "Do ye not know how tae obey a man?"

"I do not know," she said. "I've never had a man give me a command."

"If ye truly intend tae wed someday, then ye'd better learn."

She put her hands on her hips, frowning. "Is that so?" she said. "I *am* capable of making a decision. I do not need to be ordered about."

He scratched his ear. "Ye truly dunna know what I mean," he said, dropping his hand and looking at her. "The Book of Ephesians instructs a wife tae obey her husband as she obeys the Lord. Surely ye know that."

His use of scripture set her back a little. "I do," she said reluctantly. "But I will find a husband who respects me. Who values my opinion. And who does not try to order me about."

She was serious. She was also very pretty. Estevan found her quite charming when she was being stubborn. With a smirk on his face, he walked right up to her and patted her gently on the cheek.

"He'd be a fortunate man tae have ye," he murmured.

Giving her a wink, he walked past her and on to the portcullis, where Titan and Rodion were discussing something. He entered into the conversation with ease, leaving Anaxandra standing there, her heart threatening to beat right out of her chest. She couldn't catch her breath.

But… God's Bones, it was the best feeling in the world.

CHAPTER FIFTEEN

T HAT NIGHT, THE phantoms came.

A mist had moved in just after sunset, swathing the earth in a white shroud. Everything was damp, coated with the mist, and the moon was mostly blocked, which meant the only lights were those of torches as the sentries went about their duties. But everyone seemed on edge, even those who passed by Estevan, Titan, and Rodion as they stood near the gatehouse, watching the fog.

Waiting.

Somewhere, an owl hooted in the darkness.

Then it was silent again.

But the entire day hadn't been filled with the same apprehension they were feeling now. In fact, the day had passed uneventfully as the warriors wandered every inch of St. Margaret's. It was the first time they were able to see how big the place was. As Estevan had noticed the first time they arrived, Whiteside Castle had become something strange because of all the odd construction that had gone on to create the walkways and corridors and even some outdoor space that used to be part of the original bailey. That section was in the southwest corner of the ward and someone had tried to turn it into an outdoor cathedral because there were stones in circles that, once, were meant to be seats. Beyond that were derelict outbuildings, half collapsed and forgotten.

Curious about the stone circle, Estevan had asked an old nun who had been following them around. He didn't know her name when he asked about the stones, but once they'd had about an hour-long conversation, she told him that her name was Sister Hildegarde and she did not approve of the men inside the compound. Estevan had promised to behave himself if she promised to reevaluate her disapproval. That comment had brought a smile from her, though she tried very hard not to show it. She'd called him cheeky and a few other names and then stomped off.

But Estevan was pretty sure she hadn't meant it.

As he wandered the complex, making note of anything that he considered a weakness, he had only seen Anaxandra a couple of times. She had her duties and he respected that, but he had wished more than once that she would come and talk to him again. It was true that he had more questions about the complex, but it was also true that he just wanted to talk to her. He found that he liked talking to her. But she had work to do and he let her do it.

Still, he found himself hoping for a glimpse of her.

By the time evening rolled around, Estevan and Titan and Rodion had a pretty good idea of what St. Margaret's strengths and weaknesses were. Because it had been a castle before, it was already built for protection, so there really weren't any great failings as far as that went. The women of St. Margaret's had kept it up very well, walls included, so all things considered, they were in a good position. The only thing that Estevan didn't like was the fact that the wall walk didn't have a parapet.

The wall walk, for almost all castles, was usually guarded by a short stone wall to protect the defenders from flying projectiles. He had asked Sister Hildegarde if St. Margaret's had ever been attacked, and she had told him that it had never been, at least not in her lifetime. Perhaps their peaceful existence had given them a false sense of security and no parapet had ever been built. In any case, if they did get into a skirmish, they were going to have to be very careful about using the wall walk for defense. One wrong move and someone was going to get pierced by a bolt or they were going to slip and fall over the side. It was a good twenty feet to the ground below. That was a long fall, time enough for a man—or woman—to think about their coming death.

Tonight, the three men found themselves on that wall walk, looking into the fog, wondering if the Ormsfolk were out there. They heard more than one owl now, as the birds were territorial and their calls warned each other not to come into their domain. There seemed to be at least three, perhaps more. It only added to the uneasy mood that had settled.

Mists were always full of ghosts.

"I had a pet owl as a child," Rodion said quietly.

Estevan and Titan looked at him. "How did ye come by it?" Estevan asked.

Rodion smiled weakly. "My father found it in the forest, wounded," he said. "He brought it home to eat it, but I begged him to have it for a pet, so he did. That owl was about as tall as I was at the time, with great, taloned feet. It was rather terrifying for a four-year-old child, but I made a home for it and nursed it back to health with the help of my nurse. When the bird became well, he followed me everywhere. He never left my side."

"What happened to him?" Titan asked.

Rodion sighed. "One morning, I awoke and he was gone," he said. "Oh, I was so very heartbroken. As heartbroken as a child can be. But I saw him later and he'd found a mate. I suppose a lady owl was more attractive than I was. But sometimes I would find little dead mice or birds on my windowsill. I knew they were a gift from him. I even wrote a poem about it called 'My Owl Friend.'"

Estevan smiled. "Ah," he said. "I'd expect nothing less from the poet. Do ye remember the poem?"

Rodion had to think a moment. "I wrote it so long ago, I do not remember much of it, but it went something like this—

In moonlight's embrace,

An owl whispers secrets,

And a boy listens close.

Underneath a starlit sky,

Their friendship takes root,

And a love only they two share.

A boy.

His owl friend.

And a sky full of dreams."

It was a sweet little poem. Estevan and Titan returned their attention to the mist, hearing the owls in the distance. "Mayhap that's him," Estevan said. "He's looking for ye, Rody."

Rodion laughed softly. "I'm sure he's long dead by now."

"Who is dead?"

The three of them turned to see Mother Michael coming

out of the mist. Anaxandra was behind her, wearing a long leather robe against the damp night, something that would keep the dampness off her. A crossbow was slung over one shoulder while a quill of several bolts was slung over the other.

The woman had come for a battle.

"I was speaking of an old pet, my lady," Rodion said. "I used to have a pet owl, and we've been standing here listening to the owls call to one another."

Mother Michael's thin face turned in the direction of the mist. "That is what I came to tell you," she said softly. "We have never heard owls here before. Nightbirds, we have. But never owls."

That had Rodion and Estevan standing straight from where they'd been leaning against the gatehouse's second-floor wall. Those few words, calmly delivered, had the surge of battle rushing through their veins. They were already in full battle attire, with both Titan and Rodion in full armor and protection, so they were ready.

Ready and waiting.

We have never heard owls here before.

The spooky night had just gotten spookier.

"Men sometimes communicate in battle with whistles and birdcalls," Titan muttered. "I've heard it before. The Gordon have been known to do it."

Estevan nodded faintly, his focus on the darkness before them. "If it is men communicating, we need tae remove the torches from the wall," he said. "They can see everything we're doing."

Mother Michael swiftly turned to Anaxandra. "Tell every-one to douse their torches and stay where they are," she said. "I do not want someone misjudging a step and falling to their death. No light in the bailey, either. *Hurry!*"

Anaxandra nodded and fled the wall, walking too quickly for Estevan's liking as she made it to the stairwell and disappeared. He peered over his shoulder at the bailey below, watching her emerge from the tower and run to the first person she came across. After a brief conversation, that person ran off, as did Anaxandra, and they disappeared into the mist, carrying the message. Soon enough, the torches around the wall began to go out one by one. There were torches down in the bailey also, and those went out as well. Soon enough, everything was nearly black. There was no way to see anything.

Estevan returned his attention to the area in front of the gatehouse and waited. The owls were still calling to one another, only not as frequently as before. As he listened to them, an idea occurred to him.

"I'll be back," he told Titan. "Keep a sharp eye."

Titan could barely see him in the darkness. "Where are you going?" he said. "You should stay put, Es. If you go over the side, you'll break your neck."

He grunted. "If I land on my head, it willna matter," he said. "My da says my head is as hard as a rock. I willna hurt myself."

Titan grinned, white teeth standing out in the mist. "You idiot," he said. "Stay here."

"I'll be back," Estevan said again, moving around Mother Michael. "I have an idea."

"What idea?" Titan called after him. When there was no answer, he called again. "Estevan?"

But Estevan didn't answer. He'd managed to find the tower with the stairwell and took the steps down to the bailey. Once there, he felt a little better because the truth was that he wasn't fond of heights, and most especially heights without protection to keep him from falling. In the darkness, he quickly made his way over to the sanctuary.

The big, heavy entry door creaked as he pushed it open. Inside, there was some light as a few of the nuns moved around, mostly tending Leonore over near the wall. To Estevan's surprise, Mateo was sitting on his bed, though his face was in his hands. Not that Estevan blamed him. Being sick in a strange place was never a pleasant experience. Making his way over to Mateo, he put his hand on the man's forehead.

"Has yer fever abated?"

Mateo's head came up, his eyes red and his face pale with illness. "I think so," he said, his voice hoarse. "I do not feel as if I still have it. Why? Do I feel warm?"

Estevan took his hand away. "Nay," he said. "But ye look terrible, Matty. Have ye eaten something?"

Mateo nodded wearily. "Some kind of pea stew," he said. "It is giving me a belly ache."

"Keep it down if ye can," Estevan said. "Ye may need yer strength."

"Why?"

Estevan lowered his voice. "Because we're hearing sounds outside of the walls," he said. "Like owls. Mother Michael says they dunna have any owls around here, at least not ones they hear."

Mateo's eyebrows lifted. "Birdcalls?"

"Aye."

"That is how men communicate in battle so the enemy will not know."

"I know," Estevan said. "The Ormsfolk may already be here."

Mateo drew in a long, pensive breath, ending with a couple

of coughs. But his attention moved to the other side of the sanctuary.

"I think I know of someone who might know," he muttered.

Slowly, Mateo stood up and staggered across the floor to Leonore's cot. One of the nuns had just given her warm goat's milk, so she was lying down, ready for sleep. Sometime during the day, someone had taken her mildewy, torn clothing, sponged her down with lavender water, and dressed her in a clean pair of breeches and a tunic like the other women were wearing. It wasn't fashionable or even appropriate for a queen, but she was cleaned up and that was what mattered. When she saw Mateo and Estevan approach, she struggled to sit up.

"Great lords," she said in Latin. "I am honored by your presence."

Mateo took a knee in front of her, gently telling her to sit down when she tried to stand up. He forced a smile at her, though he'd never felt less like smiling in his life. He was weak and exhausted, but he didn't have time for that.

He needed answers.

"May I ask a question, my lady?" he said.

She nodded. "Ask."

"You know something of the Ormsfolk in battle, do you not?"

Her pleasant expression faded. "I have seen them fight," she said. "When they made war on a village to the south, they took me with them and forced me to serve the men. But there have been other times."

Mateo didn't want to get into what she did when she "served" them. It was probably something unsavory that would only make him mad and further upset her were she forced to explain, so he ignored that part of her statement.

"Do they use bird sound to communicate in battle?" he asked.

She blinked, startled by the question. "Why do you ask?"

"Will you tell me?"

She was starting to quiver. He could see it. "Bird sounds," she muttered. "I have heard them. Crows. Gulls."

"Owls?"

"I've not heard owls, but it is possible."

Mateo nodded, thanking her with a genuine smile, before standing up to face Estevan. "They *are* here," he whispered, his expression deadly. "You had better tell Titan and Rodion."

Estevan nodded. "We already suspected, so all of the torches have been doused," he said. "They are already on alert. But if they are here, why have they not come tae the gate? They dunna know if she is here or not. Why not come and ask?"

Mateo shook his head. "I do not know," he said. "Mayhap they will in the morning. We must be ready."

"Aye," Estevan said, determination in his tone. "Can ye take charge of the sanctuary and make sure it is fortified and ready?"

"I will," he said. "We can bring any wounded here."

"I would suggest having the sisters help ye," he said. "Ye'll need tae bring in water and food and anything else that wounded need."

"I'll make sure of it."

Regardless of the state of his health, Mateo was a damn fine knight, so Estevan left him in the sanctuary to organize it as a fortified area as he fled outside, into the fog and the cold. He had a thousand things to do and little time to do it. He was just getting his bearings when he heard a soft voice off to his left.

"Estevan?"

He turned to see Anaxandra coming out of the darkness.

She had an oilcloth cloak over her shoulders and head, covering the crossbow and quill so the wood wouldn't swell with the water.

"Ye put the torches out quickly," he said. "Well done. Are ye going back tae the wall?"

She nodded. "Aye," she said. "Mother Michael has asked me to be part of the night watch. She says that she needs her best warriors alert tonight, so that is where I will be."

He simply nodded. Thinking she wasn't going to get a reply out of him, she forced a smile and tried to move past him, but he reached out and grasped her by the arm.

"Wait," he said huskily. "Just wait a moment."

She paused, turning to look at him curiously. They were fairly close to one another, close enough that he could see the mist on her eyelashes. The longer he looked at her, the more protectiveness he began to feel, which wasn't healthy. Not at this moment. This was a woman who had been raised by other women to be strong and independent, yet obedient. She'd already told him that she didn't want to marry anyone who would order her about, so he wasn't about to tell her what he wanted her to do. She'd probably break his ribs if he tried. But he truly didn't want her on that wall tonight. It simply wasn't safe.

But he wasn't sure how to tell her what he was thinking.

What he was feeling.

And he was feeling a lot.

"We are fairly certain that it is, indeed, the Ormsfolk out there," he murmured. "In the mist. Watching us as we are watching them. I have a great concern about that wall, lass."

Her brow furrowed. "What about it?"

He tried to think of a way to explain it to her that wouldn't make her defensive or angry. "Have ye never seen another castle?" he asked. "Ye've fought other battles, but have ye seen another castle when ye did?"

She thought about it. "In the distance," she said. "I've never been to another castle if that is what you are asking."

He shook his head. "Nay, I'm not asking that," he said. "I'm asking if ye've ever seen the wall around a castle, up close. What I'm trying tae explain is that wall walks all have a parapet around them, which are short walls tae protect those on the walk. It prevents them from falling off the wall, or it protects them from projectiles fired at them from an enemy."

She wasn't sure why he was bringing it up. "I've not seen such a thing."

He pointed in the direction of the gatehouse. "Yer wall doesn't have a parapet," he said. "I dunna know why, but it is very dangerous. And it's wet up there, lass. Ye must be careful that ye dunna slip over the edge."

She looked at him as if she had no idea why he'd just said that. "I am careful," she said. "Do you think I am clumsy, then?"

He just snorted, seeing that this conversation could easily go in the wrong direction, so he chuckled as he put his hand gently on her face. "Of course not," he said, touching her softly before dropping his hand. "Lass, do ye not know when someone is concerned for yer health and safety? When someone is showing… care?"

The puzzled expression on her face seemed to be permanent as she tried to work through what he was telling her. But soon enough, the clouds began to clear and her eyes widened.

"Y-you mean… *you*?" she stammered.

He nodded. "If it makes ye angry, I'll not show it again."

That only made her eyes widen further. "Why would you

show it at all?"

"Because I am concerned for ye."

"Why?"

He could see that she didn't have any idea what he was driving at. Truth be told, he wasn't sure what he was driving at himself, only that he was feeling… something.

He couldn't stand the thought of her being in danger.

Throwing caution to the wind, he did something he probably shouldn't have done. It was impulsive, but it felt right. So very right. Grasping her by both shoulders, he pulled her against him and planted a sweet, hot kiss right on her lips. Squarely on the mouth. She tasted so good that he did it again before quickly letting her go.

"Because I'm going tae court ye, ye silly wench," he said into her shocked face. "Ye want a husband? Ye may have just found one, so get up on that wall, watch yer step, and dunna slide off or I'll have tae come and rescue ye and ye probably wouldna like that. But if I court ye, I have every right tae tell ye tae be cautious, so ye'd better get used tae the idea."

With that, he left her standing there, mostly because he didn't want a fist in his face or a kick to the groin should he remain any longer. The woman had never been kissed and he'd just done it in a most inopportune way.

And he wasn't sorry about it in the least.

Truth be told… neither was she.

CHAPTER SIXTEEN

THE TORCHES HAD gone out.

That was unfortunate because up until that moment, they had been able to see their enemy perfectly clear.

Now, they were looking at darkness.

Bastijn and Willem were close to the gatehouse, just inside the line of trees. The fog was so heavy that they knew they were concealed from anyone looking out from the wall or the gatehouse. They could barely see anything themselves. The fact that the torches went out was concerning, but they knew they hadn't been seen. Perhaps it was simply a method of conserving fuel.

Perhaps they didn't need the fires any longer.

But Bastijn suspected it was more than that.

In any case, his men were spread out around St. Margaret's, inspecting the landscape and gaining intelligence that would eventually help form a plan of attack. This was usual when they were considering an assault on unknown territory. They'd found the place easily earlier in the day, staying out of sight and watching the activity. The even saw the Templar nuns on the wall walk, though they weren't sure why they were called that.

They didn't dress like nuns, but rather like warriors. Perhaps that was why they had their name.

But it didn't matter.

The Serpent People could defeat them.

Men could always defeat women. They were confident in that. As they scouted the area around the abbey, they were communicating with each other with owl sounds because there was nothing more normal than birds of prey hunting in the dark. They usually communicated with birdcalls in a situation like this, and they chose the owl sounds because those birds were particularly active in the nighttime. There should be nothing unusual about that.

Or so they thought.

But the truth was that they'd been biding their time since their arrival. They had been in the trees since dusk, when the gates were still open or, at the very least, there were people milling about the portcullis. At that time, they could have very easily have walked up to the gatehouse and asked if they had seen a strange woman who had come from the sea, but given this was an abbey, they were fairly certain that even if she was within the walls, the nuns would not allow them in, and they probably would not let the woman walk out. Especially since she had probably already told them why she had fled.

And *whom* she had fled.

No, they didn't see any successful scenario in asking about her at the gatehouse.

That meant they had to come up with an alternative plan.

It was only an abbey, after all. At least, that was what they thought until they actually got there and saw women armed with crossbows upon the wall walk. That, in and of itself, was confusing enough, but what made it worse was that any woman they did see was dressed like a man. They were in breeches and tunics, with their hair tied back. The men started to think that they were in the wrong place until the bell tolled for evening prayers and they could even hear song upon the air. That told them that they were in the right place.

Even if the right place did seem… rather strange.

Further complicating the issue were the armed women on the walls. That didn't look like a normal abbey to them, which possibly negated an easy attack. Surely nothing would be easier than breaching the walls of an abbey, but not when those nuns had crossbows. It was anybody's guess as to whether or not they knew how to actually use them, but something told Bastijn and Willem that they wouldn't be carrying such weapons if they didn't know how they worked.

Nobody wanted to be impaled by a bolt fired by a nun.

That would be most embarrassing.

So, they waited.

"I've never heard of nuns defending an abbey like this," Willem said. "This looks more like a fortress."

Bastijn's gaze was on the gates, nearly the only thing he could see in the darkness, and even at that, it was simply a dark spot. "It does," he said. "That woman in the village did call them Templar nuns, and it is clear that it is some kind of fortification. That was obvious when we could actually see it. Now…"

"Now, it is a great mystery wrapped in the fog and darkness," Willem finished for him. "They've doused the torches and there is nothing for us to see."

"Mayhap we have seen enough."

"What do you mean?"

Bastijn sat back against a tree trunk, arms wrapped around his body for warmth. The smell of mildew was pervasive in the air, coming from him, from Willem, and any number of unwashed bodies nearby.

"I mean that I believe those nuns are defending the abbey because they know we are coming," he said. "Leonore must have alerted them. She would know that we were following her. She would know we are coming for her. She has put them on the defensive, which proves she is inside."

Willem couldn't disagree. "She must be in there or they would not be on such alert," he said. "Some of the men have suggested we make ladders and mount the walls, overpowering the women on guard duty."

Bastijn grunted. "We can try," he said. "But the same mist that would shield our movements would also make us vulnerable because we could not see the nuns well enough to place the ladders. We could put a ladder up right next to one."

That was true. The mist was both a help and a hindrance in circumstances like this. Willem was looking out over the grass, seeing the shadows of trees through the fog, thinking of another way to breach the abbey.

Only one came to mind.

"If we could just get one man inside, he could get to the gates and open them," he finally said. "Or we can simply remain in hiding. They'll have to open the gates eventually. When they do, we can rush the gates and gain entry."

Bastijn leaned his head back against the bark of the tree. "They would not be expecting it," he said thoughtfully. "It would make it easier for us."

"The would not have time to produce their weapons."

Willem looked off toward the east. "I noticed a vale in that direction when we came down the road," he said, pointing. "If we retreat back to the vale, we can have men watching the road so we will known when people approach."

"And the gates will open."

"Precisely."

It seemed that a plan was set. As the night deepened and the mist seeped into their clothing, making them feel cold and wet, they kept their focus on the gatehouse and on the structure in the distance, waiting for dawn and knowing that once it came, hopefully, their path forward should be clearer.

The queen was so close that Bastijn could smell her.

God help her when he finally got his hands on her.

Now, all they could do was wait.

CHAPTER SEVENTEEN

THE FOG HADN'T lifted by morning, but at least there was some light to see by now.

It was very little light, but it was enough. The women could move about the bailey without running into anything, but the land was still coated in mist. It touched everything, wet and cold.

The morning meal was being prepared and the smell of smoke, trapped by the fog, was heavy in the air. The children were up and moving, carrying water and supplies into the sanctuary under Mateo and Sister Hildegarde's supervision, while Mother Michael and Anaxandra were handling the general protection of the abbey. Unfortunately, that ran counter to a few things that Estevan and Titan wanted to do, so at present, Estevan was trying to prevent a battle from breaking out.

Literally.

"Mother, I mean no disrespect, but have ye ever had tae defend St. Margaret's?" Estevan asked as politely as he could. "Because it is different from being summoned tae fight another man's battle. When yer home is attacked, ye must have certain protocols in place."

Mother Michael was in full battle regalia this morning, which surprisingly consisted of chain mail that had been passed down from one mother abbess to the next. It was old, but it was serviceable. Her white hair was cut close to her scalp, wet with the mist, but her face was red with displeasure. She didn't like these men telling her what to do when it came to the protection of the abbey.

Mother knew best.

"The abbey has stood for over one hundred years, young lord," she said pointedly. "It can stand against a group of men from the sea just as it is."

Estevan was struggling with his patience. "All I need ye tae do is open the gates and let the mist soak intae the portcullis," he said. "We need the wood tae be wet so it canna burn should the enemy decide tae light it afire. It's an older portcullis and the wood is splintering. We must soak it so it canna burn."

Mother Michael's solution to shoring up the security of St. Margaret's was to keep everything closed, including the big gates, which were already soaked from the mist. They protected the portcullis, which had seen better days. Estevan was just trying to make the gatehouse less vulnerable, but she didn't seem to like that.

"I will think on it," she finally said. When he opened his mouth to argue, she put her hand up to silence him. "I know you are trying to help, but this place has stood for a very long time. We do have some experience in protecting it."

Estevan sighed heavily and looked at Titan, who simply shook his head. He'd already had his own argument with Mother Michael about bricking up the postern gate. There were stones in an unused outbuilding that were from the building of the walkways and corridors decades ago, along with barrels of lime and sand. It was old, and some of it had already hardened, but they still had enough to use to block up the postern gate, which was not particularly stable.

But Mother Michael wouldn't hear of it.

"Mother, we're not contesting your ability to protect your women and children," Titan finally said. "We are simply offering a fresh eye to what may be a weakness in your defenses. Both Estevan and I have years of education and experience in this matter. We are trying to help you."

Mother Michael eyed the big knight. "I realize that," she said. "And I further realize that you are a de Wolfe. Your family practically rules the north of England and southern Scotland right along with it, so you are accustomed to being in control. However, I am telling you that we do not need your suggestions. If you are to remain, I would appreciate it if you would simply do as I command. Can you do that or not?"

Estevan mumbled something that sounded like an affirmative, but Titan simply cocked an eyebrow.

"We can follow commands," he said in a low voice. "But a good commander knows when to take the advice of his seasoned men. A good commander does not shut out reasonable suggestions. A commander who does not to do these things risks catastrophically failing, so aye, we will follow your commands, but if your command will risk my life or the life of my friends, I will not follow it. And you will know why because I will tell you. I hope we are clear on that because you are traveling down a dangerous path with your inability to listen to anyone other than yourself."

With that, he turned away and headed toward the sanctuary that was a hive of activity at the moment. Estevan's gaze lingered on the woman, who seemed somewhat humbled by the scolding, but when she saw that Estevan was looking at her, she quickly walked away.

That left Estevan and Anaxandra alone.

"She has been doing this for a long time," Anaxandra said softly, offering up an excuse. "She has never taken orders from anyone. It is difficult for her to do so."

Estevan looked at her. She was still clad in the clothing she'd had on the night before, her hair and ponytail wet from the mist, her face pale but her eyes bright. She'd been up all night, like the rest of them, but Estevan swore he'd never seen a more beautiful woman. His desire to keep her safe was like a runaway bull, almost uncontrollable, and Mother Michael's refusals were frustrating to say the least.

"No one was giving her orders," he said. "We were simply suggesting a few minor things that may be very helpful in the end. 'Tis a stubborn woman who refuses help."

Anaxandra nodded. "I know," she said. "It is simply her way."

"I hope her way doesn't get us all killed."

Anaxandra nodded weakly, feeling his frustration, but there was also something else she was feeling.

His lips on her mouth.

Whatever he'd done to her yesterday had started a fire inside of her. It was difficult to describe because she'd never felt anything like it before, but the best way she could explain it was that her lips were still hot where he'd touched her. His heat against her heat, so hard and so firm, had left a mark, like a branding.

His lips had branded her.

Truth be told, Anaxandra didn't even really know what a

kiss was. She had only seen it once or twice, and that had been between some of the older women. They were kisses of friendship, or of greeting, but that wasn't something she had ever done herself or had ever personally experienced.

Until last night.

Now, it was all she could think about. Even as she'd patrolled the wall last night, in the mist, her entire body may have been cold, but her lips were still warm with his touch. Estevan had been around all night, but any eye contact between them had Alexandra blushing so furiously that she was positive her head would go up in flames. He simply smiled at her while she had stood there and reeked of embarrassment. But it wasn't that she was embarrassed he had kissed her. It was the fact that she had *liked* it. Even now as she looked at him, she wanted him to do it again.

"Estevan," she said quietly, "may I ask you something?"

"Anything."

"Did you mean what you said last night?" she said. "About courting me?"

The mere mention of it caused a smile to spread across his lips. "And if I did?"

She wasn't sure how to answer that at first. "What does it all mean?" she said. "You never did tell me what a courting is."

His smile grew as they veered onto a far more pleasing subject than battle defenses. "It is very simple," he said. "It means that I want tae come tae know ye, and ye want tae come tae know me, and we spend time together before we're married."

"Time together doing what?"

He shrugged. "Anything," he said. "I've thought a little about this. In fact, I was thinking about it last night when I should have been thinking about the owl sounds that stopped around midnight. But I was thinking of taking ye tae the Hydra, where my family lives, where ye could live with my mother and sister and learn how tae be a lady. No offense tae the skills ye have now, but when I marry, I'd like my wife tae manage my home. Do ye know how tae?"

She frowned. "Nay," she admitted. "What do I do?"

"My mother would teach ye," he said. "Would ye be willing tae learn?"

Anaxandra simply stared at him. He could see the emotions rolling through her eyes, finally rippling across her face. She wasn't any good at concealing her thoughts because she'd never needed to. She was delighted, she was afraid, she was in disbelief. Estevan could read them in turn, one at a time.

Finally, she shook her head.

"Sir," she whispered, "are you truly serious about this?"

He nodded, his eyes glimmering with warmth. "Very much," he said. "Dunna ask me how or why, because I dunna know. All I know is that I see something in ye that is rare. Ye're unlike anyone I've ever known. I could leave today, but I'd never forget about ye, Anaxandra. I'd always wonder about ye and I'd make it a point tae return, just tae see ye. I know ye dunna know anything about men, or what happens between men and women, but I promise that if ye'll give me a chance, I'll show ye. Maybe we can both learn how wonderful it can be."

Anaxandra didn't know what to say, but his words made her cheeks flush again. With the cold weather, it was obvious. He started to laugh because she was flushing a deep red, so she giggled and lowered her face, trying to cover it with a hand. Reaching out, he took that hand away from her face and held it.

"Just think on it," he said. "I'm not asking for yer agreement now, but I want ye tae think on it. I can offer ye everything ye have dreamt of, Anaxandra. A home, children. And a husband who would be loyal tae ye, and only ye, until the day he died."

With that, he kissed her hand tenderly, causing her to gasp as if he'd stung her. He looked at her with concern only to see utter, complete awe in her expression. That was all he needed to pull her to him again and slant his mouth over hers, gently.

Oh so gently.

Until she threw her arms around his neck and nearly strangled him.

"*Estevan!*"

A shout drove them apart quicker than the blink of an eye. Suddenly, they were standing a few feet away from one another, breathless, startled. Estevan's head was swimming with the taste and feel of her, but he quickly regained his wits. The shout had come from the wall, which was barely in view as the sun rose.

"What it is it?" he called.

It was Titan. "The mist has lifted enough that we can see a massive party approaching," he said. "You'd better come."

Estevan was on the wall in a split second.

⅓

"WHAT *IS* THIS place?" Zora asked. Wrapped up in a heavy cloak that her mother made her wear, she was riding alongside her brother on a sturdy palfrey. "It looks like a place where people go tae die."

Kaladin snorted at his sister as the walls of St. Margaret's finally came into view in the distance. Shrouded by remnants of fog, it did indeed look dark and gloomy.

"It's an abbey of fighting women," he told her. "I've told ye they are called the *Na Ban-Teamplairean*. The Lady Templars."

Zora's expression was full of distaste as she looked at the gatehouse looming at the end of the road. "Fighting nuns," she muttered. "That's *not* what God intended."

Kaladin continued to snort. "How do ye know?" he said. "They're much feared, lass. They're good at what they know. If I were ye, I'd not insult them. Ye might be on the wrong end of a beating."

Zora shrugged and turned her nose up at him. Grinning, he turned to Caelus, who was riding slightly ahead of them, on point. "Cae," he said, "I'm going back tae speak tae Papa. Watch the bairn over here and make sure she doesn't get intae any trouble."

Caelus growled. "I was forced tae watch over her yesterday," he said. "It's yer turn."

"It's no one's turn!" Zora said angrily. "I dunna need watching over. Focus on yer own hides and leave me alone."

"Ungrateful wench," Caelus rumbled. "I hope yer horse runs off with ye still on it."

"I hope it does also!"

"This is why no one likes ye, Zora."

"Mama!" Zora suddenly reined her horse back for the carriage where her parents were. "Mama, tell Caelus tae stop being so nasty!"

She was shouting all the way down the column, causing the men in Lares' army to start laughing. But that was usual with Zora, who was brave in her bullying until someone gave it to her in return. Then she ran to her mother to punish the offenders. Being the youngest of ten children meant she should have had a thicker skin than most, but she didn't.

And her brothers knew it.

"Zora?" Caelus called after her. "Dunna go away angry. I

was only jesting with ye."

But Zora ignored him. She was back at the carriage now, complaining to her mother, who told her to stop her moaning and either get in the carriage or go back to the front with Caelus. Kaladin, who had been in conversation with his parents in the carriage, was pushed aside when Zora interrupted. He stuck his tongue out at her when she didn't get the answer she wanted from her mother. Angrily, she headed back toward the front of the column, but not before she made a detour to a nearby tree and yanked a switch off it.

"Mae," Kaladin said casually, "Zora has a stick with her. If she strikes Caelus, ye know he'll spank her with it."

Mabel sighed heavily. "I cannot always be there to discipline her," she said. "Tell Caelus that he may spank her if she strikes him, but leave no marks."

Kaladin had to lower his head, laughing, as his father chimed in. "Kal, tell Caelus he's *not* tae lift a finger tae her," he said. "Tell him now."

Kaladin tried to wipe the smile off his face. "In a moment," he said. "We must discuss our arrival. I'm not entirely sure the mother abbess will allow all of these men intae her bailey, so ye must be prepared tae negotiate with her. She's a stubborn women and she doesn't like men."

"I will speak to her," Mabel said. "It may be better coming from me."

"Agreed," Kaladin said. "She's a strong woman, Mama. But so are ye."

Mabel tipped her head at the compliment. "What else do we know about her?"

Kaladin mulled over the question. "Only that she's been trained for this role since she was a wee bairn," he said. "This is the only life she's ever known. This is her world. She's very protective about her women, and the women are warriors. Oh, and she goes by Mother Michael."

Mabel nodded as she digested the information. "Then I shall deal with her appropriately," she said. "She simply must understand that we are here to help."

A shout came from the front of the column, and Kaladin turned in time to see Caelus yanking Zora off her horse, across his lap, and begin spanking her. She still had the switch in her hand and she was trying to hit him in return.

He chuckled.

"Caelus is beating Zora," he said. "She is trying tae beat him back."

Mabel rolled her eyes. "Good God," she muttered. "Kal, go up to the front and bring her back here. We are nearly at the gates and I'll not have her embarrass the entire family. Go, now. Fetch her."

That was true. They were at the gatehouse and Caelus was demanding entry. He thought he might have seen one of the gates move, preparing to open. Still laughing, Kaladin started to rein his horse forward to break up the fight between his brother and his sister. Those two together were like oil and water. Always volatile, but always entertaining. The entire army had been front and center to the show.

Just as Kaladin started to proceed forward, the entire world exploded.

CHAPTER EIGHTEEN

E STEVAN RECOGNIZED HIS mother's carriage. In fact, he recognized his father's men, all of them bearing the dun Tarh sash. It was a strip of red-and-yellow cloth that they wore somewhere on their body, usually across the chest. Additionally, the red-and-yellow bull standards of the Earl of Torridon were flying from the carriage. How his parents were here, at this time, was a complete mystery to him, but he also caught sight of Kaladin's black-and-white horse, so he knew his brother had somehow fetched his father.

It was a miracle.

Or, more than likely, it was because his father got homesick when he and Kaladin had departed for the Hydra. Estevan knew his father well and knew the man always longed for his home in the Highlands of Scotland, so when he saw his sons departing early, he wanted to go as well. It had happened before. Mabel, unable to put up a fight, simply went along with it.

And that was exactly why he had been so paranoid about going to The Butcher's.

He grinned when that thought popped into his head. He had been paranoid for a reason, as it turned out, because his parents were not more than a few days behind him. If the whole situation with St. Margaret's hadn't come up, his mother could have very well found him and Kaladin and the rest of them at The Butcher's and there would have been the devil to pay. Perhaps finding Leonore on the banks of the River Nith had been a gift from God, ensuring that none of them would get into trouble with Mabel the Masher. A terrible nickname, but one that made sense when one was on the receiving end of one of her punishments.

Estevan thanked God for watching out for him in avoiding his mother's flying hand.

With fond thoughts of Mabel on his mind, Estevan estimated that the carriage was about quarter of a mile out. They could see it approaching in the fog, which was starting to lift now that the sun was rising. It wasn't nearly as thick as it had been. There were just patches of it, mostly, but everything was still quite wet. Alexandra had followed him up to the wall and now stood a few feet away, watching the carriage approach along with him. All of them were watching Zora, his youngest sister, ride down the column and ending up at the carriage. As Estevan watched, he could see Zora waving her hands around, clearly conversing with somebody inside the carriage, which Estevan knew to be his mother.

But that brought about another issue.

Now his mother and sister were arriving at an abbey that was under the threat of an attack. He was certain that Kaladin had told his father what was happening, so they knew the danger going in. However, since they were heading home from Ashkirk Castle, Mabel and Zora were naturally going to be with them. Everyone was heading home. The only saving grace was the fact that it was a large escort, at least two hundred or more men, and they would provide ample protection. Estevan felt better just looking at them, and he was finally beginning to feel some relief. When they reached the gatehouse and the guards began the process of opening the wooden gates, he turned for the stairs leading down to the bailey. He was looking forward to greeting his brothers and parents.

And possibly Zora, too.

Unfortunately, he didn't get very far. He heard a noise behind him and turned to see the forest bordering both sides of the road come alive with men. Men with clubs and weapons, all of them charging for the dun Tarh party.

It was a shocking moment.

The danger they'd been waiting for had finally begun.

Ↄ

FOR KALADIN, A brief moment of surprise gave way to his training. The thrill of battle filled his veins, his nostrils, and everything about him. Projectiles started to fly from the trees on either side of the carriage and men rushed out of the foliage, bellowing and waving clubs and swords. The first thing Kaladin drew was his own weapon to face the charge.

"Papa!" he boomed. "Stay inside the carriage!"

Realizing they were under attack, Mabel screamed to him. "Zora!" she cried. "Protect your sister!"

Kaladin knew that. God help him, he knew that, but he also knew that she was with Caelus, who was a tremendous fighter. No one would get the better of him.

"Caelus has her, Mama," he said steadily. "She will be fine. He'll not let her come tae harm."

"A horse!" Lares shouted, already trying to open the carriage door. "Bring me my horse, Kal! *Now!*"

"No time," Kaladin said. "Stay in the carriage, Papa!"

He was already charging toward the incoming wave of men. At the rear of the column, Lucan gave the order to engage, and suddenly, over two hundred men were rushing out to meet the onslaught.

It was chaos.

Fortunately, Kaladin was wearing his usual battle protection. Anyone participating in an escort always wore full battle dress for moments just like this—unexpected attacks. Therefore, he charged into the fray with complete confidence, swinging his sword, kicking men who got too close.

He noticed quickly, however, that Caelus was at the gatehouse of the abbey, demanding that they take Zora. When he wasn't shouting at them, he was fighting off attackers, with Zora screaming because she was vulnerable and terrified. That brought Kaladin, pushing through clumps of fighting until he reached Caelus and Zora.

"Estevan!" he bellowed. "Open the gates!"

Estevan was on the gatehouse overhead, looking down at them as women on either side of him launched crossbows into the fighting. There were bolts flying overhead, their sickening song filling the air. But Estevan didn't answer—instead, he lay on his belly, reaching over the side of the wall walk and extending the end of a rope.

"Grab the rope!" he shouted. "They willna open the bloody gates and chance letting the enemy inside, so grab the rope. I'll pull her up!"

Truthfully, Kaladin and Caelus understood why the gates had to remain shut. It was their fear for Zora that was making unreasonable demands. With Kaladin and a few other soldiers shoving back any attackers, Caelus managed to right Zora on the saddle and help her stand up. The rope was dangling overhead, almost out of her reach, and she was terrified she was going to fall even with Caelus steadying her legs. Estevan lowered the rope as much as he could, but it wasn't quite enough.

Zora began to weep.

"I canna reach it!" she cried.

Estevan could see that. He was sick to his stomach with what was going on, desperate to help his family, but this was the best he could do because Mother Michael refused to open the gatehouse to them. He understood that from a defensive standpoint, but as the brother who was watching his family being attacked, he was struggling. There was coiled rope near the gatehouse's second floor, used to repair the rope that raised and lowered the portcullis, so he grabbed a length of it with the intention of pulling Zora to safety. But it simply wasn't long enough.

He had to think of something else.

Suddenly, Anaxandra was next to him.

"Lower me down," she said, grabbing the rope from him and proceeding to tie it around her waist. "Lower me down and I'll take hold of her. But you'll need help pulling us up."

Estevan didn't argue with her. He didn't have time. She already had the rope around her waist and was ready to descend. He shouted at Titan, who had just emerged from the stairwell onto the wall walk, and the man nearly killed himself running over to help. Rodion was down in the bailey, watching the postern gate, so it was just the two of them, but they easily lowered Anaxandra. With a battle going on around them, she grabbed Zora by the hands. With a little more effort, Estevan and Titan managed to pull both Anaxandra and Zora back to the wall.

Weeping loudly, Zora threw her arms around Estevan, who hugged her briefly before peeling her off him and turning her for the stairwell.

"Get off the wall," he told her, trying to protect her from the bolts that, having been launched at the enemy, were now starting to fly back at them. "Come, lass. Hurry!"

He half pushed, half pulled Zora to the tower. He then helped her down the stairs and into the bailey, where Estevan pointed at the sanctuary, all the way across the ward.

"See those doors?" he said.

Zora was sniffling, wiping her nose with the back of her hand. "Aye."

"Go there," he said. "Run. Bang on the doors and tell Matty tae admit ye. He's inside."

For once in the entirety of her life, Zora did exactly as she was told. Estevan watched her run, her red hair blowing behind her like a banner, until she reached the doors and began pounding. He could hear her shouting to Mateo, and the door abruptly flew open with Mateo on the other side. He looked at Zora in surprise, but when he saw the chaos of the bailey, he pulled her in as he came out. The door slammed behind him as he ran in Estevan's direction.

"Where do you need me?" he demanded.

Estevan frowned. Mateo still wasn't well, but at least he wasn't feverish any longer. He'd tried to keep him in the sanctuary, but it was clear the man wasn't going to stay put with a battle going on.

Not that he blamed him.

"Do ye fell well enough, Matty?" he asked.

Mateo had his sword on his hip. "Tell me where you need

me to go."

That was his way of saying nothing short of death would keep him from aiding in this attack. That was the determination of a knight. Estevan's frown turned into a smile, though it was a wry one. Wry because he understood Mateo's attitude perfectly.

He would have done the same thing.

"The wall," he said, pointing up. "Hurry, now. My family has arrived and they're being attacked at the gate."

Mateo nearly beat him up the stairs. Together, they ran to the second floor of the gatehouse, gathering with Titan and Rodion as they watched the fighting below.

"Listen," Rodion said. "Do you hear them?"

No one was quite sure what he meant. There was so much noise from the battle that it was difficult to single out one sound or word.

"What is it, Rody?" Estevan asked.

Rodion pointed to a foe fighting against a smaller dun Tarh man. "Listen," he said. "He's saying something every time he strikes."

They listened. As the men exchanged blows, it became clear what Rodion was pointing out. A strange, haunting sound was coming from the attackers, like a song. A prayer.

A curse.

"I hear it," Estevan said. "They speak before they strike. Every time."

"What are the saying?" Mateo asked. "I do not hear it."

Estevan looked at him. "That is because yer ears are packed due tae yer illness," he said. "Ye should be back in the sanctuary."

Mateo cocked a dark eyebrow. "Yet I am not," he said. "What are they saying?"

Estevan looked around for the rope he'd used to rescue Zora. "It sounds as if they are saying *döda*," he said. "It means tae kill in the language of the Northmen."

That had Mateo and Titan and Rodion looking at the men below with realization. "Then we have confirmed the Ormsfolk," Mateo said quietly. "I wonder if they are blaspheming us when they say it?"

Estevan shook his head. "I dunna know," he said. "Whatever it means, I intend tae help my family."

He tied off one end of the rope to the mechanism that raised, and lowered, the portcullis, which was exposed on this level. Gripping the rope with one hand, he went over the side, essentially rappelling down the wall until he could rappel no more.

Then he jumped.

They all did.

The drop from the end of the rope to the ground was about ten feet, but they took that easily, except for Rodion, who was shorter than the rest of them. He had further to fall. But he leapt to his feet and, suddenly, there were four heavily trained knights now fighting off the horde of Ormsfolk who had decided to attack the dun Tarh escort. But the fighting was quickly dwindling as the Ormsfolk rushed back into the trees, leaving their dead but taking their wounded. There were a few wounded dun Tarh men, also, but no dead, fortunately. When the Ormsfolk faded back into the foliage, Estevan turned around and shouted to the gatehouse.

"Open the gates!" he said. "All is clear! Open the gates!"

There was a slight hesitation, but the portcullis went up and the gates opened. Very quickly, the dun Tarh escort moved into the safety of the bailey, and it wasn't graceful by any means.

They simply poured in, any way they could, so the gates could be closed again. The knights and the dun Tarh brothers tried to calm everyone down, at least moving them out of the way, so they could start focusing on assessment and recovery.

It was difficult for men who had just faced battle to ease their nerves, but ease them they did. They had to. Kaladin and Lucan were given the task of assessing the wounded while everyone else was still trying to take care of any needs the men might have—bandages or water or just a word of praise on a job well done. As all of this was going on, the women of St. Margaret's, in their battle finest, watched with trepidation and suspicion.

Men.

Everything they'd been warned against.

Mother Michael met Estevan as he was walking in beside the carriage.

"How many wounded?" she asked.

Estevan turned directed the carriage to turn for the sanctuary before answering. "Four so far," he said. "Nothing life-threatening, I dunna think. I told them tae take the wounded intae the sanctuary. I hope I did right."

Mother Michael nodded. "Of course the wounded are welcome," she said. "But *who* is this?"

"My parents," Estevan told her. "The Earl and Countess of Torridon."

Mother Michael's eyes narrowed. "Ah," she murmured. "Lucifer in the flesh."

Estevan ignored the comment, mostly because he'd heard it before and it didn't bother him. He'd long gotten used to what his father was called. "My mother is here also," he said. "I'd be honored tae introduce ye."

He was already on the move before she could answer, opening the rear door of the carriage when his father unbolted it. Lares stepped through, hugging Estevan tightly in greeting. Then he moved on before Estevan could stop him to find Zora to ensure she'd not been injured. Behind him, Mabel stepped out, looking like she'd just been tossed around within an inch of her life.

She was moving slowly.

"Estevan," she greeted him, straightening her wimple as he kissed her on the cheek. "You are well?"

"I am," he said. "And ye?"

"Well enough," she said, though she was more disheveled than she would have liked from the rough ride. "I must say, I'm surprised to find you here."

His brow furrowed. "What do ye mean?"

"I was certain I would find you at The Butcher's."

Estevan's expression shifted to one of complete innocence. "Of course not," he said. "Ye dunna like us tae gamble. I wouldna disappoint my favorite mother."

"Your *only* mother," Mabel said, eyebrow cocked. But then she started to look around. "Where is Zora?"

Estevan pointed to the sanctuary. "In there," he said. "Papa has gone after her, but she is without a scratch, I swear it."

Mabel exhaled in relief. "Praise the saints," she said. "I would see my daughter, please."

Estevan could see that she was shaken, but he needed to make an introduction before he connected his mother with Zora and the scolding began.

"In a moment," he said, taking her by the arm and gently pulling her with him. "Mama, this is Mother Michael. She is the mother abbess of St. Margaret's."

Mabel straightened up, unwilling to show weakness in front of another woman of power. "Your Grace," she greeted her. "I hear we have you to thank for giving my sons and the others shelter when one of them became ill. You have my gratitude."

Mother Michael dipped her head in acknowledgment. "My lady," she said. "We are honored by your visit."

Mabel grunted. "'Tis not a visit," she said. "From the welcome we received just now, I would say you have a problem. May I be of assistance?"

Mother Michael wasn't sure how to take that. Criticism? Or was the countess simply stating the obvious? There was something strong and icy about the woman, something Mother Michael recognized.

She, herself, had those very same traits.

"It is possible," she finally said. "Your son brought an injured women to us and, evidently, she has a past."

"So I was told," Mabel said. "And those men we just saw?"

Mother Michael shrugged. "The very men who held her captive, we think," she said. "I am grateful for your assistance in sending them away, but I suspect they may be back."

"May I see the woman they seek?"

Mother Michael led her away, toward the sanctuary, where Zora also happened to be so Mabel could also see to her daughter. She was nearly to the door when someone else caught her attention over near the carriage. Her eyes narrowed at the sight.

"Mateo de Wolfe!" Mabel called. "Come to me this instant."

Mateo had been helping with the horses who had been pulling the carriage, but a command from Lady Torridon was not meant to be disobeyed. Promptly, he went to her, smiling as he bowed his head respectfully. He genuinely liked Lady

Torridon, who was a friend of his mother's.

"My lady," he said. "It is good to see you."

"Cease your flattery," Mabel snapped softly, putting her hand gently on his forehead, his cheek, feeling for a fever. "Kal said you were ill. Well? What are you doing out here?"

On the spot, Mateo cleared his throat quietly in preparation for speaking but ended up coughing a little. His chest was very congested. Mabel heard it and so did everyone else within earshot.

"You are not well enough to work," Mabel said, taking him by the arm. "Come inside with me this very moment."

Mateo didn't want to go, but he didn't dare dispute her. "Truly, Lady Torridon, I sound worse than I feel."

"You sound like you're dying."

"I am not dying, I assure you," Mateo said, his protests falling on deaf ears. "I am well enough to fight, my lady."

Mabel fixed on him. "Get inside before I do something you will regret," she said sternly. "Your mother would never forgive me if I did not tend to your health, so you will do as you are told. *Go.*"

Mateo did. Lady Torridon was known to spank full-grown men who displeased her, and he didn't want that embarrassment, so he went inside, followed by Mabel and Mother Michael. What he left in his wake were a bunch of grinning men, glad it was Mateo in trouble with Lady Torridon and not them.

That included Estevan.

"That is your mother?"

The question came from behind him and he turned to see Anaxandra standing there. He nodded.

"That," he said, "is the famous Mabel, Countess of Torridon. I will introduce ye."

Understandably, Anaxandra was timid after what she'd just witnessed. "Mayhap later," she said. "Is it safe to go outside the walls and collect any bolts that we find?"

"Now?"

She nodded. "We will need them if they attack again."

She had a point. Estevan wasn't keen on her going outside of the walls so soon, but he conceded. "Quickly, then," he said. "I'll send men tae stand guard while ye do it. Grab a few lasses tae go with ye, but move swiftly."

He headed over toward the gatehouse with her in tow, collecting about ten soldiers as he went. Anaxandra motioned to a few women who had come down off the wall, all of them with crossbows, and they dashed outside with the armed escort to collect any loose bolts. Weapons, and ammunition like the bolts, were expensive and precious, so anything that hadn't embedded itself in a man would be collected and reused. Unwilling to leave Anaxandra's safety to a few soldiers, Estevan headed out with them.

By now, the fog was completely gone and it was a bright day overhead, but Estevan couldn't relax. He watched the trees diligently, as did the soldiers he'd brought with him, while Anaxandra and the other women quickly gathered the bolts they could find. Some were in perfect condition, simply embedded in the ground, while others were twisted and broken. Estevan gave the women just a few short minutes to gather what they could before he was herding them back into the compound. Only when the gates were closed and the portcullis lowered did he feel safe enough to breathe.

But there was no rest for him.

Only duty.

Once back inside, he caught sight of Caelus and Lucan and went to embrace his brothers. Neither one of them had a scratch from the battle and were, in fact, rather excited about the entire fight. Since Kaladin had told them everything about the situation at St. Margaret's, they knew what had happened and why. But much as Estevan had been when he first arrived at the abbey, they were curious about the Templar nuns.

A great curiosity, indeed.

They watched the women with the crossbows and how they took all of the gathered bolts over to what used to be the smithy stall and began cleaning them up. There was also a group of women who had spears and shields, who had made it up to the wall during the battle, but who had been called off by Mother Margaret because bolts were already flying and she didn't want to accidentally kill any dun Tarh soldiers. Estevan couldn't tell them very much about the nuns, or the way St. Margaret's functioned, because he didn't know much about it himself. He hadn't been there long enough to learn more than Anaxandra had told him or what he'd observed personally.

Around him, soldiers were finally being organized against the wall in groups and the carriage and two provisions wagons were lined up over by the sanctuary. There were no horses at St. Margaret's other than the ones Estevan and the others had brought, and the stables themselves weren't large enough to hold the conveyances. As the brothers headed back over to the wall to help the sergeants with the men, Lares emerged from the sanctuary and made his way over to Estevan.

"This is quite a situation," he said to his son. "And it all started with finding a woman on the riverbank?"

Estevan nodded. "It was by accident," he said. "Rody found her."

"Where *is* Rody?"

Estevan looked around, finally spying him over by the gate-house. "There," he said. "With Titan. The portcullis is in rough shape, Papa. I think they're trying tae figure out how tae strengthen it somehow."

Lares could see the knights studying the wooden grate. Scratching his head, he looked around the bailey, inspecting it. It was worn, and not particularly well appointed. There was nothing impressive about it.

"Ye know this attack was simply tae test our strength," he said quietly. "They'll be back."

Estevan nodded. "Probably," he said. "Have ye fought against the Ormsfolk before?"

Lares drew in a long, pensive breath. "Aye," he said. "There used tae be more of them around, especially on the outer isles. I remember my grandfather speaking of them and how they'd wear shells on their clothing and shave their heads. There was a time when they'd paint themselves with the blood of their enemies before tossing the bodies tae their eels. As a child, the elders used tae frighten us with tales of the Serpent People."

Estevan scrutinized his father for a moment. "Ye still seemed frightened."

"I am," Lares said, looking at him. "There is nothing good about these people, lad. The only way tae defeat them is tae destroy all of them. Otherwise, they'll keep coming back tae the last man."

Estevan considered that very real possibility. "They followed their captive all the way here," he said. "We thought they'd come tae the gate and ask if we knew anything about her, but they never even asked. They simply attacked when yer escort reached the gatehouse."

"They were trying tae get in," Lares said. "They waited until the gatehouse was being opened and they struck. That is when a fortress is most vulnerable."

"But we closed it before anyone could get in."

"Aye, we did," Lares said. "But it was opened tae admit us. Someone could have slipped in then in the crowd of men."

Estevan frowned. "'Tis not possible," he said. "Only dun Tarh men entered."

"Are ye sure?"

He wasn't. Estevan couldn't guarantee it. He began to look around at all of the soldiers inside the bailey and a feeling of dread swept him.

"I'm not," he said. "Ye must line up every man here and make sure he belongs in yer army. Ye know all of yer men, dunna ye?"

Lares nodded. "I know every one of them because I invited them tae join me," he said. "I'll have Kal and Caelus and Lucan line them all up now. We'll identify everyone."

"Good," Estevan said. "But meanwhile, we'd better not say anything tae the women. I dunna want tae upset the mother abbess and have her order us all out."

Lares understood. "Not a word."

As he wandered off to find his other sons, Estevan found himself looking for Anaxandra. He couldn't go two minutes without thinking about her, and given what they'd just gone through, his concern was justified. He couldn't help but be impressed when he remembered her selflessness at pulling Zora out of danger. He found himself looking at her through new eyes because the woman wasn't just talk. She didn't just fire bolts from overhead and stay out of any real fighting. She had exposed herself greatly by doing what she did for Zora.

He hadn't even thanked her for it.

Anaxandra was over in an old smithy stall with several other women, all of them going over the bolts they'd collected. She had her head down, cleaning dirt and grass out of some grooves in the head of one of the bolts and didn't see him approach, but the women around her did. In fact, they began to scatter, startled that a man had entered their orbit. Anaxandra only looked up when she realized everyone was leaving. A glance over her shoulder showed her why.

"Do you always have that effect?" she asked.

He smiled as he came near. "What effect?"

"Chasing people away with your mere presence?"

He nodded seriously. "It happens every day," he said, watching her grin. "Did ye not see the enemy run when they saw that I was in the battle?"

She chuckled. "Come to think on it, they did leave very quickly," she said. "It must be a talent you have."

"Something I've worked hard at," he said, but soon enough, his face took on a warm expression. "And there's a talent ye have also."

"What's that?"

"Bravery."

She wasn't quite sure what he meant. "We were all brave today."

"True," he said. "But ye were the only one I saw lowering yerself with a rope tae save my sister. Thank ye for doing that, Ana. Ye dinna have tae do it, but ye did. Ye saw a woman in trouble and ye risked yerself tae help."

Anaxandra was back to flushing brightly for two reasons— he'd called her by a diminutive, something only Mother Michael or Sister Hildegarde did, and he'd also complimented her on her courage. No one had ever done that before.

"Is your sister well?" she asked.

He nodded. "She seems tae be quite well," he said. "She's strong. Any daughter of Mabel dun Tarh is strong, but Zora has the issue of my father being overly sympathetic tae everything that happens tae her. He still sees her as a small child in need of a father's overwhelming protection."

Anaxandra grinned. "And you do not believe she still needs her father's protection?"

He nodded quickly. "She does," he said. "Especially since she manages tae enrage or annoy nearly everyone she comes intae contact with, including her brothers. She needs for my father tae protect her from them."

Anaxandra giggled. "I'm afraid I did not grow up with a family or brothers, so I would not know," she said. "You are the closest thing I've ever experienced in that regard."

His smile faded. "I dunna want tae be yer brother, lass," he said in a low, seductive voice. "Ye do understand that, dunna ye?"

She was back to flushing bright red again. "I do."

"And ye're agreeable?"

She couldn't even voice the words. It was too… *something*. Overwhelming? Embarrassing? But she was absolutely agreeable, so she nodded eagerly, eyes averted.

Estevan laughed softly.

"Good," he said. "Because I plan tae tell my parents so they can approach Mother Michael for permission. That means my mother must meet ye. She'll appreciate ye, I promise."

Anaxandra's gaze lifted, meeting his. "I do not know why," she said. "In many ways, I am ignorant. I know nothing of the Outworld."

"Ye're going tae live with my family and learn. We've discussed this."

She nodded, lowering her gaze again. "I find that this all seems like a dream," she said. "It does not seem real. Does it feel that way to you, too?"

He couldn't keep the smile off his face. "I dinna think when I brought an injured women to the lair of the Templar nuns that I would find a wife here," he said, his gaze drifting over her lovely face. "But I think I did. I hope I did. But she's never said that she is excited about this. All she's ever done is ask me if I'm certain I want tae go through with it."

She grinned, both a modest and coy gesture. "I said that I was agreeable."

"Did ye ever say, 'Estevan, ye're a handsome devil and I'm fortunate tae have ye'?"

She put her hand on her face, snorting, completely unused to the gentle flirtations between men and women. Still, she was taking quickly to it, or at least trying to.

"Estevan, you are a handsome devil and I feel very fortunate," she said, watching him laugh. She chuckled with him before quickly sobering. "I've never wanted to become a nun. I told you that. But I did not know how I would leave this place, or what I would do, or if I would actually ever leave at all. God brought you here, Estevan. He left that wounded woman on the riverbank for you to find so that you would come here. I will believe that until the day I die."

The humor faded on Estevan's face. "I think they call that destiny," he said. "I'm yer destiny and ye're mine."

Anaxandra thought on that for a moment before a smile spread across her lips. "I like that," she said. "I never knew I had a destiny."

"Nor did I."

"I certainly never knew it was you."

"Are ye glad?"

Her smile widened and she nodded, yet again, agreeing with him but unable to voice it, yet again. She would have to practice her responses to him, but he was giving her the courage to try. His response was to reach out and pull her to him, gazing deeply into her eyes before kissing her most sweetly.

"Finish yer duties," he said huskily as he released her. "When ye're finished, I'll introduce ye tae my mother."

Breathless from his kiss, Anaxandra nodded unsteadily. "I look forward to it."

Knowing how his mother could be, especially with women where her sons were concerned, had him give a little snort. He wanted to say something like, *I hope you feel that way once the introduction is over,* but he bit his tongue. He didn't want to frighten her.

Mabel could do that all by herself.

But something told him that his mother was about to meet her match.

CHAPTER NINETEEN

I N THE CHAOS of the battle and subsequent retreat, Willem had managed to do what he'd set out to do.

He'd made it inside the abbey.

It had been a shockingly simple thing. When his people were fleeing the battle and the incoming escort was crowding into the gatehouse, which was open to admit them, he'd simply managed to rush in with the rest of the army, no questions asked. Everyone was focused on getting inside and getting the wounded to the building that was surely the great hall, so no one noticed him at all. There were so many men that it was easy to lose himself in the crowd, and when the timing was right, he simply slipped away and ended up hiding in some unused outbuildings by a weird stone circle.

He considered himself quite fortunate.

The battle, of course, had been purely opportunistic. They had seen the incoming party about an hour before it made its way down the road to the abbey. Then they'd waited until the party made it to the gatehouse and the gates started to open. They should have waited until the gates were completely open, but a few of their men became too eager and broke rank before the order was given. That meant they all had to move, and they had to move quickly, because the escort was at least three or four times larger than their group.

They had to strike.

When it came to the Serpent People, however, that didn't matter. They had always boasted that one of their men was worth five of any other man. However, in this case, the opposing army proved to be formidable. They also had several knights with them, something that hadn't been anticipated, and those knights were nothing to fool with. They were fearsome and they were highly trained, and Willem had seen at least seven or eight of his own men cut down fairly quickly. When they realized they were in over their heads, they'd called a retreat, but not before they left eleven men dead on the field of battle. They couldn't carry them because they couldn't move fast enough, and there was a real fear that the party they attacked would try to pursue them.

Therefore, they fled and took the wounded with them.

All but Willem.

Surely by now, Bastijn would have realized that Willem wasn't with them. He would send men to scrutinize the dead to see if Willem was among them, and when he discovered that he wasn't, he would assume that Willem had made it inside the complex. Willem knew Bastijn extremely well, and he knew the man would not move far away. He knew that Bastijn would linger somewhere nearby, waiting for Willem to emerge with the very thing they sought.

The queen.

She was here, somewhere.

And Willem was going to find her.

Now, Willem watched from his hiding place, observing the

army settle down and the women of the abbey going about their duties. St. Margaret's seemed to be a vast place, but it was also an unconventional place. The construction of the interior was strange and, in some places, not particularly sturdy. There were outbuildings and stalls that were not in use, which had provided him with a convenient hiding place. But the women seemed to be traveling in groups, each of them assigned to a particular task or duty, and no one seemed to be drifting in his direction, which was good for him. It gave him time to gather his thoughts and formulate a plan.

He had to face this logically.

The wounded were being taken to the large building that he had assumed to be the great hall. He kept watching the people coming in and out, wondering if he would see the queen, but he never did. But in his mind, logic would dictate that after spending so long at sea and having the boat run aground, the queen was probably not in the best physical condition. She might even be ill or wounded herself for all he knew. It therefore stood to reason that she was probably in that great hall also. If that was where the sick and injured were being kept. He simply hadn't seen her yet.

He needed to get inside that hall.

There were only two ways he could make it inside there— the first way would be to sneak in somehow. But given all of the people going in and out, he doubted that was an option. The second way, of course, was if he was wounded. He wasn't wounded at all, but he could certainly injure himself to a believable degree while still retaining his senses and his strength. But the only way to accomplish that would be if they believed he was part of the incoming army. No one would believe a wounded enemy had wandered in and begged for help.

Perhaps they were risky plans, but they were all he had at the moment.

Unless…

There was another way.

Perhaps if he were to take a hostage of one of the women and exchange her for the queen, he could get them both out alive. He had a big dagger with him and could use it as leverage. But he wasn't a fool. He'd been fighting since he'd been old enough to speak because his people were a fighting people, fighting and winning any way they could. They used methods that more civilized armies wouldn't use, but those methods were successful. The queen he sought was the result of those methods.

So, perhaps what he needed to use was one of those brutal methods. Use and abuse until he got what he wanted. Until he was allowed to leave unharmed with the queen in his possession. That was all he really wanted, just the woman who had escaped the Ormsfolk, which was an embarrassment in and of itself. Perhaps that was why they were so desperate to get her back. If she succeeded in escaping home, then it would diminish their terror in the eyes of their enemies.

And Willem wasn't going to risk it.

Therefore, he'd find a hostage to exchange for her.

And God help the woman he chose.

☙

"Mae, I must speak with ye."

Mabel had been supervising the cleaning of a wound on one of the dun Tarh soldiers, a young man who had taken a club to the face. It had split his brow, and the left side of his forehead, and one of the nuns was tending to it while Mabel stood over her and made sure all was done to her liking. But the softly uttered question, from Estevan, had her turning to look at the man.

"Where did you come from?" she asked her son. "I did not see you enter."

Estevan gestured to the entry door, which was open because of the people going in and out. "I'm not needed in the bailey," he said. "Caelus and Lucan have that well under control. And I can see ye have everything in here well under control, too."

He was teasing her because Mabel was a woman of action. She liked things done her way, even in an abbey that she had never visited in her life. But these were her husband's men and she had a responsibility to them, so much so that Mother Michael had fled the hall. Mabel wasn't sure she'd offended the woman by insisting on tending her husband's men, but if she had, it couldn't be helped.

She had a job to do.

"Of course I have control of the situation," she said, looking over at the other wounded. "Fortunately, no one is terribly injured."

"That is good tae know."

Standing a few feet away was none other than Leonore herself, helping a wounded man drink from a cup. Mabel gestured in that direction. "The woman you brought here seems to have recovered well enough also," she said. "Matty said she is a decent woman with an undeserved fate."

Estevan nodded. "I think he's spent some time speaking with her, so he would know," he said. "Were ye introduced?"

"Briefly."

"Good," Estevan said. "Matty caught the poison in his chest from her. Did he tell ye that? He seems tae have taken the worst of it."

Mabel's gaze lingered on Leonore. "He will recover if he listens to me," she said. "But what will become of the lady, I wonder?"

"She wants tae return home," Estevan said. "Would ye be opposed tae taking her with us on our journey north? We can find her an escort in Glasgow tae take her the rest of the way tae her home."

"Where is home?"

"Jura, I'm told."

Mabel considered the request. "We'll ask your father's opinion on the matter," she said, looking to the wounded again. "But it seems that none of us will be leaving this place anytime soon. We should simply be grateful that everyone survived."

Estevan completely agreed. "It could have been worse."

"It certainly could have," Mabel said, shifting her attention back to her son. "But the soldiers aside, thanks to you, your sister also survived. Zora told me what you and Titan did. That was incredibly brave of you, my son."

Estevan caught sight of his sister over by Mateo, who was sitting on his bed with a bored expression on his face. "It wasn't just Titan and me," he said. "There was a lass involved, one of the Templar nuns. She risked her life tae pull Zora tae safety. She is the one ye should thank."

"I will," Mabel said. "Who is she?"

That was the question Estevan had been waiting for. He suddenly felt a little nervous because that question had more than one answer.

Who is she?

The woman I want tae marry, Mae…

"She's the woman I first met when we brought the injured woman tae St. Margaret's," he said, which was the truth. "As I was approaching the gatehouse, she fired a few warning bolts tae keep me at a distance. She's the best shot I've ever seen, and that's saying a good deal. I've seen many talented archers in my time."

Mabel was listening with interest. "I see," she said. "And what is her name?"

"Anaxandra," Estevan said as if it were the most beautiful name in the world. "That's what I wanted tae speak with ye about. Firstly, not all of the women here are nuns. That's something I dinna know. Some of them are just widows or women who joined the order for shelter and protection. There's only eight nuns here, Mae. The rest are not. Anaxandra is not. She… she's very special, and I'd like ye tae come tae know her."

Mabel wasn't stupid. She could hear something in Estevan's voice when he spoke about the woman who'd saved Zora.

An eyebrow lifted.

"Because…?"

"Because I want tae marry her."

There it was. The spoken truth. Mabel had to admit that she was surprised. Not shocked, but surprised. Estevan didn't have women following him around like some of her other sons did. He was too sensible for that. He focused on his duty and on his family, so for this young woman to charm him as she evidently had was unheard of when it came to Estevan. He'd never fallen for a woman in his life.

Until now.

Mabel could see it in his eyes.

"Does she know that you want to marry her?" she asked.

Estevan nodded, pleased his mother hadn't outright denied him. "She does," he said. Then he lowered his voice. "She's been here since she was a bairn. She's the bastard of the Earl of

Teviot and a lady-in-waiting tae his wife. They brought her here, so she was raised by the nuns. Mae, she's of good stock. She's intelligent and beautiful and brave."

Mabel smiled faintly. "It sounds as if you admire her already."

"I do," Estevan said. "It was her idea tae save Zora the way she did. I've never known a woman like that in my life. I dinna have time tae be frightened because I was too busy being awed by her."

Mae chuckled, softly. "She has impressed you."

"She has," he said. "But she doesn't know where she comes from, so dunna mention it when ye speak tae her. I dunna think it matters, anyway, but I wanted ye tae know that she comes from noble bloodlines. I'd want tae marry her even if she dinna."

"It sounds to me as if you are serious."

"I am," Estevan said. "Will ye speak tae her?"

Mabel nodded. "I will," she said. "Where is she?"

"Outside," Estevan said. "She's with some other women cleaning the bolts they collected from the battlefield. I'll introduce ye."

Mabel stopped him. "No need," she said. "You remain here. Go over and save Matty from your sister's incessant chatter. I will find this young woman and speak with her myself."

Estevan couldn't help it. He leaned over and kissed her on the cheek. "Thank ye," he murmured sincerely. "And… be kind tae her, please? She's been raised by women who have no warmth, no love as a family does. She's never really spoken tae anyone else but them, so she may seem cold. But she's not, I assure ye."

Mabel eyed her son knowingly. "I assume you have discovered this personally?"

Estevan wasn't known to blush, but if he was, he would have done it at that moment. Instead, he started laughing, his hand over his face.

"Not as much as I'd like tae," he said to her prying question. "She's an innocent, Mae, in all ways. Dunna fear. Nothing untoward has happened. Yet."

Mabel cracked a smile. "Cheeky devil," she muttered.

Estevan just stood there and grinned. But it soon became apparent that Mabel wasn't in any hurry to meet Anaxandra, but rather, she was still watching the care of the soldier with the damaged eye. Since the soldier wasn't in any immediate danger, Estevan was becoming restless.

"Will ye go now?" he asked.

Mabel looked up from the wounded soldier. "Is there a rush?"

Estevan sighed sharply. "Nay, but…"

Mabel took the hint. "But you want me to do it now," she said. "Very well, if you insist."

Estevan was back to smiling again. "Thank ye, Mae. I love ye."

Mabel snorted softly, giving her impetuous son a wink before heading for the sanctuary door. She passed near Mateo as she walked, noting that he wasn't doing what she had told him to do.

"I will not tell you again to lie down," she told him, pointing a finger at him. "You had better be on your back when I return or there will be a row you cannot win. Zora, sit on him if you have to."

Zora smiled gleefully while Mateo rolled his eyes and fell back on the bed, feeling persecuted by a ruthless woman and her annoying daughter. Mabel continued to the door as Estevan went over to save his friend, but what he really wanted to do was send Zora away so he could tell Mateo about Anaxandra. He was fairly bursting with it.

And Mabel knew it.

The last she saw, Estevan was trying to force Zora to tend to the other wounded, but Zora was more interested in bothering Mateo. Mabel smiled to herself as she headed out into the sunshine of a new morning, taking in a deep breath of the fresh air and thankful that a bad situation hadn't turned out too horribly. As Estevan had said, it could have been much worse. But now, she was on the hunt for a young woman she didn't know. All she had was a name and a location.

She struck out to search for a group of women cleaning bolts.

Like everyone else who visited St. Margaret's, Mabel immediately noticed how odd the place was. The bailey was vast, but some of the buildings were connected by walkways that looked as if they were ready to collapse. As she continued on, she caught sight of a large and well-tended vegetable garden and stables that were small, given the size of the complex.

In fact, she could see her husband and two of her sons in the stable, speaking to Mother Michael as they tried to figure out how to feed all of the horses. Mabel briefly wondered if she should go and help Lares, as Kaladin had suggested she might be better in dealing with the mother abbess, but she decided against it. She'd already chased the woman out of the hall. Besides, Lares was a man of tact and understanding when he wanted to be.

She hoped this was one of those times.

As Mabel continued on, she could see groups of women

around the bailey. Some were sitting down, cleaning swords, while still others were over by the kitchen yard. She couldn't quite see what they were doing until one of them moved aside and she could see that they were handling bolts, which were fired from crossbows.

She headed in that direction.

"Who is Anaxandra?" she asked as she came upon the women.

Seven or eight pairs of eyes looked at her, startled, but one young woman set down the bolt in her hand.

"I am Anaxandra," she said. "How may I be of service, Lady Torridon?"

So the woman knew her name. Mabel found herself facing a tall young woman, taller than she was, with long blonde hair, tied back, and the face of an angel. She could immediately see what had Estevan smitten, at least on the surface.

She didn't blame him.

"You know me?" she said.

Anaxandra nodded. "We all do," she said. "We saw you come in with the carriage. Estevan told me who you were."

Mabel nodded, looking the young woman over, evaluating her. But Anaxandra didn't flinch, instead, facing her the way she faced everything.

With bravery.

That impressed Mabel.

"I would like to speak with you, my lady," Mabel finally said. "Will you walk with me?"

Anaxandra didn't hesitate. The two of them started walking toward the abandoned outbuildings on the south side of the bailey where the stone circle was. Anaxandra was struggling not to look directly at Mabel, or speak to her, instead waiting to be spoke to first. She wasn't the type to start up a conversation, anyway.

Nervously, she waited.

"I understand that you are to thank for saving my daughter's life," Mabel finally said. "Estevan said that you were very brave."

Anaxandra flushed that familiar shade of red. "I saw a problem, my lady," she said. "I only wanted to help."

"You did," Mabel said. "My daughter is unharmed and you are to be commended. You have my gratitude."

"I was glad to do it, my lady."

"My son also tells me that he wishes to marry you," Mabel said. "Has he told you that?"

It was a bold question, right to the point, and one that had Anaxandra's cheeks predictably flushing. They had come to the abandoned stalls, which was away from the activity in the main part of the bailey. It was wet and muddy and cold because of the heavy mist, and the derelict buildings gave the area a spooky quality. Anaxandra had to steer Mabel away from a particularly nasty mud slick before she answered.

"I know, my lady," she answered honestly. "He has spoken of it to me."

"And what do you say?"

"I am agreeable."

Mabel had been expecting more of an answer. "And… how do you feel about it?" she said, trying to elicit more of a response. "Are you happy? Sad? Repelled?"

Anaxandra could see that Mabel was a strong woman. That was obvious. But given that she dealt with Mother Michael and Sister Hildegarde on a regular basis, she was rather used to strong women. She wasn't intimidated, but she couldn't help the nerves she felt. Deep down, she did want to be liked. Especially by Estevan's mother.

The moment was as unexpected as it was important.

"Anxious," she finally said.

Mabel's brow furrowed. "Why do you feel anxious?"

Anaxandra took a deep breath. She'd never wished more in her entire life that she'd been schooled in the social graces, because standing before her was a cultured woman. A great woman who presided over a great house, who was well respected by her peers. From her short observations of Mabel, she could already see how much her sons esteemed her. Estevan spoke so fondly of her.

Now, this gracious lady was asking her why she felt anxious.

Honesty was the only thing Anaxandra could give her.

"I simply meant that I was not raised in a fine home," she said. "Surely you can see that."

Mabel nodded. "I can," she said. "That still does not explain why you feel anxious."

Anaxandra struggled to put her emotions into words. "Because I do not know anything of the Outworld," she said. "I have told Estevan this and he does not seem to care. He said that I could live with you and that you would teach me how to be a fine lady."

Mabel cocked her head curiously. "Outworld," she repeated, making it sound mystical. "What is that?"

"It is what we call the world outside of the abbey."

"Ah," Mabel said in understanding. "Truthfully, there is not much to know. Can you do your sums?"

"I have been taught such things, my lady."

"Can you read?"

"I can, my lady."

"Then learning the Outworld, as you have called it, will be a simple thing," she said. "You can learn to manage a home. You already know how to command the people around you, don't you?"

Anaxandra nodded. "I am the leader of the Bow Pack."

"What is that?"

"The archers of St. Margaret's."

Mabel smiled. "See?" she said. "You already know how to properly command women. You can easily direct servants with that knowledge. And what you do not know, you will learn. Estevan believes you are very bright, and I think that I agree with him."

Anaxandra looked at her doubtfully. "You do?"

Mabel nodded. "Are you willing to learn?"

Anaxandra was bobbing her head in an affirmative gesture before Mabel was even finished speaking. "Indeed, my lady," she said. "I would be willing to learn anything Estevan wishes for me to learn. I... I told him that I never wanted to remain here at St. Margaret's forever. I always felt there was more for me in the Outworld, but I never truly believed it until now."

Mabel's smile faded. "Then you see my son as your way out of the abbey?" she said. "Do you seem him as a savior to give you a better life?"

Anaxandra sensed suspicion in that question, though she wasn't sure why. "I have felt that way since I was a child, my lady," she said. "If you mean did I wait for a man to come and take me away, the answer is that I did not. I would have left whether or not Estevan came to St. Margaret's. Mayhap I would have become a servant somewhere, or herded sheep, or scrubbed floors, but I would have found a life to lead on my own."

Mabel didn't seem convinced. "Did you tell Estevan this?"

Anaxandra nodded. "I did," she said. "I have not been dishonest with him. Or you."

"Do you love my son?"

"Love?" Anaxandra seemed confused by the question. "My lady, we have only just met. I have grown very fond of him. He is a kind and generous soul. He sees things in me that no one else does. Love has not existed in my life before now, but I am certain that love can be built on such things. Admiration and friendship, to start."

"Love takes more than that."

"Did *you* know that you loved your husband within the first three days of knowing him, my lady?"

It was a clever question, but Mabel felt like it was a challenge. Her eyes narrowed. "We are not speaking of me," she said. "We are speaking of you and of my son, who seems to have presented you with the chance you have been looking for."

"That is not true, my lady."

"Will you swear this to me?"

"Upon all that his holy, I will."

Mabel still wasn't certain. She was coming to wonder if the girl was simply an opportunist and Estevan had fallen for it. As she was considering that very thing, hoping her son hadn't been foolish in his assessment of Anaxandra's character, she wandered toward a stall that had a buildup of mud and debris around the base. It was crumbling, but she wasn't paying attention to it. She was thinking on what Anaxandra had said. As she reached the stall, she turned around to say something to Anaxandra, but the strangest thing happened before she could get the words out of her mouth.

Hands grabbed her, digging into her flesh, and she let out a yelp. Then she had visions of Anaxandra charging in her direction.

After that, it was pandemonium.

CHAPTER TWENTY

S OMEONE HAD GRABBED Lady Torridon.

At first, Anaxandra wasn't sure she was seeing the situation correctly. Hands came out of the derelict stall, grabbing Mabel by the arm and by the neck. It was Mabel's cry of fear that jolted Anaxandra from her shock, and suddenly, she was rushing forward, yanking on Mabel and trying to pull her from what turned out to be a rather skinny but surprisingly strong man. He had hair all over his face and shaggy hair on his head, and there wasn't one inch of him that wasn't covered in filth.

Something was very, very wrong.

Anaxandra couldn't stop to think about who, or what, he was. Even after Anaxandra tried to pull Mabel away, the man had hold of Mabel's wimple, pulling it off her head, but it was tightly pinned. That meant Mabel was falling backward into him.

Anaxandra jumped over Mabel and shoved her open palm right into the man's nose. He fell back in agony, blood immediately flowing from his face, and Anaxandra was all over Mabel, stepping on her, pushing on her, pulling on her, as she tried to get her away from her attacker. When that didn't work,

Anaxandra balled a fist and hit the man in the face again, twice, before he was startled enough to release Mabel.

Now, the real fight began.

Anaxandra had the man by the hair with both hands, yanking on him as she used her right foot to kick him brutally in the hip and left knee. Mabel fell to the ground but managed to crawl away as the fight became between Anaxandra and the brute who had attacked her.

And what a fight it was.

Having been trained in combat, Anaxandra knew how to stay on a level playing field with a man who was stronger and bigger than she was. She had to go for the vulnerable areas. The hair was a perfect example—she yanked on it until a handful came out and the man grunted in pain, but she wouldn't let go, even when he began striking her on the arms and torso. She was in the process of kicking him in the groin when he pulled forth a wicked-looking dagger and plunged it right into her back, just beneath the left armpit.

Anaxandra went down in a heap.

It was a shocking end to a violent fight. Beaten, and a little bloodied, the man kicked her when she was down for good measure before turning his attention back to Mabel, who had just managed to get to her feet. He started to come toward her, but she put up her hands as if the gesture alone would stop him.

"Come no closer," she said, sounding strong and fearless. "If you do, I will scream and every man in this compound will come running. Do you understand me?"

He did. But he still came. The first thing he did was cover her mouth with the hand that wasn't holding the bloodied dagger. He put the weapon to her neck.

"Do you understand me?" he said in stilted English. "*Un-*

derstand?"

Trapped, Mabel nodded. That caused the man to poke her neck with the tip of his dagger, drawing a little blood. "Aye," she said.

"Good," he said, angry and snarling. "Where is the queen?"

By the look on Mabel's face, she knew exactly who the man was and what he wanted. What an entire battle couldn't accomplish, a single man with a single hostage probably could. Mabel began to feel real fear as she realized the predicament she was in.

"I know where she is," she said against his dirty palm. "If you kill me, you will never know."

He pulled his palm back. "Scream and I will drive the dagger through your neck," he muttered. "Where is she?"

The man was so focused on Mabel that he had no idea that Anaxandra was stirring on the ground. But Mabel did. She was trying hard not to look at her for fear the man would turn around and kill the woman before she could defend herself, so she kept her eyes fixed on him. But in her periphery, she could see Anaxandra rising unsteadily to her feet. She had to give her time to get help.

She had to stall.

"In the sanctuary," she said after a moment. "But there are people in there with her. You will not be able to get to her."

The man snorted, a rude sound. "I do not need to," he said. "We will walk to the sanctuary together and you will demand they release her to me. Her life for yours. That is the bargain we will strike. We will—"

He never had the chance to finish the sentence. Anaxandra, bleeding heavily from the wound in her back, had collected a rock that she'd fallen on, a big rock, and she came up behind the man and smashed him as hard as she could on the back of the skull. As he faltered, Mabel jumped away from him, screaming loudly. Anaxandra had managed to knock the man silly, but he didn't go out. He still managed to bring the dagger around low, stabbing her a second time in the left side of her torso. That caused Anaxandra to take the rock and smash him again, in the face, a second time. When he fell to his knees, she hit him in the head twice, thrice, until he finally fell to the ground, unconscious.

With Mabel's screaming bringing a charge of men and weapons, Anaxandra fell to her knees beside the man, pulled the knife from his hand, and, with both hands, plunged it deep into his chest. She did it twice before falling beside him, limp and comatose from the wounds she'd received.

And that was how Estevan found her.

CHAPTER TWENTY-ONE

"**P**UT HER DOWN! *Estevan, put her down!*"

Mabel was shouting at him. Mother Michael was shouting at him. Everyone was shouting at him as he carried Anaxandra's limp, bloodied form into the sanctuary. He was holding her so tightly that he couldn't seem to let her go, fearful that if he did, she would die. As long as he was holding her, she wasn't dead. He could still feel her warmth.

She wasn't dead.

She's not dead!

Mateo and Titan were there, trying to separate them. In fact, every knight at St. Margaret's was there, trying to figure out what in the hell was going on. Mabel was bloody, Anaxandra had been stabbed, and there was a dead man no one had ever seen lying in the corner of the bailey.

"Es," Titan said in Estevan's ear. He was pressed up against him from behind, his arms around the man, trying to force him to loosen his grip. "Release her, Es. Let your mother look at her wounds. Be a good lad—let her go."

Estevan was trying. He really was. But he was terrified to. He didn't know when he realized that he was weeping, but suddenly, he heard a sob and was aware that it had come from him. Somehow, Titan managed to force him to relax his grip and Mateo pulled Anaxandra from his arms, laying her on his bed.

There was blood everywhere.

"Matty, Kal?" Mabel motioned. "Quickly, now. Roll her onto her right side. *Carefully*. I must get a look at the wounds."

The knights did as they were told, and Anaxandra was gently rolled onto her side as Mabel and Mother Michael both cut away the fabric that had been tattered and stained. Between the two of them, they managed to expose the wounds. The were wide punctures that were still seeping.

"Your Grace," Mabel said calmly and quietly, "we need rags for the bleeding. Also, we must remove her tunic and you must piece it together to see if any fabric has been pushed inside the wounds. Will you do this quickly, please? Before the wounds seal?"

Mother Michael was already moving. "Indeed," she said, motioning a weeping Sister Hildegarde forward. "Find something to cover her with. And get all of these men out of the sanctuary, please. They should not witness this."

Sister Hildegarde wiped the tears from her cheeks as she turned around and began shouting at the people crowded into the sanctuary. Along with a few of the other women, they managed to herd every man that didn't belong there out of the sanctuary. When they tried to herd Lucan and Caelus out, they received some resistance until Kaladin told them that they could remain, as dun Tarh brothers.

And they would need all of the brothers to keep Estevan calm.

Lares was another story, however. He stood at the end of

the bed, watching the activity going on, admittedly more concerned for his wife than the woman bleeding on the bed. Mabel seemed well enough except for some blood on her neck, but given the status of the woman on the bed and the dead man in the bailey, it could have been much worse.

Lares was deeply thankful that it wasn't.

"Mabel?" he said quietly. "Yer neck is bleeding, love."

Mabel knew that. It was staining the top of her dress and she could see it. "Were it not for this young woman, there would be considerably more blood," she said, pausing to look at him. "That man in the bailey attacked me. Had it not been for the bravery of this young woman, he would have killed me. I owe her my life, Lares."

Lares didn't question that. But he did want to know what happened. "What did he do?" he asked. "And who is he?"

Mabel was peering closely at the wounds, which were trying to clot. "I do not know," she said. "But he asked me if the queen was here. I can only assume he was part of the army that attacked us at the gate."

Estevan, by this point, had stopped weeping, though his face was still damp. When he heard his mother's explanation, he turned to his father as they silently relived the conversation they'd had earlier.

Only dun Tarh men entered the gatehouse.

Are ye sure?

As usual, Lares was right. He was almost always right in situations pertaining to the nature of men and battle. He'd seen a good deal in his lifetime and had dealt with a variety of situations, so in this case, he had correctly surmised what had happened.

And it had almost cost Mabel and Anaxandra their lives.

Guilt swept Estevan. They shouldn't have agreed to keep their suspicions private. They should have told everyone so they could be on their guard. That judgment call might have cost him everything, because as he watched, Mother Michael returned to the bedside bearing metal instruments for probing the wounds for foreign substances. Anaxandra's tunic was carefully stripped off by Sister Hildegarde and another nun, who promptly took it away to inspect it for missing pieces. Meanwhile, another nun brought a blanket to cover Anaxandra's nudity from the waist up. Between Mabel and Mother Michael, she was carefully covered and wrapped.

There was nothing to do now but wait for Anaxandra's wounds to be assessed.

Far calmer than he had been only moments earlier, Estevan sat at the end of the bed with Titan, Mateo, and his father, watching Mabel and Mother Michael inspect the wounds with long, sharp tweezers. It was a good thing that Anaxandra was unconscious, because the pain would have surely been too great for her to bear. One wound appeared to be clean, with no fabric pushed into it, but the one on her torso seemed to have a bit of cloth pushed deep. Mabel was the one who used the pointy tweezers to dig in and pull forth a tiny piece of material. Fortunately, that seemed to be all.

After that, Mabel and Mother Michael cleansed the wounds with copious amounts of wine before tightly stitching them up. As this was going on, Estevan felt in control of himself enough to stand up and pull his father aside for a coherent conversation on the situation.

"What do ye intend tae do with that bastard who did this?" he asked. "Where is he? I want him made an example of, Papa."

Lares, who hadn't been told directly of Estevan's affection

for Anaxandra, started to figure it out the moment his son collected her bloodied body and carried it back to the sanctuary. The way he carried her and the emotion he displayed pointed to something more than simple concern.

Something much more.

Therefore, he wasn't surprised by his son's passionate request.

"The body is still where we found it," he said as Titan, Mateo, Kaladin, Rodion, Caelus, and Lucan crowded around. "He is clearly one of the Ormsfolk. He must have slipped in with my army and we did not notice."

Estevan's face was tight with emotion. "They left their dead behind when they fled the battlefield," he said. "How many of them are there?"

"Thirteen," Rodion said. "That is how many I counted from the wall."

"Thirteen," Estevan muttered. "Plus one in our bailey. Papa, correct me if I am wrong, but I have heard that the Northman believe that if a body is buried without eyes or a tongue, he canna enter their heaven. Have ye heard that?"

Lares nodded. "Also, if the hands are removed, they canna eat or drink. They will go through eternity like that."

Estevan looked at the men around him. "The Ormsfolk are known for their brutality," he said. "Attacking two women as they did proves it. Papa, they know their queen is here, which means these attacks aren't over. We know that. They'll return, again and again, if we dunna stop them."

Lares inhaled deeply, pondering that statement thoughtfully. "What would ye suggest?"

Estevan's pale eyes glittered. "Do ye truly want tae know?"

"I asked. Tell me."

Estevan didn't hesitate. "Slay them," he hissed. "Slay them all."

"I agree," Mateo spoke up. He'd been listening to everything and had something to add. "Leonore told me of a prisoner the Ormsfolk had, a man who was a Scottish warlord. They cut a piece off him every week, cauterizing the wounds, until the man was nothing but a head and body. They even took his ears and his tongue. Then they left him in a hole for eight days, waiting for him to die. Now… think what you will, but I agree with Estevan. I do not want to end up in a hole with no arms and legs. We *must* slay them before they slay us. Or worse—make us wish they had."

The decision was made on the spot.

They had to end it, once and for all.

Later that day, Lares took all of the knights, his sons, and his entire army out of the walls of St. Margaret's to hunt down the Ormsfolk. It was a ruthless task, but a necessary one if they wanted any peace. As Estevan had said, it was time to slay them.

And they did.

No mercy.

But before they went, they collected the dead, including the one killed by Anaxandra, and all of them had their eyes, tongues, and hands removed. Then they were hung from the wall of St. Margaret's as a warning to those who would try to attack the abbey again. When the bodies were on display, Lares and his men charged into the trees, following the paths of the Ormsfolk, paths that were not difficult to follow, and spent the next two days chasing down every last man and killing them. With no one left, they hauled the bodies down to the mouth of the River Nith, where their boats were still grounded, and made several funeral pyres.

Bodies were burned, including the bodies from the walls of St. Margaret's, and the boats were burned right along with them. Ashes were combed down to the shoreline of the Solway Firth, and when the tide came in, those ashes became part of the sea. No trace was left of the Ormsfolk from the Isle of Mann, for they had tangled with the wrong people. Dun Tarh, de Wolfe, and de Velt had seen to that. The men who lived by violence, and died by violence, returned to the place they came from—the sea.

When Estevan told Leonore, she wept.

Finally, she was free.

As were they all.

CHAPTER TWENTY-TWO

Three days later

ESTEVAN HAD NEVER sat at the bedside of someone who was so ill. This was a new experience for him and not one he was particularly fond of.

It was agony.

Anaxandra had been unconscious for almost five days and Estevan had hardly left her side. At this point, his mother thought she was merely in a deep sleep as her body strived to recover from her injuries. There was no fever, thankfully, due to the careful care of Mabel and Mother Michael, but still, Anaxandra wouldn't awaken.

Estevan was struggling not to become despondent.

"Es?" Mabel had entered the sanctuary, wrapped up in a heavy shawl against the early morning chill. "How did she fare during the night?"

Estevan's gaze was on Anaxandra's pale face. "She did not awaken," he said. "But she was peaceful."

"Good," Mabel said, leaning over Anaxandra and lifting an eyelid, watching her pupil react to the light. "As I said, I do believe she is only sleeping now. She will awaken soon."

"Are ye certain?"

"I am," Mabel said. She smiled at Estevan because he looked so worried. "Do not be troubled, my son. Women like Anaxandra are meant to live long lives with the men they love. She will be well soon, I promise."

It took Estevan a moment to realize what she was saying. He tore his gaze away from Anaxandra, looking at his mother.

"I never did ask ye if ye had the chance tae know a little about her," he said. "I know that ye were together when ye were attacked, but I never asked ye how the conversation went. Did ye learn what ye wanted tae know?"

Mabel's smile faded. She had been thinking on the discussion between her and Anaxandra since nearly the moment it happened. When they were attacked, she was on the verge of questioning the woman's motives with Estevan. But... she shouldn't have. She also thought about the way Anaxandra had defended her and fought to save her. A shallow woman who was an opportunist would not have risked her life so, she decided. In fact, Anaxandra's actions had been most selfless.

"Aye," she said after a moment. "I learned what I wanted to know."

"And what is that?'

Mabel shrugged. "That she is a woman of honor," she said. "Her manner was cold, as you said, but she does not seem to *want* to be, if that makes sense. I do not think she knows any better. And she very much wants to please you."

A weary smile creased Estevan's lips. "Then ye approve?"

Mabel's attention moved to Anaxandra. "How can I not?" she said. "Your young woman risked her life for me. She saved me, Estevan. We must return the favor. We must save *her*."

Estevan snorted softly. "From St. Margaret's?"

"From a life she does not want nor deserve," Mabel said. "We must give her a better one. With you."

Estevan reached across Anaxandra, taking his mother's hand and kissing it. As he sat there and held her hand, smiling at her, they both heard a faint, breathy voice.

"How… dare you."

It came from Anaxandra. Startled, Estevan dropped his mother's hand and put his palm on Anaxandra's cheek in a tender gesture.

"Are ye awake, love?" he said. "Can ye hear me?"

Anaxandra moved her head slightly, her eyes rolling open. "I can hear you," she muttered haltingly. "I can also see you. How dare you kiss your mother's hand and not mine."

Estevan burst into soft laughter. Even Mabel was smiling. He picked up Anaxandra's right hand and kissed it sweetly before holding it against his face, gazing lovingly at her.

"Better?" he asked.

A small smile appeared on her lips. "Much," she said. Then she sighed wearily. "Where am I?"

"Ye dunna recognize yer sanctuary?"

Anaxandra moved her eyes slightly as her surroundings became clear. "Aye," she whispered. "I do now."

Mabel leaned over so Anaxandra could see her without moving her head too much. "How do you feel?" she asked.

Anaxandra had to think about the question. "I am not sure," she murmured. "Weak, I think. What happened?"

Mabel put a gentle hand on Anaxandra's forehead, just to make sure the fever had stayed away. "What do you remember?" she asked.

Anaxandra sighed and closed her eyes. She didn't say anything for quite some time, and they thought she had fallen back asleep until she spoke again, soft and mumbled.

"A man," she finally said. "He grabbed you. Did he hurt you?"

Mabel couldn't believe the woman was thinking of someone other than herself after what she'd been through. "I am perfectly well, dearest," she said. "Thanks to you, I am unharmed. But you have some recovery ahead of you. Do you recall what happened after the man grabbed me?"

"A little," Anaxandra said. "I tried to help."

Mabel wasn't sure how much she truly remembered, so she wasn't going to remind her about the stabbing or the brutality. She didn't see the need. "You did splendidly," she assured her. "The threat is over. You needn't worry about anything other than getting well now, I promise. All will be well."

Estevan kissed Anaxandra's hand again. "I'll be with ye the entire time," he said. "I'll not leave yer side, not for a moment."

Anaxandra squeezed his hand. "You will be the best medicine for me," she said. "But how is everyone else? The men injured in the battle? Did the Ormsfolk return?"

"Nay," Estevan said. He didn't want to delve into what had ultimately happened to the Ormsfolk, at least not now. "No more battles. There is no more threat."

"But what of Leonore?" Anaxandra said. "Won't the Ormsfolk come back for her?"

Estevan shook his head. "Nay," he said. "Not any longer. In fact, she is feeling much better and I believe Mateo is going tae escort her home. She is a queen, after all, and requires a proper escort. My father believes it is a good idea."

"Will she be safe with only one knight as protection?"

Estevan's eyebrows lifted. "Have ye *seen* Matty?" he said.

"The man is an army all by himself. Of course she'll be safe. He'll make sure she gets home."

"That is good," Anaxandra said. Then she moved her head a little, looking around. "Where is Mother Michael?"

Estevan shook his head, looking to his mother, who answered. "In her chapel," Mabel replied. "I just left her there. She and Lares are discussing the possibility of the Earls of Torridon becoming patrons of St. Margaret's. We would make donations to help repair your portcullis and supply new equipment. We would help feed the foundlings. St. Margaret's does important work, you know. The Templar nuns' reputation has clouded their true purpose, but I have spent time with Mother Michael. I have seen the good work that goes on here. It is to be commended."

Anaxandra smiled weakly. "I am glad you have noticed," she said. "I had always hoped someone would. We need a patron badly. I had always hoped the man I married would donate money to the abbey to provide things that we need."

Mabel patted her on the shoulder, very gently. "Not only will the man you marry donate money, but so will his family," she said. Then she looked at her son. "Well? You *are* going to marry her, aren't you? The woman risked her life to save me, Estevan. The least you can do is marry her for her efforts."

She was beginning to bully him, and he started laughing. "Am I tae understand that ye approve?"

Mabel grunted. "I approve of her more than I approve of you," she said. "*You* may not be good enough for her, but I suppose you'll do."

"Thank ye, Mother," he said, miffed. "How kind of ye."

With a gracious nod to her son, she bent over and kissed Anaxandra on the forehead. "Hurry and get well, my dear," she said. "Zora is already planning your wedding, so we must not disappoint her."

With that, she headed out of the sanctuary, which was nearly void of people except for the few men still recovering from their war wounds. That left Estevan and Anaxandra alone, holding hands, smiling as the rising sun began to stream in through the sanctuary windows.

"Ye heard what she said," Estevan said. "We must hurry and get married."

Anaxandra held his hand as tightly as she could. "Is this real?" she murmured. "Are we truly to be married?"

"That is what my mother said. And we dare not disobey her."

Anaxandra managed a chuckle, weak as she was, but the sunrays streaming in through the windows caught her attention. The had landed just a few feet from Estevan, lighting up the floor of the sanctuary like beams from heaven.

It was a life-changing moment.

It was a life-changing day.

"Everything looks different," she said softly. "The sanctuary, the world. I said once that I believed God put Leonore on the riverbank for a reason. Had she not been there, you would have never come to St. Margaret's. She was the catalyst for greater things to come."

Estevan nodded. "Life is strange sometimes," he said. "It brings ye things ye never know ye needed."

"And you needed me?"

Leaning forward, he kissed her gently on the mouth. "It has brought me my destiny," he whispered. "My destiny is ye."

Lifting her hands, weak as they were, Anaxandra pulled his face to hers once again, kissing him with what remaining strength she had. Those words, and that moment, were something she would remember for the rest of her life.

My destiny is you.

On the necklace he'd bought her in Dumfries, the one she wore until the end of her life, those exact words were inscribed.

They were words to last a lifetime.

And they did.

EPILOGUE

Hollee Castle
Scottish Borderlands
Year of Our Lord 1359

"ALL I WANT is a son, lass," Estevan whispered. "That's all I ask of ye. Just one son."

He was delivering his plea in between heated kisses. But Anaxandra didn't want talk—she wanted action. They were in the small solar of Hollee Castle, a small outpost north of Ashkirk Castle that Lares had given to Estevan when he and Anaxandra were married. The castle itself had a large curtain wall, a vast bailey, a big hall, but a keep that was only six chambers over three stories and not very large at that. Still, it was their home, where they were raising their family.

Four loud, beautiful, delightful, and loving little girls.

Hence the reason Estevan was begging for a son.

"But I am already with child," Anaxandra said, trying to breathe in between his sensual onslaught. "It is already a boy or a girl. Begging me for a son at this moment will not change that."

Estevan didn't happen to think she was right.

In order to entice his wife to breed him a child of the male persuasion, he'd had to be clever. He knew what she liked. Pulling her tightly against him, he moved his mouth over her collarbone. She was unbelievably sweet and soft, and he could feel his temperature rise. The woman always had that effect on him and had since the first time he'd touched her. When his seeking mouth came to her neck, she threw her head back and he feasted on her throat. He was still sitting in his chair, as he'd trapped her against his worktable when she came in to ask him a question, but now she ended up on his lap, her head hanging back as he devoured the flesh. When he reached her earlobes and suckled tenderly, she lifted her head and slanted her mouth hungrily over his.

Hot, passionate kisses followed. Estevan's hands were in her hair, on her shoulders, stroking her back before moving to her chest. He couldn't control himself and pulled the neckline of her garment down, exposing a plump breast. When he clamped down on a tender nipple and suckled, she cried out softly.

"Upstairs," she breathed. "To our chamber."

"No time," he replied, his mouth against her breast.

The table was behind them, and it presented a perfect opportunity. Estevan cleaned it off with one sweep of his hand, clearing a path for his wife. Grasping her by the buttocks, he lifted her up and put her on the table, carefully laying her down.

Clothes were coming off or being pushed aside. Anaxandra only had her skirts to lift, and she did, pulling them up as Estevan yanked off his tunic. He probably didn't need to disrobe, given the situation, but he did anyway. As he was doing that, Anaxandra fumbled with the tie of his breeches. He was still pulling his arms out of his tunic when she scooted off the table, pulled his breeches to his knees, and put her mouth on his throbbing, engorged manhood.

Estevan nearly lost his mind.

"Christ," he hissed as her mouth worked him. "This is going tae be over before it starts if ye keep that up."

He put a hand down to stop her, but her response was to move that hand to her hair. She liked it when he pulled her hair, something the years of sexual discovery between them had revealed. His repressed, isolated wife had grown into an adventurous woman who would try anything in bed, or let him do anything he pleased. He'd taught her how to pleasure him with her mouth, and she did it so well that Estevan was dizzy with it. His hands were in her hair as her mouth plunged down on him, again and again.

But he could only take so much. He could feel himself quickly building to a release, so he stopped her, firmly this time, and lifted her onto the table again, wedging his muscular body between her legs. Anaxandra's arms went around his neck, her mouth seeking his, and he kissed her deeply while his hands moved to intimate places. He stroked her thighs, experiencing their soft texture, before his fingers moved to the fluff of blonde curls between her legs. He discovered, with pleasure, that she was hot and ready for him.

Estevan didn't make her wait.

Pulling her hips to the edge of the table, he mounted her and thrust deep, her slick body closing in around him. He continued to thrust into her, listening to her grunts of pleasure as his hands loved her up. Every coupling was like the first time, only better, which was why they'd had four children in six years. He was hers, she was his, and they couldn't get enough of one another.

But this time, he really did want a son.

Anaxandra's orgasm came with swift pants and a stiffening body, and he prolonged her pleasure as he suckled her breasts. Unable to hold it back any longer, Estevan thrust hard and released himself deep into her body, feeling every last spasm, every last ripple. He simply held her buttocks against his groin, plunged as deep as he could go, and ground his hips against hers because he knew that if he did it enough, she would climax again. She was very sensitive at this point in their lovemaking, and, as predicted, she experienced her pleasure once more as he continued to rub against her.

When it was finally over, he pulled her up from the table, still joined to her, and held her tightly. Anaxandra's legs were wrapped around his hips, holding her against him, her head on his chest as she slowed her breathing. He was just about to say something to her when there was a knock on the solar door.

"Es?" It was Cruz dun Tarh, his youngest brother, who now served him at Hollee. "Es, are ye in there?"

Anaxandra's head came up, her eyes wide as she looked at her husband. He put a finger to his lips, asking for her silence, as he answered.

"I'll be out in a moment," he said. "What do ye need?"

"The escort is prepared for the journey tae Castle Questing," Cruz said, muffled through the door. "Do ye want tae inspect it?"

"I'll come in a moment."

They could hear Cruz's footsteps fading away. With a grin, Estevan pulled Anaxandra off the table before pulling up his breeches and securing them.

"At least he did not walk in this time without knocking," Anaxandra said, fixing the bodice of her garment. "He's done that before."

Estevan grunted as he picked up his tunic. "Never again," he said firmly. "The last time he did it, I threatened tae send him back at the Hydra and tell my mother what he'd done. That convinced him tae be more cautious when the door is closed and he knows ye're in the keep."

Anaxandra burst into soft laughter. "Poor Cruz," she said. "He's only just gotten away from your mother. He does not want to go back."

"Not anytime soon."

Anaxandra continued to chuckle as she finished smoothing her clothing and pulling on a shoe that had fallen off when Estevan lifted her onto the table. Once she was finished re-dressing, she put her hand on her belly, which was barely rounded at this stage. She still didn't look pregnant, not like she would look toward the end. Estevan finished dressing also and put his hand over hers, feeling the gentle hardness of the life they'd created together. He kissed her again.

"It will be a lad and his name will be James," he declared. "Mark my words, love. I will have my son."

Anaxandra didn't argue with him, nor did she mention that he'd said the same thing for their first four children, all daughters who looked, to varying degrees, like Mabel—with the exception of Paloma, who was the image of her beauteous mother. Truthfully, Estevan didn't mind so many girls. He rather liked girls, and he particularly liked his own. But he was starting to feel outnumbered.

"As you wish," Anaxandra said. "Now, we've a journey to prepare for and we should probably get to it. We told Titan we would arrive next week, you know. Everyone is going to be there—Matty, Rodion, your brothers Aurelius and Darien, and many others, I'm sure. It will be a big gathering."

"I know."

"Are Matty and Leonore coming?"

"Nay, but that's a story for another time."

Anaxandra accepted that. "Then we really should depart."

They were already heading for the door. Estevan had Anaxandra by the hand, using his free hand to open the solar door.

"I might mention that we are going tae visit Titan tae celebrate the birth of his new son," he said. "The new heir tae the House of de Wolfe."

Anaxandra nodded patiently. "You've told me that every day since we received the missive."

"Did I mention that he has a son?"

Anaxandra rolled her eyes, her patience thinning. "Then why not ask him if we can trade one of our girls for his son?" she said. "Our girls are bright and beautiful. Surely he would consider it."

He could see her annoyance and knew he'd pushed her to her limit, so he grinned and took her in his arms, pulling her against him and gently kissing her cheek. He was about to kiss her on the mouth when a noise from the stairwell caught their attention and they turned to see a gang of little girls emerging from the steps in the care of their nurse.

Sister Hildegarde made an excellent nurse.

"Sophia, Paloma," the old woman said firmly, "I've told you not to come down those stairs so quickly. If you do it again, I shall hold your hand the entire way. Is that what you want?"

Sophia, the eldest at seven years, and Paloma, younger by eighteen months, faced Sister Hildegarde, or "Hildie," solemnly.

"Nay, Hildie," they said in tandem.

Sister Hildegarde was holding on to the youngest girls, Catalina and Isabella, one in each hand. "You are not babies any longer," she said. "But you must listen to me, still."

"Aye, Hildie."

"You *will* obey the next time or there will be punishment."

The older girls nodded. But then they turned around and saw their father, and the scolding was forgotten.

"Papa!" they cried.

Estevan smiled and opened his arms to his children, who hugged him fiercely. Catalina, the three-year-old, also ran to him, but Isabella, the baby at nearly two years, went straight for her mother. Anaxandra cradled her youngest as the older three hugged and kissed their father, who lavished affection on them. He may have wanted a son, but he absolutely doted on his daughters.

"Now," he said, looking at the three little faces, "are ye ready tae go for a visit tae see Uncle Titan? He told me that he has ponies for ye tae ride."

The girls began jumping up and down, cheering. The idea of ponies excited them greatly. But then Uncle Cruz came back into the keep and they immediately ran to him because they knew he would play with them. True to form, Cruz got down on his hands and knees and the girls tried to jump on his back and ride him like a horse. Estevan had to help Catalina because she was too small to climb on. He continued to hold her steady as Cruz walked around the entryway on all fours, pretending to be a horse, pretending to rear up and make noise.

The girls loved every minute of it.

And Anaxandra watched it all.

This was her life. This was the one she'd always dreamt of, but one she never truly thought she'd have. Sometimes, in moments like this, it was positively surreal. If growing up at St. Margaret's had taught her one thing, it had taught her to be brave. To not fear what was to come. It taught her to have faith in the smallest things because, in the end, the reality would be more than she could have ever dreamt of. The family before her was proof of that.

Her family.

Finally, she had one.

It was the greatest achievement she could have ever hoped for.

And it was Estevan's achievement, too.

He never did tell her about her background or the circumstances of her birth. He had confided in Mabel about it those years ago, but with her help, he had decided that telling Anaxandra wouldn't make her life any better. It wouldn't enrich it. In fact, it might make her feel unloved or unwanted, given that she was sent away the moment of her birth, never to know her real mother. Certainly, her real father couldn't have anything to do with her.

But it was Mabel who had told the Earl of Teviot that her son had married his daughter.

Jaime, or James, de Longley, Earl of Teviot, had wept when Mabel told him, but he, too, agreed that telling Anaxandra the truth of her birth would not have enriched her. It wasn't as if de Longley could acknowledge her and keep his political marriage intact. It wasn't as if he could welcome her into his family. But the truth was that he had loved her mother, and the first time he saw Anaxandra at a tournament at Berwick, he could see that she looked exactly like her mother, who had returned to Aragon those years ago and now had a family of her own.

Nay, telling Anaxandra was not the right thing to do.

She was far better off living in her own world.

And what a world it was.

As Cruz and Sister Hildegarde finally took the little girls out into the sun, to a small garden that was safe from the rest of the bailey where they could play, Estevan stood in the keep entry with his arm around his wife and surveyed his empire. There was work to do, but Anaxandra knew that Estevan would join the children, eventually. He couldn't stay away from them for long. The qualities that made him a wonderful and attentive husband also made him a wonderful and attentive father.

She was blessed.

When a beaten, injured woman was found in the silt those years ago, there was no way of knowing she would be the gateway for bigger and better things for so many people. Reclusive nuns and gambling warriors came together to ensure life, health, and happiness was preserved, giving way to a future that was bright for everyone. But the brightest future of all was of the woman who had fired the bolt at the man who would, one day, be her husband.

It was the best thing she'd ever done.

Destiny, for Anaxandra and Estevan, had come full circle.

Forever.

Ᏸ THE END Ᏸ

Children of Estevan and Anaxandra

Sophia

Paloma

Catalina

Isabela

James

Richard

Vincent

Leonore

Kathryn Le Veque Novels

Medieval Romance:

De Wolfe Pack Series:
Warwolfe
The Wolfe
Nighthawk
ShadowWolfe
DarkWolfe
A Joyous de Wolfe Christmas
BlackWolfe
Serpent
A Wolfe Among Dragons
Scorpion
StormWolfe
Dark Destroyer
The Lion of the North
Walls of Babylon
The Best Is Yet To Be
BattleWolfe
Castle of Bones

De Wolfe Pack Generations:
WolfeHeart
WolfeStrike
WolfeSword
WolfeBlade
WolfeLord
WolfeShield
Nevermore
WolfeAx
WolfeBorn
WolfeBite
WolfeHound

The Executioner Knights:
By the Unholy Hand
The Mountain Dark
Starless
A Time of End
Winter of Solace
Lord of the Sky
The Splendid Hour
The Whispering Night
Netherworld
Lord of the Shadows
Of Mortal Fury
'Twas the Executioner Knight
Before Christmas
Crimson Shield
The Black Dragon

The de Russe Legacy:
The Falls of Erith
Lord of War: Black Angel
The Iron Knight
Beast
The Dark One: Dark Knight
The White Lord of Wellesbourne
Dark Moon
Dark Steel
A de Russe Christmas Miracle
Dark Warrior

The de Lohr Dynasty:
While Angels Slept
Rise of the Defender
Steelheart

Shadowmoor
Silversword
Spectre of the Sword
Unending Love
Archangel
A Blessed de Lohr Christmas
Lion of Twilight
Lion of War
Lion of Hearts
Lion of Steel
Lion of Thunder

The Brothers de Lohr:
The Earl in Winter

Lords of East Anglia:
While Angels Slept
Godspeed
Age of Gods and Mortals

Great Lords of le Bec:
Great Protector

House of de Royans:
Lord of Winter
To the Lady Born
The Centurion

Lords of Eire:
Echoes of Ancient Dreams
Lord of Black Castle
The Darkland

Ancient Kings of Anglecynn:
The Whispering Night
Netherworld

Battle Lords of de Velt:
The Dark Lord
Devil's Dominion
Bay of Fear

The Dark Lord's First Christmas
The Dark Spawn
The Dark Conqueror
The Dark Angel

Reign of the House of de Winter:
Lespada
Swords and Shields

De Reyne Domination:
Guardian of Darkness
The Black Storm
A Cold Wynter's Knight
With Dreams
Master of the Dawn
One Wylde Knight

House of d'Vant:
Tender is the Knight (House of
d'Vant)
The Red Fury (House of d'Vant)

The Dragonblade Series:
Fragments of Grace
Dragonblade
Island of Glass
The Savage Curtain
The Fallen One
The Phantom Bride

Great Marcher Lords of de Lara
Lord of the Shadows
Dragonblade

House of St. Hever
Fragments of Grace
Island of Glass
Queen of Lost Stars

Lords of Pembury:
The Savage Curtain

Lords of Thunder: The de Shera Brotherhood Trilogy
The Thunder Lord
The Thunder Warrior
The Thunder Knight

The Great Knights of de Moray:
Shield of Kronos
The Gorgon

The House of De Nerra:
The Promise
The Falls of Erith
Vestiges of Valor
Realm of Angels

Highland Legion:
Highland Born
Highland Destroyer
Highland Slayer

Highland Warriors of Munro:
The Red Lion
Deep Into Darkness

The House of de Garr:
Lord of Light
Realm of Angels

Saxon Lords of Hage:
The Crusader
Kingdom Come

High Warriors of Rohan:
High Warrior
High King

The House of Ashbourne:
Upon a Midnight Dream

The House of D'Aurilliac:
Valiant Chaos

The House of De Dere:
Of Love and Legend

St. John and de Gare Clans:
The Warrior Poet

The House of de Bretagne:
The Questing

The House of Summerlin:
The Legend

The Kingdom of Hendocia:
Kingdom by the Sea

The BlackChurch Guild: Shadow Knights:
The Leviathan
The Protector
The Swordsman
The Tempest

Guard of Six:
Absolution
Insurrection

Regency Historical Romance:
Sin Like Flynn: A Regency Historical Romance Duet
The Sin Commandments
Georgina and the Red Charger

Gothic Regency Romance:
Emma

Historical Fiction:
The Girl Made Of Stars

Contemporary Romance:

Kathlyn Trent/Marcus Burton Series:

Valley of the Shadow
The Eden Factor
Canyon of the Sphinx

**The Eagle Brotherhood (under the
pen name Kat Le Veque):**
The Sunset Hour
The Killing Hour
The Secret Hour
The Unholy Hour
The Burning Hour
The Ancient Hour
The Devil's Hour

Sons of Poseidon:
The Immortal Sea

**Pirates of Britannia Series (with
Eliza Knight):**
Savage of the Sea by Eliza Knight
Leader of Titans by Kathryn Le
Veque
The Sea Devil by Eliza Knight
Sea Wolfe by Kathryn Le Veque

Note: All Kathryn's novels are designed to be read as stand-alones, although many have cross-over characters or cross-over family groups. Novels that are grouped together have related characters or family groups. You will notice that some series have the same books; that is because they are cross-overs. A hero in one book may be the secondary character in another.

There is NO reading order except by chronology, but even in that case, you can still read the books as stand-alones. No novel is connected to another by a cliff hanger, and every book has an HEA.

Series are clearly marked. All series contain the same characters or family groups except the American Heroes Series, which is an anthology with unrelated characters.

For more information, find it in **A Reader's Guide to the Medieval World of Le Veque**.

ABOUT KATHRYN LE VEQUE

Bringing the Medieval to Romance

KATHRYN LE VEQUE is a critically acclaimed, multiple USA TODAY Bestselling author, an Indie Reader bestseller, a charter Amazon All-Star author, and a #1 bestselling, award-winning, multi-published author in Medieval Historical Romance with over 100 published novels.

Kathryn is a multiple award nominee and winner, including the winner of Uncaged Book Reviews Magazine 2017 and 2018 "Raven Award" for Favorite Medieval Romance. Kathryn is also a multiple RONE nominee (InD'Tale Magazine), holding a record for the number of nominations. In 2018, her novel WARWOLFE was the winner in the Romance category of the Book Excellence Award and in 2019, her novel A WOLFE AMONG DRAGONS won the prestigious RONE award for best pre-16th century romance.

Kathryn is considered one of the top Indie authors in the world with over 2M copies in circulation, and her novels have been translated into several languages. Kathryn recently signed with Sourcebooks Casablanca for a Medieval Fight Club series, first published in 2020.

In addition to her own published works, Kathryn is also the President/CEO of Dragonblade Publishing, a boutique publishing house specializing in Historical Romance. Dragonblade's success has seen it rise in the ranks to become Amazon's #1 e-book publisher of Historical Romance (K-Lytics report July 2020).

Kathryn loves to hear from her readers. Please find Kathryn on Facebook at Kathryn Le Veque, Author, or join her on Twitter @kathrynleveque. Sign up for Kathryn's blog at www.kathrynleveque.com for the latest news and sales.